I0597992

THE GIVING SEASON

Rebecca Brock

PEARLSONG PRESS
NASHVILLE, TN

Pearlsong Press
P.O. Box 58065
Nashville, TN 37205
www.pearlsong.com
www.pearlsongpress.com

© 2009 Rebecca Brock
www.rebeccabrockonline.com

ISBN-10: 1597190187
ISBN-13: 9781597190183

Cover & book design by Zelda Pudding

No part of this book may be reproduced, stored in or introduced
into a retrieval system, or transmitted, in any form or by any
means (electronic, mechanical, photocopying, recording,
or otherwise), without the written permission of the publisher,
with the exception of brief quotations included in reviews.

Library of Congress Cataloging-in-Publication Data

Brock, Rebecca, 1970–
The giving season / Rebecca Brock.
    p. cm.
ISBN-13: 978-1-59719-018-3 (trade pbk. : alk. paper)
ISBN-10: 1-59719-018-7
1. Women teachers—Fiction. 2. Overweight women—Fiction.
3. Self-esteem—Fiction. I. Title.
PS3602.R6235G58 2009
813'.6—dc22
                                    2009038352

To my mother, Leah,
and my brothers, Matt and Dave.
Thank you for encouraging me to keep trying.

Chapter One

"*PLEASE* TELL ME you're kidding—"

"No, ma'am." The old man behind the counter paused a moment to pick his teeth with a matchbook cover. "Storm's caught near 'bout everybody by surprise. I'd say there ain't an empty motel room within ten miles of here. And with tomorrow being Thanksgiving and all, there might not be one in the whole county."

Jessy Monroe stared at the wrinkled little man, her whole world collapsing while a rerun of *Andy Griffith* blared on the countertop TV. So this was where her little cross-country odyssey would end: in the office of a cheap motel in Bear Paw, Minnesota, trapped by an unexpected blizzard. *Way to go, Jess.*

Melting snow dripped down her neck and back, chilling her to the bone. Great. She was wet, she was tired, and she was cold—and now this guy was telling her that there weren't any empty rooms. For about the millionth time since packing up and leaving Kentucky, she mentally kicked herself in the butt. When it came to making brilliant life decisions, she really couldn't be beat.

"I really am sorry about all this, ma'am—" The old man looked almost embarrassed, which made Jessy feel even worse. She forced a brittle smile despite herself.

"That's okay," she said quietly, straining to sound like she wasn't about to collapse into tears. "Thanks anyway—"

Before the old man could mumble another apology Jessy headed for the door, suitcase cradled in her arms as she stepped out into the night. An icy gust of wind slapped her in the face, pellets of snow blinding her for a moment as she trudged through the ankle-deep drifts. The achy feeling she'd had since leaving Kentucky was finally turning into a cold, and she coughed explosively, her throat already raw. Great. With her luck, it'd turn into walking pneumonia by morning.

Jessy winced as another wave of numbing wind sliced through her too-thin coat. *And who do you have to thank for all this crappiness,* she thought as she climbed onto the bus again. *Charlie? The bimbo he started living with?*

Nope. It's all you, babe. You made the decision to drop everything in your life and follow him to Minneapolis. You made the choice to believe him when he said he loved you.

Idiot.

If one of her friends had come to her with the situation, she would have told her that no man was worth giving up your independence. And if one of her friends had even considered leaving her job to follow her boyfriend to another state in the vague hope that it would lead to true love and marriage, she would have laughed in her face and told her to wake up and smell the reality.

But no. No, no, no. Jessy couldn't take her own advice. She was too busy mooning over Charlie Wilks, too busy being grateful that he had looked beyond the fact that she was a "big girl" and was willing to be seen in public with her. And too busy dreaming of silly romantic fantasies with a guy who obviously hadn't reciprocated her feelings. Hindsight was a wonderful thing, and now she could see that Charlie had liked her well enough, but he hadn't loved her. She served a purpose to him, kept him entertained.

And all it had taken was one drunken phone call to make her turn her life upside down and go running to him. She didn't like to think she was that gullible, that desperate.

Apparently, she was.

If she'd had more experience with relationships she would have immediately realized that she wasn't in one with Charlie. She thought that just because they had a million things in common, because they could have serious conversations and laugh at the same jokes, because they felt so utterly comfortable with each other, it was love.

Well, it was on her part, at least.

The last few days seemed like a bad dream. When Charlie had called her late one night she'd known he was drunk, but the things he said were all the things she'd ever wanted to hear. She was worth her weight in gold to him. He wouldn't have been able to get through the past few years without her. She meant more to him than she'd ever know.

And then the final knock-out blow to her common sense: He was lonely up there in Minnesota without her, and he missed her so much he couldn't stand it sometimes. He said he had plenty of room at his place if she ever wanted to come up and visit—or anything else. Even now, replaying the conversation in her mind, she was sure he had wanted her to move in with him. He didn't come right out and say it, but he insinuated it.

Just like he'd never told her he loved her. But he insinuated it plenty. She wasn't stupid. She would have known if it had *all* been a lie.

God, how happy she had been at first. Usually she considered and reconsidered and considered yet again every decision she had to make, especially the big life-changing, earth-rattling decisions. She had been raised by her Aunt Amelia to question every motive of other people, especially when those other people happened to be men. All that had flown out the window. In a burst of misplaced idealism she decided it was time for a change in her life.

It seemed like a sign. She had just lost her job teaching third grade due to budget cuts and her apartment was turning into a wildlife preserve for mice due to a landlord who didn't like to deal with actually maintaining the apartment building. If ever there was time for a change, it was now.

So she did all the things she would have advised her best friend not to do. She decided to throw caution and common sense to the wind and, for the first time in her life, do something exciting and impulsive and crazy. She bought a plane ticket and decided she would just show up on Charlie's doorstep. He'd welcome her with a kiss and be thrilled to see her and proud of her brave decision to take a chance, since he always told her she was too staid and boring, and then they'd live happily ever after.

Idiot.

When she showed up at Charlie's doorstep that fateful morning, it wasn't Charlie who had opened the door. It had been a gorgeous redhead. In a nightie. She'd taken a look at Jessy and smirked, then called for Charlie.

He came out of the bedroom with a towel wrapped around his waist and an instantly guilty look of surprise on his face when he saw Jessy.

Turned out that all that talk about being lonely and wishing she were out there with him was just that: talk. He hadn't wanted to hurt her feelings by telling her about Kirsten. The night he'd called, Kirsten had broken up with him and he'd gotten plastered to try to get over her. He didn't even remember half the things he had said. But now he and Kirsten were back together and planning to be married.

Throughout his whole confession Jessy had remained calm and unreadable. She didn't cry. She didn't speak. She just let him talk. He told her the story of how he met Kirsten the first day he'd moved into his apartment. He told her about their first date and how he realized he was in love with her a week after they met. He told her everything, and she listened. If he stopped talking, then she'd have to speak. And if she spoke, she didn't think she'd be able to hide the agony she felt.

It all came down to his cowardice, in the end. He simply hadn't known how to tell her the truth—that even though he really liked Jessy and thought she was a great person and a wonderful woman, he just wasn't attracted to her physically. He wished he could get over it, but he just couldn't.

And that was the final body blow that she just could not absorb. Those were the words Jessy knew she would play back in her mind for the rest of her life, even though she had known deep down that Charlie had felt that way. The few times he had kissed her he had seemed like he was forcing himself to do it, like he was trying to make himself enjoy it. He'd never shown any signs of affection when they were in public—never held her hand, never put his arm around her. She had heard her aunt's voice in her mind, warning her not to fool herself about Charlie's sincerity when he'd told her that her weight hadn't mattered to him. At 220 pounds, Jessy realized that if a guy had to choose between her and someone half her size, the skinny gal would usually win every time; personality and character had nothing to do with it. She had just thought Charlie was different. She thought he could see beyond her shyness and her quiet nature. She thought he could see past her weight.

Before he came into her life she had been perfectly content alone. She was happy teaching, and she thought nothing of spending her evenings at home with a good book and a bag of popcorn. But it was the same old story. She took a chance and fell for him, and Charlie had broken her heart.

And now she was trapped in a blizzard, with five bucks to her name and nothing to go home to.

Happy Thanksgiving to me, Jessy thought, taking a deep breath as she leaned her head against the cold glass of the window. She wiped at her eyes, angry to be crying over him again when he so obviously wasn't worth it. Aunt Amelia would have tut-tutted over her crying and told her Charlie wasn't even worth the salt in her tears.

God, how she missed Amelia. It had just been six months since she'd died, and Jessy missed her more and more every day. Amelia had been her only family, and now she was totally alone.

Fresh tears burned Jessy's eyes as another series of wracking coughs tore through her, leaving her weak. She closed her eyes, willing her memories of Charlie and Amelia and everyone else she had lost to fade away. Her entire body ached as the slight case of sniffles she'd fought for weeks finally blossomed into a full-fledged chest cold. But a cold was nothing. She could survive a cold.

She tucked her nose and chin beneath the collar of her coat, struggling to stretch her legs out in front of her. So it wasn't the most comfortable of positions; as exhausted as she felt, a bed of nails would have been perfectly cozy. After a few minutes, she finally managed to drift into a thin, dozy sleep.

"HEY—WHAT ARE YOU DOING out here?"

Jessy jerked awake, a sharp gasp catching in her throat, choking into a cough. For a moment she forgot where she was, unable to adjust her eyes to the dark.

"Who's there?" she rasped, too weak to sound tough or confident.

"And you're sick, too," the man said, the faintest hint of disapproval in his husky voice. He took a few shuffling steps forward. "Have you got a death wish or something? It's freezing out here."

He stepped into a slant of light from the motel sign and Jessy instantly recognized him. Seat 2A: The scruffy, stubbly guy who had snuck stares at her over the top of his book for the last three hundred miles like she was the featured attraction at a freak show. He'd introduced himself as Michael Forrester when they'd boarded the bus in Illinois after a dinner stop, then asked if he could use her empty overhead compartment for his multitude of luggage. He'd gone a little overboard Christmas shopping, he'd explained with a way-too-charming dimpled grin that had immediately set off her insincerity alarms. Jessy had given him a vague smile and tuned him out after that.

Stifling a groan, she turned on the seat light and wearily glared at him—dark hair dusted with snow, piercing gray-green eyes, wide, slightly smirking smile. *Now* she remembered why she'd kept her distance from him: He was too damned good-looking. And if there was one thing she trusted even less than a drinking man, it was a handsome man.

"Thanks for the weather report," she said and cleared her throat, wincing as she did so. "Good night, Mr. Forrester."

"You're not staying out here, are you?"

"Looks that way," she said, closing her eyes as she settled back against the cushions again. Maybe he'd just take the hint and leave her alone.

"Fifteen below and you're going to sleep on the bus. Lady, you're either trying to kill yourself or you're as dumb as a box of rocks."

Jessy pried one eye open. He was staring at her again, trying to goad her into a response. God, how she disliked arrogant, know-it-all men.

"There aren't any more rooms left at the motel," she said quietly. "Now if you'll please leave me alone—"

He smiled slightly as she spoke, as if she were just amusing the hell out of him. Jessy began to tell him exactly what she thought about that arrogant look, then crumpled in another coughing fit, this one worse than before. By the time she managed to raise her head to look at him again, he was watching her with an odd mixture of worry and sympathy.

"Listen," she croaked, "why don't you just go back inside and let me get some sleep, okay? And quit looking at me like that."

"Like what?" he asked, a faintly teasing smile in his eyes. "Like I'm waiting to see how long it'll take until you freeze solid?"

"Would you *please* just leave me alone?"

He folded his arms over his wide chest, smile slowly fading. "No."

Jessy clenched her teeth, dropping her chin to her chest as she groaned in exasperation. She wasn't usually so combative, but she was too cold, too tired, too sick to deal with this man right now.

"Like you said earlier, you don't have too many options." Michael leaned against the seat in front of her. "If you stay out here, you're going to get sicker. And you already sound like you're going to choke on your own snot before morning."

"Gee, thanks," Jessy muttered.

"So why don't you just make things easier on yourself and bunk in my room with me." He smiled again, wider this time. "I'm perfectly harmless. I promise."

Jessy stared at him, too surprised by his offer to speak. He honestly expected her to stay in his room with him? This guy she'd never met before? This total stranger?

"How dumb do you think I am?" she asked, unable to keep from laughing. "Thanks, but I'm fine out here."

"It's supposed to dip down to twenty below tonight." The smile in his eyes disappeared. "How 'fine' will you be then?"

"I *said* I'll be okay."

"Good Lord," he muttered, turning away to open the overhead baggage compartment. His leather jacket opened as he reached up, revealing a flannel shirt pulled taut over his broad chest. Jessy stared despite herself.

"Just what is your problem anyway?" The unexpected frustration in his voice startled Jessy out of her reverie. She raised her gaze to his and saw something like anger in his eyes. "You know, I'm trying my damndest to be a decent guy and you're acting like I'm some kind of pervert. What is it with people nowadays that you can't even try to do something nice for somebody?"

Caught off guard, Jessy couldn't immediately respond to that. To her dismay, another round of gut-deep coughs ripped through her, leaving her breathless and weak.

"Listen," Michael said quietly, his expression softening as he looked at her. "I realize that you don't know me and that as far as you're concerned I could be a serial killer, but I'm just a dairy farmer from upstate Minnesota—and I hate to be the one to break it to you, but dairy farmers just aren't interesting enough for that kind of thing."

"Wasn't Ed Gein a farmer in Wisconsin?"

Michael smiled slightly and Jessy's instincts got the better of her. She didn't want him to be this nice. It made things that much harder for her.

"I would really appreciate it," he said softly, "if you'd do me the favor of coming in from the cold. You can trust me. Honest."

Jessy studied him for a few moments. Yeah, he looked like a decent enough guy—but then again, so had Ted Bundy.

"Besides," he added, "if you don't come in, I'll worry myself to death. I've got three kids. Worry is coded in my DNA."

He smiled at her again, and as much as Jessy wanted to see something devious and insincere in that smile, she couldn't. She couldn't even pretend. And maybe she'd live to regret it, but she sensed that she could trust him—for one night, anyway. She'd just sleep lightly and keep her guard up. And since she figured she probably outweighed him, she was fairly certain he wouldn't attempt to try anything. Besides, it was *her*. When had a man *ever* attempted to try anything with her?

"Fine," she said as she rose, faltering as the bus seemed to tilt and rock beneath her feet. She staggered slightly and Michael instantly grabbed her elbow, steadying her as she regained her balance. Jessy tried to ignore the gentleness of the gesture.

"But I've got one condition," she said as she took her arm back. "I'm paying you back for half the room. That way I don't owe you and you don't owe me. Deal?"

"Sure thing." Michael grinned as he allowed Jessy to step in front of him, following her down the bus aisle. "But I call dibs on the little bars of soap."

Jessy stopped in her tracks and turned to face him again, shaking her head slightly when she saw the wide, teasing smile on his face.

She had a feeling it was going to be a long night.

Chapter Two

THE LOCK CLICKED SOFTLY as Michael closed the door, plunging the room into darkness. Jessy instantly stiffened, suddenly all too aware that she was alone in a locked room with a strange man. God—how did she manage to get herself into these situations?

"You wouldn't happen to be close to a light, would you?" Michael's voice in the darkness was followed by a solid thud—his shin against a table, from the sound of it—and a muttered curse. Jessy found the bedside lamp, turning it on to find Michael sitting in one of the molded vinyl chairs, gingerly massaging his right shin.

"Found the dresser," he said with a crooked grin.

Jessy nodded, managing a faint smile as she forced herself to look away from him and study her new surroundings. It was a motel room like every other motel room she had ever seen in her life, filled with bad artwork, cheap fabrics, and cigarette-scarred furniture. She hefted her threadbare suitcase onto the dresser, setting it beside the bolted-down television. At least the place didn't have a mirrored ceiling.

"Not bad for twenty bucks," Michael said, smiling as he put his suitcase on the small table centered between two plastic chairs. "What do they call this decorating style anyway? Early American Fugly?"

"I think it's stuck in the '70s." Jessy had to smile, glancing back at him as he shrugged out of his coat. In his flannel shirt and jeans he appeared sturdy and strong, the classic farm-boy look. He glanced up and caught her staring, and Jessy quickly averted her eyes, huddling in the safe depths of her coat.

Damn it, why was he making her so nervous? It wasn't *just* because he was a stranger. It was because Michael Forrester was a good-looking man, and she knew all too well how good-looking men tended to react to her. Once they saw how overweight she was, they either ignored her or pitied her or, in some cases, ridiculed her. If given the choice, Jessy would rather be ignored. Especially since the whole Charlie fiasco.

She couldn't look at him, so she focused her attention on the room instead. "Tacky" was about the kindest thing she could say about it. The orange and green polyester bedspread shared the same zigzag pattern as the curtain. The lamps, in the shape of chubby, gold-plated cherubs, were sorely in need of a paint job. The shag rug, an unnatural shade that managed to blend every color in the spectrum into a sickly gray-green, was bare in patches, a path worn between the bed and the closeted bathroom.

And in the middle of all this splendor, she noted with a sudden jolt, there was only one bed.

One bed. Two people. She didn't have to be Einstein to do the math on that one.

"You're going to keel over if you don't get out of those wet clothes," Michael said as he pulled off his heavy work boots. "That cough sounds bad enough as it is. You don't need it to get worse."

Jessy nodded, but made no move to get out of anything as she sank down on the foot of the bed. Her heart pounded hard and fast, her palms slick with cold sweat. Oh Lord, but she hated to feel this way. She knew from long years of painful experience that it did her not one iota of good to let herself be aware of attractive men—especially a man as handsome as Michael Forrester. He probably had that all too typical male mentality that decreed a woman should have a chest the size of Texas and a wasp waist—with an I. Q. to match her age. On that standard, Jessy knew she failed big-time. A supermodel she was most definitely not—although lately she'd been questioning her own intelligence. She hadn't exactly been making the wisest of decisions.

"Listen," Michael said, startling her into looking up at him again. He was unbuttoning his flannel shirt, revealing a black thermal undershirt beneath. "I know we didn't exactly get off on the right foot—"

Jessy smiled faintly, not quite able to maintain eye contact with him. "I think that's pretty much safe to say."

"So let's start again." Michael sat beside her on the bed and she immediately tensed. She couldn't look at him, staring at the rug at her feet while her cheeks burned with embarrassment and her entire body trembled. She silently cursed at herself; now she was just being ridiculous. She was far too old to be acting like such a child.

"I'm Michael Forrester," he said and smiled, extending his hand. "And you are—?"

Jessy hesitated a moment, gazing at his offered hand. She had to admit it was one of the nicest she'd ever seen: long fingers, neatly trimmed nails, and wide, almost delicate wrists. His forearms, exposed by his pushed up sleeves, were sprinkled with dark hair and nicely muscled. He had the hands of an artist, not a farmer.

"Uh—Jessy," she finally stammered, managing a very faint smile as she quickly met his gaze. "Jessy Monroe."

Tentatively, she slipped her hand into his. His palm was warm, with a wonderful texture that fell somewhere between soft and rough. Touching others, even in such a casual way, had never come easily to Jessy, but she found herself relaxing as his fingers enveloped hers and they shared a smile.

"I'm glad to know you, Miss Jessy Monroe." His dark eyes shone with an almost teasing glint as he studied her, and Jessy suddenly felt acutely self-conscious. Reluctantly, she slipped her hand out of his grasp and stood, crossing the room to the clothes rack bolted to the far wall. Distance was good. Distance was very good.

"So," she said, and laughed nervously. "Mr. Forrester—"

"Please," he said, and smiled. "Call me Michael." He leaned against the headboard of the bed, folding his arms behind his head as he crossed his long legs at the ankles. "'Mr. Forrester' just makes me feel old."

"Okay—" Jessy returned his smile, glancing over her shoulder to him as she fumbled with the buttons on her coat. Her skin felt as cold and slick as ice, but she dreaded shedding the one crucial layer that skimmed over the bulges without clinging, almost disguising the extent of her size. The only person she fooled was herself—after all, no amount of 'slimming' black could disguise a hundred extra pounds—but she took her comforts where she could. Right now Michael was treating her, more or less, like any other woman he might meet, but Jessy knew that once he saw how big she really was his whole attitude towards her would change. One glimpse of her less than perfect body and the smiles would stop as she ceased to exist in his world.

Suddenly angry that she should even care what he thought, she kept her back to him and peeled off her sopping coat. She wore a baggy green sweatshirt over loose jeans—both of which made her look even bigger and dumpier, she thought grimly. It was too late to do anything about it now anyway. She turned to face him again, expecting to see disgust or surprise or disappointment—or all three.

But instead he was watching her with an unsettling intensity, one corner of his wide mouth curled up in a half-smile. Jessy didn't know how to react to that. And it made her even more nervous than before.

"So—" Jessy cleared her throat, fighting back a cough as she sat in one of the plastic chairs, careful to keep a good distance between herself and the bed. She smiled pleasantly and forced herself to keep eye contact with him. "I guess we should try to get to know each other, huh?"

He nodded, an amused glint in his eye. "Yep—I guess so."

"Yep—" Jessy absently chewed on her lower lip, eyes darting from his steady gaze to the bed to the ceiling to the floor to any-thing but those smiling dark eyes. What was his problem? Why was he staring at her like that? Didn't he get the memo that said he should be ignoring her by now?

"So what do you want to know about me?" he asked as he leaned sideways on the bed, stretching out as he propped his head up on his fist. "Should I start with my prison record or the time I spent in South America as a soldier-of-fortune?"

Jessy laughed despite her nervousness, triggering another round of whooping coughs. "Just the basics," she managed to gasp as the worst of it had passed.

"I can't believe you think I'm joking," he said with mock-seriousness, unable to hide the teasing smile in his eyes. "Okay—basics. Let's see, I'm thirty-eight—no, wait a minute—thirty-nine. Forgot about that last birthday. Anyway, I run a small dairy farm up north, and I have three kids, five horses, and two dozen cows."

"What about the partridge in a pear tree?" Jessy asked with a smile.

"Give me a while. I've still got a few weeks before Christmas."

Jessy leaned back in the chair, crossing her legs awkwardly; she settled on resting her ankle on her knee. "So what about the rest of the basics?" she asked, eyeing his ringless left hand. Kids usually meant a wife lurked somewhere at home, didn't it? Not that she was about to come right out and ask.

"Hmm—well, I enjoy painting, riding horses, and taking my kids fly-fishing—" He suddenly batted his eyelashes and smiled brightly. "And when I become Miss America, I hope to end starvation and make the world a better place for all the little children."

Jessy couldn't help but laugh. "You'd never pass the swimsuit competition, buddy."

"Ah, well, I don't think I could survive the bikini waxing anyway." He lifted one jean-clad leg and flexed it, grinning as Jessy smiled again. "Actually, that's about it for me. I'm a dairy farmer in Minnesota. I can't think of anything more boring than that."

"Did you grow up on the farm?" Jessy winced inwardly at the inanity of the question, but her brain seemed to be taking a coffee break. She couldn't remember ever being so antsy around a man.

"Yep—" Michael's smile softened, growing almost sad. "I left home for college so I could be a painter or graphics artist or *something*. Anything but a farmer." His smile quirked downward, almost fading completely. "But Dad died a few years back and left

Mom the spread. She asked me to come home and help her run it and—here I am. A farmer, just like Dad wanted."

Jessy heard the regret in his voice. "What about the rest of your family?"

Michael smiled again, seeming to regain some of his good mood. "My older brother, Frank, is a sheriff in a small town up north. All I do is milk the cows and slop the pigs and clean the stalls."

"Sounds thrilling."

Michael shrugged, a mischievous smile curling his lips. "Most people would think it was *udderly* boring."

Jessy winced even as she smiled. "Oh, boo—bad, bad joke."

"Sorry." His grin spread even wider. "When it comes to bad jokes, I just get a *bovine* inspiration."

"Please—" Jessy said as she laughed. "You're milking this thing to death."

Michael lost his semi-straight face and laughed with her. Their gazes caught for an instant and held, the smiles lingering just a moment longer than they should have.

Jessy sobered instantly. This wasn't good. Not good at all. She was starting to like this man, and she knew from past experience exactly what road that would lead to. First, she'd start *liking* liking him, then she'd start acting really dumb and stupid around him—and then she'd say something that would send him screaming for the hills. After all, what man wanted a 220-pound woman interested in him? None that she'd ever found. Charlie had taught her that much.

"What about your wife?" she asked quietly. Not the most subtle approach, but she was too tired to be discreet. She dreaded his answer almost as much as she wanted to hear it. "How does she like living on a dairy farm?"

"She didn't." Michael smiled, but his eyes were strangely flat. "It was the whole *Green Acres* thing—I loved the farm, but she loved the city. She's still in Chicago, a reporter for the *Tribune*. The kids are with me at the farm."

"Oh," Jessy murmured, slowly nodding. So he wasn't married. She wasn't sure how she felt about that—despite the fact that every nerve in her body was doing a quiet little happy dance.

"And I think I just got a little too up close and personal," he said abruptly, changing the mood with a grin that was just *way* too cute for Jessy's comfort. "So what's your story, morning glory?"

Jessy's smile held a few moments longer. She really didn't want to get into the whole sorry saga of her trek North. What could she say? *I uprooted my entire life and moved hundreds of miles away from home for a guy who didn't bother to tell me he was engaged to somebody else?* Bad enough that she already thought she was an idiot for being so naïve; she couldn't stand the thought of Michael thinking the same thing.

"Okay," she said quietly, hoping she sounded casual enough. "Let's see—I'm from Kentucky, I'm a third grade teacher—and, well—I guess that's about it. The end."

"So you're a teacher from Kentucky." Michael's smile widened. "Hold on while I try to process that overload of information."

"I told you I was boring."

"Well—where are you going?"

Jessy shifted slightly, uncomfortable with the conversation's sudden change of direction. "I'm just—*going.*"

"I suppose that's your polite way of saying it's none of my business, right?"

"Guess so." Jessy abruptly stood, absently pulling at her sweatshirt to loosen it. She caught a glimpse of herself in the mirror over the dresser and grimaced. Dear Lord, but she looked horrible. Her hair hung in lank chunks around her puffy face, and the rest of her looked as wide as a house. It was a reality slap that she hadn't particularly needed at just that moment. But it brought her back to Earth, like it or not.

She turned away from her reflection and busied herself by digging through her small suitcase, coughing harshly into her balled fist. She felt as bad as she looked—if not worse. All she wanted was to take a hot shower to clear her aching sinuses and unkink her muscles. Then she wanted to sleep—preferably for days. She wanted to forget about the last few days of nonstop traveling. She wanted to forget that Charlie Wilks had ever existed. More than that, she wanted to forget that she could possibly be as gullible and dumb as she had been over him.

"Something tells me that you'd rather I change the subject," Michael said quietly, sitting up. Jessy forced herself to casually look at him again. Something about his expression confounded her; he actually seemed to be interested in what she had to say. He actually seemed to *want* to listen to her.

For a moment she wanted very badly to confide in him, to trust her instincts and allow him to be her friend—but she couldn't. The past few months had been an education she could have done without. People she thought she could trust had turned out to be hiding behind masks. The experience with Charlie Wilks had been a hard lesson, but one she'd taken to heart. Now she didn't want to trust anyone—especially handsome men with big, bright smiles.

"There—" she took a deep breath and forced a false smile. "There just isn't anything else to talk about. That's all."

"One more question," Michael said, his friendly smile slowly replaced by a growing expression of concern.

Jessy nodded. "Okay. One more."

He gazed at her for a few long, unnerving moments. "Who have you been crying over?"

Jessy automatically turned away from Michael to the mirror. Her eyes were still red and swollen. Michael gazed at her with disconcerting intensity, his silence demanding that she answer. Only problem was, Jessy didn't know what that answer would be.

So instead of speaking, Jessy lowered her eyes and fumbled mutely with the clothing in her suitcase. She really didn't want to get into her life story with this stranger. There were too many things she regretted, too many bad choices, too many missed opportunities.

"It's a long story," she finally said quietly, forcing a slight smile as she looked up again. "Too long and too boring."

Without saying a word, Michael rose and stood beside her. He didn't crowd her, didn't touch her, but she was acutely aware of his strength, his warmth. She wished she could just wrap her arms around him and cry. She wished he would hold her until she didn't feel so damn alone.

But it was foolish to wish for that. After all, why should he care about her or her problems? He didn't even know her. As soon as the snow melted, they'd board the bus and never see each other again.

Jessy kept her gaze focused on the unbuttoned collar of his thermal shirt, on the dark chest hair that peeked out at the base of his throat. She knew that if she met his eyes again, she'd say or do something she might regret.

"Jessy," he said quietly, "I'd like to help you—"

"Why?" she whispered, her eyes and throat burning as she desperately tried not to cry yet again. She hadn't expected him to be concerned. "Why would you want to help me?"

"I don't know," he said with a shrug, lifting her chin with a hooked finger. His expression was solemn, but something in his eyes smiled at her. "I like your accent. I think you have pretty hair. It's Wednesday." Now the smile slowly stretched across his wide mouth. "Who says I have to have a *reason*?"

Jessy studied him for a few moments. Maintaining her healthy distrust of the man was getting harder and harder to do. "What do you want?"

"Besides world peace and a million bucks?" His smile faltered when he saw Jessy wasn't smiling back at him. "Listen, Jess—I don't know anything about what's going on with your life, but on the behalf of all decent people everywhere, I have to tell you that not everyone is going to *want* something from you."

Jessy closed her eyes, blocking out the concern and worry she saw in his expression. She couldn't handle this. Not right now. Her instincts were divided into two screaming camps: One demanded that she trust him and allow him to be her friend—and the other refused to believe a word he said.

"I'd rather not talk about it right now," she said softly, words choking into another coughing fit. She dimly felt his hand on her shoulder, bracing her as she nearly lost her balance. His warmth burned through her sweatshirt, unfamiliar but comforting. For a moment, they simply stood there: Jessy with her head down, and Michael with his hand cupping her shoulder almost protectively.

"Are you okay?" he finally asked.

"I'm fine." She raised her head and took a deep, ragged breath. "It's just a cold."

"Yeah, that's what they said about the plague," Michael said and smiled again. He kept his hand on her shoulder, absently massaging it, and suddenly he seemed too close, too intimate. Rationally, she knew he meant nothing by the touch, but memories of Charlie's rejection still burned bright and hot. As casually as she could she stepped away from Michael, keeping her eyes downcast.

"Tomorrow's Thanksgiving," Michael said quietly. "Where are you going to be?"

Jessy stopped at the bathroom door, clutching the armful of clothes even closer to her chest. Ever since her parents died, the holidays had just been ordeals to endure. Amelia had tried her best to keep the traditions she had known with her parents, but it could never be the same. Every year, Jessy found herself missing her mother and father more and more. She missed having that sense of belonging, of family. The holidays had always been the most painful time of the year for her—and this year would be even harder. This year she wouldn't even have Amelia.

"I haven't really thought about it." Jessy finally said, half-turning back to face him again. "And to tell you the truth—I don't know."

"This is no time to be by yourself," he said quietly.

Jessy couldn't look away from him, trying to figure out his angle, what he might want from her. Another thing Charlie had taught her: Men always want something.

"Listen," she said, "Thanks for the advice, but—"

"Why don't you come home with me."

Jessy stared at him for a moment, stunned into silence. "Excuse me, but *what?*"

"Come home with me," Michael repeated. He slowly smiled, as if warming to the idea. "Spend Christmas with me and my family."

"Christmas is a month away."

Michael shrugged. "So?"

"*So* I can't just—" Jessy's voice trailed away as she shook her head. "This is crazy."

"What's so crazy about it?" Michael's smile faltered. "You don't have any place to go, and I've got more than enough room at my house—"

"But you don't even know me."

Michael rolled his eyes. "What does that have to do with anything? For Pete's sake, Jessy, it's Christmas time. If you can't do something nice for somebody now, then what's the use?"

Jessy silently studied him for a few moments. Part of her wanted to say yes, to allow herself to follow her instincts and trust him—but she couldn't. What kind of person asks a total stranger into their home for Christmas? His offer was generous, but the holidays were a time for families. And that was one thing she didn't have anymore.

"Thanks for the invitation," she managed to whisper, "but I can't—"

Before Michael could say anything more, Jessy ducked into the bathroom, closing the door before he could see her tears.

Chapter Three

WHAT THE HELL am I doing?

Michael stretched out across the bed, willing his cramped muscles to unkink, and closed his eyes as he listened to the sound of running water. Apparently he'd finally lost his mind—inviting a total stranger to come home with him! No wonder Jessy had looked at him like he was crazy. It *was* crazy.

But he'd wanted more than anything for her to say yes. He didn't know why—he just knew he didn't want her to be alone for Christmas.

Michael groaned under his breath and covered his face with his hands. Maybe *he'd* been alone for too long since the divorce. Maybe he wasn't thinking clearly enough. Or maybe he was just plain crazy. Whatever the reason, he couldn't stop thinking about Jessy Monroe—and he couldn't figure out why.

It wasn't even like she was his type—not that he'd had a "type" since Ann left. He usually liked long, cool blondes—not short, feverish brunettes. But there was something about Jessy—something gentle and kind and almost impossible for him to define. She didn't want him to think she was vulnerable, didn't want him to think she needed anyone's help, but that just made him want to help her even more. Maybe she just brought out the macho-manly-man instincts in him. What the hell did he know anymore? He hadn't trusted his own feelings since the divorce.

So what *was* it about Jessy Monroe? He'd first noticed her in

Illinois, after he'd transferred onto the bus for the last leg of his trip when his flight home had been canceled. At the dinner stop, as everyone boarded the bus again, an elderly woman had taken a nasty spill on a patch of icy sidewalk. He'd immediately started towards her, but Jessy had gotten there first, the only one who'd bothered to help the lady up again. He'd jogged to catch up with them, nearly breaking his own neck on the ice, and helped Jessy carry both her luggage and the old woman's onto the bus. His introduction had been uninspired, but she'd smiled at him, and that smile had warmed him in a way he couldn't quite understand or explain. Even though her smile had eventually faded into a guarded wariness, Michael was already hooked.

But what was he getting himself into? She obviously didn't want to trust him and he really couldn't blame her for that. Who trusted strangers nowadays? And a woman traveling alone? He was surprised she even spoke to him.

Michael heard the shower stop, then the faint shuffle and bump of movement inside the small bathroom. She'd be coming out at any moment, and the thought made his heart beat just a little faster. And what was *that* all about? Was he attracted to her, or did he just feel sorry for her? Of course he was aware of her self-consciousness about her weight, but he hadn't really paid much attention to her size—although he doubted she would believe him if he ever admitted it to her. Instead, he'd noticed her hair, a dark chestnut brown that shone like silk. And he'd noticed her eyes, the way the light caught the flecks of gold in the depths of jade. And her smile—the way just the sight of it made him want to do whatever it took to keep her looking at him that way, like he was just the greatest guy she had ever seen.

But—

He wasn't looking to be interested in anyone right now. He had too many other things to deal with, like Ann's new demands about regaining custody of the kids. The last thing he needed or wanted was the hassle of being caught up in a relationship—especially a relationship with someone like Jessy Monroe, who he sensed needed to be handled with kid gloves. He didn't have the time or the patience *or* the inclination to be anything but a friendly stranger to Jessy.

So why couldn't he stop thinking about her? And why had he been so disappointed when she'd declined his invitation to spend Christmas with him and his family? Why did he care about her when only a few days ago he hadn't even known she existed?

Jessy stepped out of the bathroom dressed in a sweatshirt and a fresh pair of jeans, and Michael slowly sat up, watching as she combed her still-damp hair, noticing that she only cast quick gazes at her reflection. He remembered how Ann used to sit at her vanity like a queen, capable of spending hours brushing her hair or studying her face. Jessy acted like she couldn't bear to face herself, keeping her eyes downcast as she drew a comb through her thick chestnut hair.

He hadn't really noticed it before, but Jessy really *was* pretty—in a fragile, quiet way. Not beautiful in the traditional sense, but— there was something in her eyes, in her smile, that transformed her from merely pretty to something more than beautiful.

But he just felt sorry for her. That's what he had to keep reminding himself. He felt sorry for her because she was alone and upset and because he had a soft spot for strays. He didn't ask her to go home with him because he was interested in her. He just wanted to help her. Just wanted to be a friend.

Putting down the brush, Jessy turned around to face him, almost startled when she saw that he was already watching her. Her long hair shone in the amber light of the room, curling loosely over her shoulders, framing her pale face in soft waves. Freshly scrubbed and completely without make-up, Jessy looked far younger than her years, innocent in a way Michael hadn't noticed before. To think of her alone in the world, vulnerable to all the predators out there—

Yeah, he was definitely doing the right thing by helping her out. No ulterior motives. He was just trying to be a nice guy.

"The—uh—bathroom's yours," she said quietly, hurrying past him. She busied herself by fumbling through her suitcase, keeping her back to him as she sorted through her clothes.

What was she like before this happened, Michael wondered. What was she like when she could smile without looking over her shoulder, when she could laugh without wondering if someone was going to hurt her? What might have happened between them if he'd met her in a different time, a different situation? Would he have even noticed her?

Michael didn't really want to know the answer to that one. Not that he had anything against overweight people, but Jessy was the first overweight woman who had ever really attracted him. If he'd passed her on the street, he really didn't know if he would have taken the time to actually look at her. Jessy was pleasant enough at first glance, but she wasn't as obvious and overstated as most of the women Michael had seen. He'd always thought the whole concept of "inner beauty" was a cliché—until he met Jessy.

She half-turned to face him just then, catching him before he could act like he hadn't been staring. Thank God she couldn't read his mind.

"I'm—um—" He cleared his throat, backing toward the bathroom. He felt as if a switch had been thrown, casting new light on Jessy. "I'll be in here—"

Jessy silently nodded, frowning faintly at his sudden awkwardness. "Okay."

"Okay—" Michael managed a smile, then ducked into the bathroom, exhaling slowly as he closed the door behind him. *No ulterior motives,* he kept repeating to himself. *You're just trying to be a nice guy. That's all.*

That's all.

THE BATH should have made her sleepy. Instead she was wide-awake as she crawled into the bed, self-conscious in her baggy sweatshirt. Not that Michael was making things any better. She felt as if he watched her every movement, evaluating her. She knew she didn't look too great, but did he *have* to stare at her like that?

Jessy curled up on the bed, making sure to keep close to the edge, and closed her eyes as she pulled the covers up to her chin. The sound of the running shower was almost hypnotic, lulling her into a light doze. Good. She wanted to avoid any more uncomfortable moments by being asleep by the time he got out.

No such luck.

Michael was one of those five-minute shower types, and he stepped out of the steamy bathroom before Jessy could even begin to relax. He'd changed clothes, trading a worn flannel shirt and faded jeans for a faded Northwestern T-shirt and a pair of baggy black sweatpants. Jessy watched him warily as he roughly towel-dried his hair and looped the towel around his neck, then brushed his teeth. She'd never seen a man's post-shower routine before, and something about Michael's mundane actions fascinated her. Probably because he looked gorgeous even with wet hair and a mouthful of toothpaste foam.

"So how are you feeling?" he asked as he rinsed his toothbrush. His dark hair stood wildly on end and he took a moment to smooth it down, barely glancing at his reflection. "Still at death's door?"

"I'm fine," she said quietly. And of course her lungs decided at that moment to spasm in a series of wracking coughs.

"Yeah, right." He studied her closely as he ambled over to the bed, sitting on its edge as he pressed his palm against her cheek, then across her forehead. His touch was so gentle, so fatherly, that for just an instant she felt like she was ten years old again.

"You feel a little warm," he said, moving his hand to her cheek again, lingering there an instant too long. Jessy felt her face grow even warmer. "Maybe we should get you to a doctor."

"I'm fine. Really." Jessy tried to smile again, but an unexpected wave of wheezing coughs took her breath away for a few moments.

"If that's *fine*, then I'd hate to see you when you're *really* sick." He studied her for a few moments, gaze tracking over her face, and Jessy felt suddenly self-conscious, all too aware of her double chin, her puffy cheeks.

"Why are you being so nice?" she whispered. "What do you want from me?"

The good humor faded from his eyes even though his slanting smile remained. He looked away from her for a moment, laughing softly to himself as he shook his head. Funny thing was, he didn't sound a bit amused.

"What kind of question is that?" he asked quietly, gaze flicking up to hers again.

"A legitimate one." Jessy spoke softly, but she could almost feel the hardness creeping into her tone. "Sorry if I offended you, but good Samaritans usually have ulterior motives whether they want to admit it or not."

Michael straightened, shoulders stiffening as he took a deep breath. Jessy instantly regretted her words—but she wasn't about to apologize for the way she felt.

Without a word he stood up and went back to the sink, leaning against the countertop for a few moments, his head down and shoulders hunched.

"All I want to do is help you out, Jessy." Michael's voice, when he finally spoke, was almost so gruffly soft that Jessy couldn't hear him. He raised his head and she could finally see his face again. Anger had given way to a peculiar sadness in his eyes. For a moment she almost felt guilty for doubting him. *Almost.*

"You might as well give up if you're looking for hidden agendas and ulterior motives. If you won't—" He cut himself off, sighing heavily as he looked away, his mouth tightening into a straight line. "I think you should get some sleep now."

"No," Jessy said as he crossed the room. "If I won't *what?*"

He settled down in one of the plastic chairs with a pillow and a spare blanket. Without so much as a glance in her direction, he stretched his long legs out and propped his feet on the edge of the bed, crossing them at the ankle as he pulled the blanket up to his chin.

"If you won't even *attempt* to trust me," he said quietly, scooting down in a futile effort to find a comfortable position, "then I don't think we've got a hell of a lot more to say to each other."

Jessy blinked, startled. "Maybe we don't," she managed to say.

"Good night," he said quietly, shifting uncomfortably, contorting his neck as he stuffed the pillow between his head and shoulder. He closed his eyes without waiting for Jessy's reply.

Jessy rolled onto her side, away from him, and pulled the blanket over her head. Fine. Let him sulk if he wanted to. Big man with hurt feelings—geez. She closed her eyes, suddenly tired of it all. Tired of thinking, tired of worrying, tired of wishing everything in her life was different. All she wanted to do was go home—

But she would never be able to do that again. The only home she had ever known had been gone for almost twenty years, ever since her mother and father had gone over a mountainside one snowy night. Amelia had tried her best to raise Jessy, but both of them knew it could never be the same. And now Amelia was gone, and the only person Jessy could depend on was herself.

She was scared to death that maybe that wouldn't be enough.

HOURS LATER, ragged coughs caught her by surprise, jerking her out of a troubled sleep. Jessy struggled to sit up, anything to ease the awful pressure in her chest. She couldn't breathe, couldn't catch her breath.

"Jessy?" Michael sat up, his silhouette outlined against the window. The sound of his voice snapped her out of the hallucination.

"Go back to sleep," she managed to stammer, finally catching her breath as she fell back against the pillows. "I'm okay—"

"Yeah, you sound just peachy," Michael murmured. Before Jessy knew what he was doing he had crawled onto the bed, settling down beside her as she leaned against the headboard. Jessy had thrown off the blankets, but he carefully covered her up again, adding his own blanket to the pile. "You need to see a doctor."

"I'm *fine*, Michael—" She took a shallow breath, then exploded in another wracking wave of coughs. After it passed she collapsed against the pillows, exhausted. "This cold just mutated on me, is all."

"C'mere." He gently pulled her against the warmth of his body, nestling her close to his chest as she coughed again. His hands stroked her hair, her back, and even though she cringed at the thought of him feeling the rolls of fat along her sides, his touch soothed her. She closed her eyes, relishing the unfamiliar feeling of security.

Michael began to hum softly, a song she remembered from her childhood. She could feel the rumble of sound in his throat, the scratch of his stubble against her skin as she nestled into the crook of his neck.

"This always works with my kids," he finally whispered, his words little more than a breath against her ear. She could almost hear the smile in his voice. His hand trailed over her upper arm, tracing light figure eights over her shoulder. "Any better now?"

"Yes," Jessy managed to whisper, not quite trusting her own voice. He touched her forehead and cheeks again, his palm soft against her skin.

"You're burning up," he murmured, pulling away from her. Confused, Jessy watched as he climbed out of bed and headed towards the bathroom. She closed her eyes again as a wave of chills washed over her, slipping into an uncomfortable half-doze as shivers wracked her. Everything felt like a dream.

Something cold pressed against her forehead and she instinctively tried to duck away.

"Shhh—it's okay. This will bring down your fever." Michael's voice calmed her almost instantly. He smoothed his hand over her hair and urged her head back to his chest. "Try to rest. I'm right here. I'm not going anywhere."

Groggy from the fever, Jessy nodded and closed her eyes as he pulled the covers up to her chin and tucked them around her shoulders, then curled his own body around hers. She drifted to sleep listening to the steady sound of his heartbeat, the soft hush of his breath, safe within the circle of his arms.

And it felt like the most natural thing in the world.

Chapter Four

By THE TIME Jessy woke up the next morning, the blizzard had passed and the sun had returned with a vengeance. Wincing at the light that streamed through the half-open curtains, Jessy was instantly aware of three things: that the television was on, soundlessly flashing manic pictures of what looked to be a Thanksgiving Day parade; that she didn't feel like she was camping out on death's doorstep anymore; and that she was now utterly alone in the room.

"Michael?" she said as she slowly sat up, still squinting against the glare of sunlight. She might not feel like she was dying anymore, but she wasn't exactly bursting with energy, either. Her head alone felt like it weighed a hundred pounds. "*Michael?*"

No response. He was gone.

Coughing as she leaned against the headboard, Jessy closed her eyes again. So Michael had left while the leaving was good. What a shocker. She'd known all along that nobody could be *that* nice, *that* generous. Maybe he was one of those sociopathic types who liked to mess with people's heads, building up their trust before destroying it completely. Maybe he liked to play mind-games with unattractive women, making them feel almost desirable and wanted, then annihilating their sense of self-worth.

Good thing she hadn't fallen for that. Good thing she'd kept her wits about her and saw through his little act. Otherwise, she might be feeling disappointed right now. Or she might actually—God forbid—miss him.

She had almost managed to talk herself into believing that little spiel until she remembered how he helped her get through the night. He'd wrapped his arms around her without a moment's hesitation, comforting her without judgment. He'd whispered soothing words into her ear, stroking her hair, until she'd finally slipped into the first good night's sleep she'd had in years.

Yeah, good thing she hadn't fallen for all that.

A key rattled in the lock and Michael stepped into the room, a grocery bag in each arm. Unaware of her surprised stare, he stomped the snow from his boots, humming "Jingle Bells" with unabashed enthusiasm. When he finally turned around and saw her staring at him, he grinned and closed the door with a nudge of his elbow. Jessy knew she shouldn't be so glad to see him again, but she couldn't help it. All at once she felt a jillion times better.

"Hey—she lives," he said, grin growing almost impossibly wide and crinkling his eyes until they nearly disappeared. What had been merely stubble the night before was a full-fledged salt and pepper beard. "Good morning, Sleeping Beauty."

Jessy nodded faintly. She was so sure that he'd left for good that she half-suspected she was imagining him. "Morning—"

"Happy Thanksgiving," he said as he put down the bags and shrugged out of his jacket. He wore a red and black flannel shirt over black thermal underwear—the classic lumberjack look—and Jessy caught herself staring. She quickly looked away, but her gaze was drawn to him again despite her best efforts.

"Hope you're hungry," he said, oblivious to her stare. "It's not my mom's turkey and dressing, but—"

He snagged one of the bags and reached into it, withdrawing a loaf of bread, a package of turkey lunchmeat, bags of potato chips and pretzels, and a six-pack of soda.

"And for ze—how you zay—dessert—" he said, mangling a faux French accent as he reached into the bag one last time and pulled out a handful of candy bars. "Gas stations, by the way, are not great places to shop for Thanksgiving dinners."

Jessy had to smile. "Looks like you did okay."

"And for you, oh plague-ridden one—" He grinned, upending the other brown bag onto the bed beside her. Boxes and bottles of cold pills, flu pills, and cough syrups fell onto the blankets. It looked like he'd bought at least one of every cold medicine on the market. The man obviously didn't believe in doing anything half-way.

"What did you do?" she asked, looking up to him again. The smile on his face made her toes curl. "Buy out the store?"

"I wasn't sure about what you needed, so I didn't take any chances." Michael grinned and sat down on the edge of the bed, flattening his palm against her forehead. The touch of his hand did strange things to her heartbeat. "How are you feeling today?"

"Better," Jessy smiled self-consciously. She ran a hand through her long hair, hoping to tame it into some semblance of order, and managed to meet his gaze again. "Where'd you get all this stuff?"

"There's a little gas station about a mile down the road." He unexpectedly reached up and brushed a strand of hair from her forehead—and that was it for her defenses. She knew herself well enough to realize when she was in trouble, and she was in serious trouble now. She liked him. She really liked him. And liking him was the absolute *last* thing she needed in her life right now.

Oh, Lord—this wasn't good. This wasn't good at all.

"I had a chance to talk to the bus driver on the way out," Michael said quietly, some of his smile fading. "Want to hear the news?"

Jessy nodded silently, not quite trusting herself enough to speak.

Michael shifted forward slightly, frowning as he laced his fingers together and rested his forearms on his knees. He didn't speak for a few seconds, staring intently at his hands instead. "The roads are clear," he said quietly, raising his gaze to hers again. "We'll probably be back on the highway in two or three hours."

"I see," Jessy said, already missing him. "So—I guess this is it, then. Isn't it?"

"I guess so." He took a deep breath and sighed, wrinkling his brow as he absently scratched at his cheek, looking away from her for a moment. "Jess—I've been thinking—"

He finally looked back to her again, trying for a smile that didn't quite reach his eyes. For the first time she noticed the sadness in them, an almost weary grief that lingered even when he smiled. It was as if life had disappointed him one too many times, a feeling that Jessy knew all too well.

It was then that—as much as she hated to admit it to herself—she realized that she trusted him. It wasn't because he was friendly and handsome. It wasn't because of his sweet smile and charming manner. She trusted him because of his eyes, because of the sadness, the shared pain.

Oh, God—she didn't want to have these feelings. She didn't want to like him, didn't want to be attracted to him—but it was too late now. She liked him. She trusted him. And she would miss him when they had to go their separate ways.

This *definitely* wasn't good. Wasn't good at all.

"So—" She cleared her throat quietly and forced a faint smile. "What were you thinking about?"

"To be completely honest," Michael's own smile fell away as he gently took her hand. "I've been thinking about *you*. A lot." He laughed quietly, shaking his head at himself. "More than I probably should."

The touch of his hand sent a ripple of shock through Jessy, but that paled compared to his words. What was *this* about?

"I have to tell you," he said quietly, gazing at their joined hands for a moment, then back to her eyes again. "I don't think I can go home knowing that you're wandering around the country by yourself."

"Michael—"

"I know, I know—it's not real politically correct of me to even admit something like that, but I can't help it. I just don't like the thought of you riding around the country alone and sick."

"I appreciate your concern, but it's not—"

"Listen, I know it's hard to let anybody do anything for you. Trust me. I know." He looked into her eyes with such sincerity that Jessy's few remaining doubts vanished. "But you can't keep running away—"

"I'll go home with you," Jessy said softly.

"—because there are some good people out there who won't hurt—" His voice trailed away as he frowned. "What did you just say?"

"I said I'll go home with you." Jessy could barely believe she was even saying the words, but there they were. Point of no return. She was actually agreeing to go home with Michael Forrester—a total stranger. "But just until Christmas, okay?"

"Make it New Year's and you've got a deal," he said and grinned.

Jessy studied him for a moment, not quite sure if he was serious. Despite his smile and comically arched eyebrows, Jessy knew he'd meant it when he said he would worry about her. *Why,* she didn't understand—but her instincts were telling her to trust him, that here was someone who could be the friend she so badly needed. She knew better than to even hope that anything else could come of the relationship. Michael Forrester was willing to take her into his home as a friend, and it didn't matter if she weighed a hundred pounds or a thousand. If there was one thing she needed more than anything right now, it was a friend.

"Okay," Jessy said and smiled, shaking his hand. "Deal."

"MY TURN already?" Michael grinned, keeping his eyes on the slushy road as he drove. "What letter are we on?"

"You're stalling." Jessy ignored the scenery to look at Michael—who was far more interesting, in Jessy's opinion, than a bunch of snowy farms. They'd been on the road since he'd rented a car at the Minneapolis bus terminal that afternoon, and now they were on the last leg of the journey. "And we're on the letter C."

"C, huh. Lemme see—state capital that begins with the letter C—"

"Give up anytime you feel like it."

"Forresters do not give up." Michael's grin slanted as he glanced over to Jessy and winked. "We just whine and pout until we get our way."

Jessy laughed and looked out the window as Michael tried to think of an answer. The sun was setting over the snowy plains, and for just an instant Jessy felt homesick for eastern Kentucky's hills.

"Who thought up this goofy game, anyway?" Michael grumbled, not a bit subtle with his attempts to make Jessy smile.

He drummed his fingers against the wheel as he drove, forehead furrowing slightly as he concentrated on the road. Watching him, Jessy realized that he had the kind of good looks that would never be boring—at least, not to her. She couldn't decide which feature she liked the most: his hang-dog, smiling eyes or his silver-laced dark hair. Or his beautiful, graceful hands. Or his wide, friendly smile—

He glanced over to her and caught her staring. Jessy managed a quick, startled smile and added one more thing to her list: his dimples. Men should not be allowed to have dimples like that.

"Charleston!" he said suddenly, a huge grin on his face. "Charleston, West Virginia—so *hah!*"

Jessy laughed, forcing the lovesick thoughts to the back of her mind. "Very nice. It took long enough, but very nice anyway."

"Thank you—I think." He glanced away from the road again, smiling at her. "You nervous?"

"Who, me? Nervous?" Jessy laughed dismissively, then nodded, suddenly sober. "Like you would not believe."

"Well, relax. They'll love you." He reached over and cupped her cheek with his hand—which might have seemed to be a romantic gesture if Jessy hadn't known he was just checking her temperature again. "How are you feeling?"

"I'm hopped up on cold pills, but I'm okay." Jessy smiled, missing the touch of his hand the instant he lowered it from her cheek. "I just hope I don't infect your kids."

"My kids are walking petri dishes. They'll be fine." Michael smiled and turned off the highway and onto a side road. As they passed beneath a snow-covered wooden arch, Jessy could see nothing but acres of rolling, snow-covered countryside.

"Don't tell me *this* is the farm," she said as she gazed out the side window, catching a glimpse of cows wandering near a huge red barn, nosing through the snow in search of grass. "Wow."

"You flatter me." Michael grinned as Jessy turned to him again. "But yeah, this is the farm. What do you think?"

"I didn't expect it to be this big. Or to have so many cows."

"We tend to have those at dairy farms," Michael said with a teasing smile.

Jessy knew she was gaping like a tourist, but she couldn't help it. She could almost imagine how the farm would look in the spring, with the willow trees in bloom and the rolling hills carpeted in thick green grass. When she realized that she wouldn't be there to see the seasons change, she felt a wholly unexpected twinge of sadness. By spring she'd be far, far away from upstate Minnesota.

"And there's the house. We're home," Michael said softly. Something in his voice, in the smile on his lips, touched Jessy deeply. Michael was finally home, and to him, *home* represented something that Jessy had not known for a very long time. Home meant family. Love. Home meant far more to Michael than it did to most people. His home was his life—and he had offered to share it with her, if only for a few weeks.

The realization was at once touching and overwhelming. She hadn't known how deeply she'd yearned for a sense of home—even if it was someone else's.

Distracted by the expression on his face, Jessy didn't notice the house itself until Michael pulled into the horseshoe-shaped driveway—and then she couldn't help but to stare. The Victorian house almost didn't seem real, suited more to a storybook than a Minnesota farm. Larger than she'd expected, the place was something out of a child's imagination, with gingerbread trim and pointed turrets and lots of oddly shaped little windows. A porch wrapped around the front of the house; rocking chairs and hanging swings and a hammock waited patiently for spring. Warm amber light spilled from the windows and onto the walkway leading up to the front steps, welcoming them home.

Michael eased the Bronco to a stop and cut the engine. "So, what do you think?" he asked quietly.

"I think this is the most beautiful place I've ever seen." Jessy smiled as she turned to him again. "It looks like a dollhouse my father made when I was a little girl."

"I'm building one for Libby," Michael said with another smile. "She's nuts for miniatures and dolls and all that stuff."

It wasn't until that moment that Jessy realized that she knew almost nothing about Michael's kids. She knew that his twins, Ben and Marie, were six and that Ben loved dinosaurs and Marie wanted to be a ballerina princess. And she knew that his oldest daughter, Libby, was a very mature ten and that she was allergic to shellfish and oranges and wanted to be a veterinarian when she grew up. But that was all she knew. She'd grown so comfortable with Michael that she'd completely forgotten that he was almost a complete stranger.

"I don't know if this is going to work," she said quietly, suddenly self-conscious. She looked down at her baggy jeans and oversized sweater and felt her cheeks burn crimson. What on Earth would his mother think of her?

And that led to another thought—

"Michael—did you happen to tell anyone you were bringing me home?"

"Ah—well—" Michael cleared his throat and shrugged. "Um—not really."

Jessy buried her face in her hands. "Oh, God—"

"Now just calm down—no need to panic—"

"I thought you were going to call home first."

"I *was*—" He smiled weakly. "I just kinda forgot."

But now it was too late. The front door opened just as a little boy's delighted shout split the silence. "Daddy's home!"

"Might as well come meet the family," Michael said, quickly scooting out of the car. Jessy glared after him for a moment, then took a deep breath and followed his lead. She could almost smell the impending doom in the air.

"Daddy!" Ben leapt off the top step and scrambled down the snowy walkway, followed closely by Marie, who wore a pink tulle tutu over her jeans. Laughing, Michael met them halfway, swooping both of them into his arms and kissing their cheeks with great, sloppy smacks, sending Marie and Ben into gales of giggles. Jessy hung back, sticking close to the car as the front door opened again and Michael's mother and a tall, muscular man stepped onto the front porch. As Jessy had expected, their welcoming smiles turned slightly puzzled when they saw her with Michael.

God help me, she thought and plastered her friendliest smile on her face. All of a sudden she wanted to do nothing but burrow into the nearest snowdrift and tunnel out of there Bugs Bunny-style.

Blissfully oblivious to his family's confusion, Michael turned to Jessy as he hefted Ben onto his shoulders. "Jessy, these rugrats are my twins, Ben and Marie. Guys, this is my friend, Miss Jessy Monroe."

"H'lo," Jessy said and raised her hand in a feeble wave, feeling her cheeks blaze as she nodded her greetings to the kids. She knew Michael was watching her with that familiar teasing smile on his lips—which did absolutely nothing to help her relax.

"And I'm the *big* rugrat's mother," Michael's mother said, smiling as she stepped off the porch. Jessy felt almost immediately at ease, seeing nothing but friendly curiosity in the woman's eyes as she extended her hand. "Lyssa Forrester. Nice to meet you."

Jessy felt awkward and huge as she shook Lyssa's hand. Michael's mother was petite and birdlike, with the same twinkling eyes as her son and a headful of curly silver hair that she pulled back with a girlish headband. She possessed an aura of warmth that enveloped Jessy and eased away her nervousness. Jessy liked her instantly.

"Jessy Monroe," Jessy said softly, forcing her smile to relax from what felt like a death's head grin. "Hello."

"Hiya, Mom." As Michael grinned and kissed his mother's cheek, Jessy caught the questioning look in Lyssa's eyes and felt the urge to explain everything to her right then and there. Oh, but this was awful. This was worse than awful.

Jessy looked up to the porch and caught the other man's eye. At first glance, he seemed to be a glowering, imposing giant of a man. Then he smiled, and Jessy recognized the same mischievous glint she'd seen in Michael and Lyssa's eyes.

"For Pete's sake, what are we doing standing out here in the snow?" Lyssa laughed and took Jessy's arm, shepherding her towards the porch. "I hope you two are hungry—I've got a twenty-five pound turkey in there with our name on it."

What'd you do?" Michael asked her, flicking a quick smile to Jessy as he put down Ben and Marie and straightened up again. "Postpone Thanksgiving for us?"

"Well—*technically* we postponed it." Lyssa looked at Jessy and winked. "We haven't started in on the leftovers yet."

Jessy couldn't help but smile, reminded of her own mother by Lyssa's teasing manner and warm eyes. As Lyssa hurried up the steps and disappeared into the house, Jessy felt a twinge of envy for Michael. He still had his mother. He had a whole family.

"And of course you skip out on the year *you* have dishwashing duty," the other man said, the gruffness in his voice contradicted by his smile.

"Jessy, this is my older brother, Frank." Michael smiled as he guided Jessy up the slippery porch steps. "Frank, this is Jessy Monroe. We met on the bus on my way up from Illinois."

"Poor thing. How'd you stand to be cooped up with him so long?" Frank smiled and playfully jabbed an elbow into Michael's side. Somehow he managed to look menacing even when he smiled, with his shaved bald head and dark, deep set eyes. He was just a few inches taller than Michael, but his huge shoulders and long legs made him seem gigantic. Jessy had to tilt her head back to smile at him as he shook her hand.

"Nice to meet you," Jessy said and smiled.

"Ditto." Frank glanced at Michael again, keeping a straight face even though his eyes gave him away. "So do you want me to run a background check when I get home?"

"Frank's a sheriff," Michael said dryly as Frank laughed and Jessy shakily smiled. "But he's more Barney Fife than Matt Dillon."

"Keep it up and you might hurt my feelings," Frank said and grinned. "Listen, I gotta go. I just got a call about some post-Thanksgiving domestic disturbances that I have to break up."

"Coming back for Christmas?"

"Hell, yes. Mom'll skin me alive if I don't." Frank looked over to Jessy, still smiling. "You'll still be here by then, I hope?"

Jessy nodded. "Unless they kick me out."

Frank glanced over to Michael again. "I think I like her."

Michael grinned and slung his arm around Jessy's shoulders, completely surprising her by the gesture. "Yeah, me too."

"Well, gotta go knock some heads together." Frank grinned as he shrugged into his jacket and jogged down the porch steps. "Take care, Mikey. See you at Christmas, Jessy."

They waved goodbye and waited until Frank's taillights were out of sight before Michael led her into the house. Her attention was immediately captured by the mouth-watering scents of roasted turkey and homemade bread. She was almost embarrassed to realize that she was starving.

They entered the foyer without speaking. Jessy took the opportunity to look around, unabashedly staring as she slipped out of her coat and followed Michael into the house. There was no television in the living room. Instead, an overstuffed couch and a set of leather wingback chairs surrounded the room's main attraction, a huge stone fireplace. Hand-crocheted afghans were artfully draped over the backs of the couch and chairs. Bookshelves lined the walls, and on the mantletop were dozens of framed photographs of Michael's family, frozen moments captured in color and black and white.

For a moment Jessy felt as if she had just stepped into one of her favorite childhood dreams, a home filled with warmth and love and happiness.

Michael knelt down in front of Ben and Marie gave them both quick kisses. "Where's your sister?"

"She's upstairs crying." Ben turned to Jessy and flashed her a gap-toothed grin. "Wanna come up and see my hamster? Miss Purty's real friendly."

"No, she isn't," Marie said and grimaced. "She poops on me when I try to hold her."

"Wait a second, guys," Michael said. "Why is Libby crying? What happened?"

Lyssa entered the living room, wiping her hands on a dishtowel as she read the sudden worry on Michael's face. "Don't worry, honey—Libby's fine. It's just that darn Christmas dance at the school."

"Oh, no." Michael managed a weak grimace. "This is something about a boy, isn't it?"

"Apparently Tommy Anderson is going to the dance with that stuck up little Kathleen McClure." Lyssa *tsked* and shook her head. "Boys that age are so silly. Can't see a diamond in a pile of coal."

"When did she get old enough to worry about boys?" Michael took a deep breath and sighed, smiling again to Jessy. "Would you like to meet my daughter?"

"Maybe I should wait until after you talk to her."

"To tell you the truth, I can use all the help I can get." Michael's smile slanted sadly. "Falling off her bike or fixing her dollhouse I can handle. This new stuff with boys and dating and clothes—" His voice trailed away as she shrugged. "Libby's ten going on forty. Sometimes I think she's more mature than I am."

"Not that *that's* such a great challenge," Lyssa said and smiled, winking at Jessy before bending at the waist to be eye-level with Ben and Marie. "How about some help making the tea? You can introduce Miss Purty to Jessy after dinner."

The twins grinned and ran full speed towards Lyssa, streaking past her as they disappeared into the kitchen. Lyssa managed to flash Michael and Jessy a quick smile before she hurried to chase after them. Alone with Michael in the living room, Jessy suddenly felt awkward again.

"Maybe you should go in to talk to Libby first," she said quietly.

"Trust me, I *need* you to be my back-up on this." Michael grinned as he led Jessy to the staircase, his hand lightly flattened against the small of her back. His touch made her feel uncomfortable, all too aware of her size. It was silly, really—obviously all he had to do was look at her and know how overweight she was—but for him to actually *feel* it—

She managed to glance up to him, surprised when she saw he was still smiling at her. Jessy only wished she knew how to interpret that smile. Was he laughing at her? Mocking her? She didn't think he was the kind of man who would do such a thing, but after so many years of dodging insults and ignoring vicious criticism, she was afraid to trust her instincts.

"Wait a second," Michael said as he stopped on the staircase, a few steps below Jessy. She turned to face him and was struck anew by the quiet warmth in his eyes. God, how she wanted to believe it was sincere. She wanted so badly to believe that he was a nice guy.

"What's wrong?" she asked quietly.

His smile held a moment as he shook his head slightly. "I just—I know all this is really weird for you, walking into the middle of my life like this, but—" His voice trailed away as he reached out and took her hand, holding it so carefully that Jessy felt as if she'd suddenly turned into spun sugar. "I'm glad you're here. I really am."

For a moment Jessy didn't know what to say or do. To her mortification tears suddenly burned her eyes. Hiding it with a smile, Jessy sniffed and swiped at her cheeks with the back of her hand. Michael wasn't fooled, but he had the good grace not to draw attention to her emotional slip.

"I know," he said softly, his voice as gentle as his gaze. He gave her hand a faint squeeze as he continued up the stairs, Jessy at his side.

Comfortably silent, they continued to Libby's room, hands still lightly entwined. For Jessy, the mere act of holding Michael's hand felt at once unnatural and wonderful. She knew that most women would take such a thing for granted, but she couldn't—and she didn't think she ever would. Human contact was unfamiliar and strange, but now she found that she craved it.

And now that she realized what she had been missing, it would make it that much harder to eventually leave.

They stopped in front of Libby's door and Michael knocked lightly. Jessy subtly slid her hand out of his; she knew that if she were Libby, the last thing she'd want to see was her father with another woman and get the wrong idea. She knew from her students that kids usually hoped that their divorced parents might get back together. And who knows, maybe Michael and his ex-wife *could* reconcile. His ex would have to be a complete idiot not to realize what she was giving up.

"Libs? Can I come in?" Michael knocked again when there was no reply. "Libby, honey—"

"The door's open." Libby's voice sounded thick with tears, and as Michael opened the door Jessy instantly understood the true cause of Libby's pain.

Libby Forrester was ten years old and extremely pretty, with long dark hair and her father's chocolate-brown eyes—and she was at least fifty pounds overweight. Jessy looked at Libby and saw herself at that age: unhappy and lonely and frustrated. Her heart went out to the girl.

"What's wrong, sweetie?" Michael asked as he sat beside Libby and held his arms out to her. Libby fell into them gratefully, her sobs renewed as she buried her face against his chest. Michael looked up to Jessy and she could see his own pain; whatever had hurt Libby was hurting Michael twice as much.

"He—he said I was too fat—" Libby moaned, her breath catching miserably as she looked up to Michael again. Jessy remained in the doorway, still unnoticed by Libby. She had to fight the urge to go to the girl and put her arms around her.

"Who did?" Michael asked, the slightest edge of protective anger creeping into his even tone. He gently wiped the tears from Libby's cheeks. *"Who,* Libs?"

"Tommy Anderson," she said quietly, looking down at her lap. Her father's presence seemed to calm her greatly. "Somebody told him I liked him, and he told a bunch of people that I was too fat to take to the dance. So he asked Kat McClure instead." Libby raised her gaze to her father's, and Jessy could see a maturity in her eyes that far exceeded an average ten year old's. "He's right, isn't he? Boys don't like me because I'm too fat."

"Oh, Libby," Michael kissed her forehead, pulling her close to him. "It's not like that at all."

"Then why—?" Libby's voice trailed away as she finally noticed Jessy in the hallway. Her expression immediately tightened, and Jessy suddenly wished she'd stayed downstairs and allowed Michael this time alone with his daughter. "Who's *that?*"

Michael took a deep breath and sighed. Apparently he'd picked up on the same note of accusation in his daughter's voice that Jessy had heard. "Libby, this is my friend Jessy Monroe. We met on the bus and—I invited her to stay with us for Christmas."

Libby stared at Jessy for what felt like an eternity, studying her with an intensity that made Jessy blush. She managed a faint smile, hoping she looked friendly and unthreatening. Some of the distrust faded from Libby's eyes, and Jessy thought she might understand why: Libby knew that her father could never be anything but friends with someone overweight like Jessy. Common sense and her own painful experience told her *that* much.

"But Dad—" Libby looked back to Michael again. "What about Mom?"

Jessy cringed. Great. She stood mutely by the door, completely bewildered by how to handle this situation. Anything she said or did now would be wrong, anyway. If she came on too strong, too friendly, Libby would think she was just trying to butter her up and get on her good side. If she remained quiet and calm, she would seem like an aloof witch who didn't care.

How did she get herself into these situations?

"Libby—" Michael's voice was firmer, but no less loving. "Your mom and I have talked to you about this. I'm sorry, baby, but I don't think we can ever go back to the way things were."

"Don't you still love her?"

Michael glanced almost guiltily to Jessy—which struck her as odd, because why should she care if he still loved his ex-wife? Of course, for some stupid reason she *did* care, but he didn't need to know that.

"I'll always love your mother because of you and Ben and Marie," Michael said softly. "But we don't love each other enough to be married. It wouldn't be fair to any of us."

"But what if she came back?" Libby asked, voice very quiet. "Like to spend Thanksgiving with us?"

Michael stiffened slightly. "What are you talking about, Lib?"

"Mom's coming home for Thanksgiving. She called while you

were gone." Libby smiled slightly, a hopeful glow in her eyes. "She *never* spends Thanksgiving with us. Maybe she's going to stay this time."

"Lib, honey—" Michael seemed at a loss for words. He helplessly glanced at Jessy, not that she could help him out. She felt just as stunned as him, if not more so.

"Libby!" Lyssa yelled from downstairs. "Time to set the table!"

Taking that as her cue, Libby scrambled off the bed and hurried out of the room, leaving Jessy and Michael to look at each other in a suddenly awkward silence.

"Your wife is coming home?" Jessy finally managed to say, hating the squeaky nervousness in her voice.

"*Ex*-wife. And I had no idea." Michael ran a hand through his hair and took a deep breath. "Usually she just calls the kids."

"Maybe I shouldn't stay," Jessy said softly. She straightened up and nodded to herself. "Yeah, I should go. This is—you should be with your family."

She hurried out into the hallway and was halfway down the steps before Michael caught up with her. He gently grabbed her arm and turned her around to face him. "Jess—wait a minute—"

"I shouldn't—" Jessy took a breath and closed her eyes for a moment, collecting her thoughts. "This is the first Thanksgiving your kids have had with their mom for a long time. I shouldn't be here."

"Yes, you should."

"I'm intruding."

"No, you're not."

Jessy gazed at him for a moment. He was so placid, so damnably self-confident with his calmness, that she could almost believe the idea of staying wouldn't turn into a horrible fiasco.

"What will your wife—ex-wife—think if I'm here?"

"I don't care what she thinks." Michael smiled faintly, deepening his dimples ever so slightly, and studied Jessy for a few moments. She could almost feel the tension floating out of her body; how someone could have so much of a calming effect on her, she'd never understand. "I want you to be here. For me."

"I don't want to cause trouble between you—"

"You won't. Trust me. Our problems were around a long time before you entered the picture." Michael's smile widened. "So will you stay? Please? For me?"

"Boy, you're really working the puppy-dog eyes, aren't you?" Jessy couldn't help but grin.

"Is it doing anything for you?"

"Possibly."

"Then yeah, I'm working the puppy-dog eyes." Michael batted his lashes and laughed. "Really, Jessy. I'd like you to stay."

Jessy took a deep breath and gazed at him for a moment, and finally nodded. "Okay. But I swear, if you two start reinacting 'Kramer vs. Kramer' I'm out of here. Seriously."

Michael laughed and slung his arm around her shoulders, a casual gesture that caused Jessy's heart to catch and stutter. "You've got yourself a deal. Now let's go eat."

Jessy allowed him to lead her down the stairs and into the dining room, wondering just what fresh hell she'd stumbled into now.

Chapter Five

JESSY FELT AS JUMPY as a cat, even though dinner was blissfully uneventful, with no sign of the mythical ex-wife. Which was fine. The longer Jessy could put off that eventual confrontation, the better. The woman was in for a potentially unpleasant surprise.

Jessy ate sparingly, even though dinner was delicious and she felt like she could demolish the entire tray of cornbread dressing by herself. She tried to relax and enjoy the dinner, but she could tell just by looking at Michael that he felt just as tense. Even Lyssa didn't seem too happy about the prospect of hosting her ex-daughter-in-law for dinner.

At least the kids were happy, and their unabashed joy helped Michael unclench his jaw and smile more as the dinner wore on. By the time all of the second and third helpings had been eaten, the atmosphere at the table was as relaxed as it was going to be. As they talked and laughed and got to know each other, Jessy realized that they made her feel more welcome than she had ever felt in her life.

And it was all because of Michael. The warmth she saw in his eyes, the quiet joy in his smile, made her feel as though she truly belonged somewhere—and that scared her. She didn't want to get too close to him and his family, but she couldn't bear to keep her distance, either. She needed this too badly.

"Dinner was great, Mom." Michael smiled as he folded his napkin and leaned back in his chair, looking over to Jessy. She returned his smile and quickly looked away. Prolonged eye contact with him still made her feel antsy and way too warm.

"Well, it wasn't *all* my doing." Lyssa looked to Ben and smiled. "I had some help, didn't I?"

"Yeah," Ben said, flashing Jessy a snaggle-toothed smile. "I helped make the tea."

"Daddy says we make the best tea in the world," Marie said proudly.

"And your daddy's absolutely right." Jessy took another sip of tea and smiled at Michael over the rim of her glass. He grinned and lazily draped an arm over the back of Ben's chair, unabashedly staring at her.

Hoo boy, Jessy thought as she struggled to swallow the tea without choking. *That man knows how to use those eyes. He's lethal.*

"Michael tells me you're a woman of mystery," Lyssa said with a teasing smile. Jessy gratefully turned her attention away from Michael's disconcerting stare, even though she had a bad feeling some personal questions were coming up. "What exactly do you do in Kentucky?"

"I teach third grade." Jessy managed to keep from glancing back to Michael, even though she could feel him still watching her.

Lyssa's smile widened—and if Jessy wasn't mistaken, she thought she could see something like approval in the older woman's eyes. "So you like children, I take it?"

"Yes, Mom," Michael said as he stood and began gathering plates. "Especially broiled and served with carrots."

Lyssa laughed. "Okay—point taken. I'm getting snoopy."

"But we love you anyway," Michael said, pausing just long enough to kiss the top of his mother's head as he passed behind her chair. Jessy, smiling, caught Michael's eye as he haphazardly stacked the rest of the dinner dishes. As he walked out of the room she forgot herself for a moment and stared at his broad back and shoulders, admiring his effortless grace, his easy strength, his jeans clinging so tightly to his—

Lyssa cleared her throat and Jessy, red-faced and flustered, looked back to the table. How could she lust after him in front of his own *mother?*

"You know, I feel like I should thank you." Lyssa glanced over to Marie and Ben to make sure they weren't listening. Instead, they were embroiled in a take-no-prisoners game of thumb wrestling. "With everything that's been going on here, it's just good to see Michael smile again."

Jessy's smile half-slanted into a frown. "Thank *me?* Why?"

"Well—" Lyssa lowered her voice and leaned forward slightly. "I'm sure Michael's mentioned his—situation."

"Situation? He hasn't really said anything—"

"No, Michael wouldn't." Lyssa sighed and frowned slightly, shaking her head. "I probably shouldn't be saying anything, but I think you should know."

The bad feeling in the pit of Jessy's stomach was getting worse by the second. "Is everything okay? Is it one of the kids?"

"Oh, no—thank God, no. It's nothing like that." Lyssa smiled faintly as her gaze went back to Marie and Ben. "It's his ex-wife, Ann." Lyssa dropped her voice to a whisper. "She's talking about asking for custody of the children."

Ben leaned against Jessy's arm. "Can I sit on your lap, Jessy?"

"Sure, honey—" Distracted, Jessy helped him crawl up to her lap, more than a little stunned by Lyssa's words. Custody?

"I want to sit on your lap, too," Marie said, climbing aboard before Jessy could say anything. Laughing, she helped Marie squirm into a comfortable spot. She'd forgotten how heavy a six-year-old could be. Two of them at the same time made her legs go almost instantly numb.

Ben cuddled close to Jessy, slinging one arm high around her neck, and cocked his head so that he could look up at her. Marie mimicked the gesture, playing idly with a lock of Jessy's hair.

"Jessy," Ben said as he copied Marie and twirled a curl of Jessy's long hair, "do you like kids?"

"Well, sure. I used to be one, y'know."

Ben grinned, his nose crinkling. "Did you like dinosaurs?"

"Like dinosaurs?" Jessy's smile widened. "I used to ride them to

school."

Libby rolled her eyes and groaned, but Ben and Marie were delighted. "Really?" Marie asked.

"Uh-huh. I even had one as a pet."

"Was it friendly?"

"Oh, yeah." Jessy leaned forward, grimacing as she wrinkled her nose. "But cleaning the litter box was *yucky.*"

Ben and Marie giggled, and even Libby cracked a smile. Jessy glanced over to Lyssa and saw whole-hearted approval in the woman's expression. Great. Once again, Jessy Monroe impresses the bejeebers out of a guy's mother. If everything goes as it's always gone in the past, that means that Michael will have less than zero interest in her.

"Hey! Anybody home?"

The unexpected voice was unbearably cheery, and as Jessy saw the look of excitement that passed between Libby and Ben and Marie, she knew there was only one person the unannounced visitor could be.

Ann Forrester stepped into the dining room, thoughtlessly shaking snow from her hair and coat onto the carpet. Jessy's heart sank as she got her first look at her. Of course Ann was gorgeous. Of course. In jeans and a sweater, with her honey-blonde hair perfectly styled to fall over her shoulders, Ann looked like the girl-next-door turned perfect wife and mom. Watching her as she hugged Ben and Marie, Jessy felt her stomach turning inside out. Here was that other shoe she'd been expecting, and it packed a wallop.

Michael stepped out of the kitchen, his expression neutral. He dried his hand on a dishtowel and slung it over his shoulder, a muscle in his jaw twitching as he stared at Ann.

But Ann wasn't aware of Michael just yet. Her smile had frozen on her lips as she fixed on Jessy, a strained politeness that didn't quite mask the unpleasant look in her eyes.

Jessy managed to smile pleasantly back to her. After all, just because the woman was beautiful didn't necessarily mean she'd be judgmental. Jessy always hated it when people made assumptions about her personality just because of the way she looked; she could at least extend that same courtesy to Ann. Even if she *was* Michael's ex.

Then in the next instant Jessy was dismissed from Ann's attention as she knelt to scoop Ben into a bear hug. "Look at you, Benny-boy!" Ann laughed as she picked Ben up and squeezed him. "You're getting so big! And Marie—you're getting prettier and prettier every time I see you!"

Libby joined them, smiling brightly. "Hi, Mom!"

Ann's reaction to her oldest daughter stunned Jessy. The smile slid away, replaced by disappointment. "Oh, Libby—you *promised* me you'd lose some weight!"

Jessy inhaled sharply, offended on Libby's behalf. The girl's smile dropped instantly, the pain in her eyes obvious to everyone in the room but Ann. Michael stepped out of the kitchen doorway and went to his daughter's rescue.

"It might be nice to say hello to your daughter before you start criticizing her," he said quietly.

"Hello, Mike." Ann's voice, husky yet soft, seemed inordinately loud in the quiet of the room. The affection in it sent an unpleasant shiver of premonition down Jessy's spine. "I've missed you."

Ann suddenly blinked, catching herself after an obvious moment of hesitation, all the better to allow the full impact of her slip of the tongue to hit home. "And the kids," she added feebly. "*All* of you. Even Mom."

"I'm not your mother, Ann." Lyssa stood and walked out of the room, surprising Jessy with her abrupt coldness. She looked back to Ann just in time to see her roll her eyes impatiently.

And at that moment, Jessy instantly knew what kind of woman Ann was.

"It's been too long," Ann said, gaze softening as she smiled wistfully. "I can only stay for dinner, unfortunately. I have to get back to Chicago to interview the mayor and—" She sighed, still smiling. "And never mind all that right now. It's just good to be home."

"This hasn't been your home for a few years now," Michael said mildly, leaning against the back of a chair. "Or have you forgotten?"

"I could never forget you. Or the kids."

Jessy had never felt so conspicuous, so overwhelmingly out of place, in her entire life. She forced herself to stand her ground, to at least have the dignity to act unaffected by the entire show. She had the distinct feeling that Ann was marking territory, letting her know exactly where she stood in the grand scheme of things. And for some reason, that triggered a stubborn streak that Jessy hadn't realized she'd possessed. If this was going to be a battle of wills, then damned if she'd be the one to break first.

"I didn't expect you to have *company*, Michael." Ann's voice was as annoyingly insincere as her smile.

"Jessy's a friend," Michael said quietly. "Jessy, this is Ann Forrester—my ex-wife."

"Dating so soon?" Ann's smile was venomous, not quite making its way up to her eyes. "She doesn't seem to be your type, sweetie."

Jessy managed a pained smile. She couldn't ever remember disliking someone quite so much on just a first impression.

Lyssa came out of the kitchen with dessert—a tray filled with pies and cakes—and, with a cool glance in Ann's direction, placed it on the table and left the room. Ann's smiling mask slipped as she watched Lyssa go, her narrowed eyes blazing for just an instant before she refocused her attention on Michael again. The whole drama happened so quickly, no one else noticed.

But Jessy had.

Libby had taken a small sliver of pecan pie, as well as a small sliver of pumpkin, and was beginning to spoon whipped cream on top when Ann reached over and snatched the plate from her hands. "Honestly, Libby—do you really think you need dessert?"

Libby's face turned crimson in humiliation, and Jessy had to grit her teeth, gripping her fork so tightly she thought she might bend it in half. She glanced across the table and saw that Michael was just as furious.

"Ann—" Michael's voice held a note of warning that Ann ignored. Jessy could see that Michael's ex was either quite good at remaining blissfully ignorant, or she just didn't care. She had a feeling it was the latter.

"Michael, Libby's already at least fifty pounds overweight. Do you want her to blow up like—" Ann's eyes cut to Jessy—a subtle, yet meaningful glance—before she continued. "Like a whale?"

"It's okay, Dad," Libby said quietly, pushing away from the table. "I'm not hungry anyway."

"Honey—"

"Let her go," Ann said. "It wouldn't kill her to miss a few meals."

On the verge of tears, Libby walked out of the dining room. Michael helplessly watched her go, then pushed himself away from the table. "I'm going to go talk to her."

"Don't," Ann said coldly. "You shouldn't go running every time she gets her feelings hurt. She's a big girl. She'll get over it."

Michael slumped back in his chair, shaking his head in disbelief. "What do you want, Ann? Are you *trying* to give her an eating disorder?"

"I just want what's best for her. She's too fat." Ann took a dainty bite of Libby's pumpkin pie and dabbed at her lips with a napkin. "And she'll *never* have a boyfriend while she looks like that." Ann looked to Jessy and smiled. "Right, Jessy? I mean, you must know."

"*Ann*—" Michael's voice rose slightly, his eyes darkening with anger.

"Anyway," Ann continued, unfazed, "you haven't even asked me why I'm here." She mock pouted, acting coy, and Jessy's dislike for the woman quadrupled.

"Well, I'd assumed you were here to visit the kids, since you've only seen them three times this year." Michael leaned back in his chair and leveled Ann with a steady, no-nonsense gaze. Jessy silently watched the exchange, feeling conspicuous and intrusive. But there was no way she'd leave yet.

"I *do* want to see the kids," Ann said with a slow, suggestive smile. "But I kinda missed you too, cowboy."

Cowboy? Jessy winced at the obvious affection in Ann's voice. Maybe it was time to make a clean getaway.

"But since you didn't ask," Ann continued, ignoring Jessy completely, "I came here to talk to you—about what we discussed earlier."

Michael cut his eyes toward Jessy, a less than subtle attempt to stop Ann from saying too much. Jessy leaned back in her seat, a sickly feeling uncurling in the pit of her stomach. As if she needed to feel more conspicuous.

"Now's not the time, Ann."

Ann abruptly focused her attention on Jessy again. "So you picked up my husband on a bus," she said with forced mildness. "What happened—was the street corner too cold?"

"Ex*cuse* me?" Jessy sat up straighter, feeling her face flush with anger. This was getting uglier by the second.

Ann flashed her a brilliant and totally insincere smile. "It's a joke. I'm joking. Mikey knows how I like to kid, don't you, sweetie?"

"Mmm-hmm—and by the way, I'm your *ex*-sweetie." Michael cleared his throat, flashing Jessy an awkward apologetic gaze as he shifted in his seat. "And Jessy did not 'pick me up.' We met—" His gaze touched upon Jessy's, the faintest of smiles on his lips. "We met during a dinner stop."

"What on Earth were you doing on a bus, Michael?" Ann laughed and tossed her hair, effectively drawing Michael's attention back to her. "I mean, really—I know the farm's in trouble, but surely you could afford to buy a plane ticket."

"The farm's fine," Michael said tightly. "My flight was cancelled and I wanted to get home for Thanksgiving."

"So let me ask my second question." Ann leaned forward, eyes narrowing slightly as any trace of forced friendliness vanished. "Why *are* you here, Jenny?"

"*Jessy,*" Jessy corrected, smiling as she forced herself to assume a posture of complete composure. She knew passive-aggressive tactics when she saw them. "And I'm here because Michael invited me."

"He *invited* you! How unbelievably sweet of him." Ann's smile was suddenly toxic as she looked to Michael. "Inviting a strange woman into my house to spend Christmas with *my* children. How wonderful."

"In case you've forgotten," Michael said, smiling easily if a bit stiffly, "those kids are mine, too. And this house hasn't been yours since the day you walked out on us. So please spare me the sarcasm, okay?"

"No, Michael. It's *not* okay. I don't know who or what this woman *is*—and I really doubt you do either." Ann looked at Jessy again, but this time she didn't even bother to hide her distaste. "Really, Michael—if you're going to have your little flings, can't you do it in private? Do we all have to see what awful taste you have in bimbos?"

Michael straightened in his chair, leaning forward as he glared at Ann. "Now that's *enough*. You have no right to walk in like you still live here and—"

"When it comes to my kids I have *every* right!"

"You haven't even bothered to call them in three months." Michael's voice lowered with anger. "And where were you on Ben and Marie's last birthday? Or Libby's, for that matter?"

"I told you—I was on assignment." Ann's expression tightened. "I had deadlines and—"

"And meanwhile you can't be bothered to make a five-minute phone call."

"Damn it, Michael—I have to have a *life!*"

"The *kids* should be your life," Michael said quietly. "Just like they're mine."

"Don't fight," Ben whispered, looking very small and very frightened. Jessy wished she could pick him up and hug him until the fear went away. "I don't like it when you fight."

"We're not fighting, baby." Ann looked almost triumphant as she glanced back to Michael. *"Are* we?"

"This is ridiculous," Jessy muttered, pushing away from the table.

"So what's *your* problem?" Ann snapped.

Jessy stood, tossing her napkin down on her plate. "My problem is the way you've managed to upset your children in the space of fifteen minutes."

"My relationship with my children is none of your business."

Ann glared at Jessy, the facade of forced friendliness gone now. "You have no right to criticize—"

"That's enough, Ann." Michael spoke softly, the anger in his voice sharp but controlled. "Jessy is just concerned about the kids."

"Someone ought to be," Jessy murmured, unable to resist taking one last swipe. "I'm going to go try to find Libby," she said, looking from Michael to Ann. "Maybe I can talk to her."

"She needs to talk to *me,*" Ann said, standing quickly. "You don't even know my daughter."

"I think you've said enough already, Ann." Michael's voice remained dangerously steady. "You've seen Libby three times in the past year. What makes you think *you* know her?"

At a loss for words, Ann's cheeks reddened with anger. Jessy took advantage of the silence to speak to Ben and Marie, smiling brightly as she gently guided their attention away from the argument.

"Hey—I'd sure like to see Miss Purty now," Jessy smiled as she gently wiped away the tears on Ben's cheeks. Ben managed a slight smile of his own.

"She won't bite or anything," he said quietly, taking Jessy's hand. "So you can hold her and pet her if you want."

"She'll poop on you," Marie warned.

"That's okay. I'm not allergic to hamster poop." Jessy smiled and stood, taking Ben and Marie's hands in hers, and allowed them to guide her out of the dining room. She glanced quickly to Michael, but he was staring at Ann, his eyes dark with anger. Ann returned his gaze as if they were the only two people in the world.

How could Michael ever love someone like Ann? Jessy had seen this kind of thing far too many times in her life. No matter how horrible, how mean, how selfish the woman was, if she had a good body and a pretty face, nothing else mattered. Character and personality had nothing to do with it.

Jessy shook her head in frustration as Ben and Marie led her up the stairs. Why did high-maintenance women like Ann always end up with all the men? Sometimes it seemed like a man wouldn't be interested in a woman unless she was difficult and touchy and bitchy to the extreme. Nice girls not only finished last, they rarely even got into the race. And if the nice girl happened to be fat—forget about it.

As they walked past Libby's door, Jessy wondered how long Ann had been nagging the poor girl to lose weight. She knew how painful it could be to feel so different, excluded from the rest of the world for the simple sin of being overweight. She remembered all too clearly how much it hurt to want to be like everybody else, even though she knew she'd never truly be accepted on their terms.

Ann was wrong; Jessy knew Libby quite well. In some ways she probably understood the girl better than Ann ever could.

"Come on, Jessy," Ben gave her hand a tug. "I wanna show you how Miss Purty plays in her wheel."

Jessy smiled and knelt again, brushing a lock of blond hair from Ben's brow.

"How about," she said and playfully swung his hands at his sides, "you go make sure Miss Purty is ready to meet me, and I'll come visit her in a few minutes, okay?"

"Okay—but don't be too long or else she might get sleepy. It's almost her bedtime."

"And she gets grouchy when she stays up too late," Marie said gravely.

Jessy nodded, matching their serious tone even as she bit back a smile. "Then I'll be there as fast as I can."

Satisfied, Ben and Marie smiled and ran down the hallway, racing to their shared bedroom. Alone in the hall, Jessy took a deep breath and knocked on Libby's door. Maybe she was intruding in matters that were none of her business, but—

But the hell with it. Libby needed a friend right now, even if she didn't want to admit it.

"Libby? Can I come in?"

Silence, then padded footsteps and the click of a lock. Jessy took that as an invitation. When she opened the door, Libby was sitting on the edge of her bed, a huge purple teddy bear in her arms. Her eyes were still red, her cheeks still wet. On the bed was a crumpled bag of potato chips.

"Hi," Jessy said softly, remaining in the doorway. "How are you doing?"

"I'm fat and ugly," Libby muttered. "I'm just fine."

Uh-oh, Jessy thought, *this is gonna be fun.* She eased into the room, gingerly perching on the edge of the bed beside Libby. Nothing was said, so Jessy assumed her presence wasn't *totally* unwanted. So far, so good.

"So are you gonna tell me how my mom's really worried about me and just wants me to lose weight so I'll be happy?" Libby grimaced as she spoke, rolling her eyes in the way that only adolescents can. "Because if you are—"

"I think your mom was wrong," Jessy said quietly, turning her head just in time to catch Libby's look of surprise. "I mean, I'm sure she's worried about you, but that's not the right way to show it. I don't think she was thinking of your feelings."

Libby said nothing, just staring at Jessy like she was a Martian fresh off the mothership. Jessy felt a twinge of self-consciousness—after all, she'd just met the girl a few hours before; what right did she have to give her opinion of the situation?—but she forced it away. Michael had been right; if they weren't excruciatingly careful, Libby could very easily become bulimic or anorexic—and being slim just wasn't worth it.

"Why are you here?" Libby finally asked.

"Your dad felt sorry for me, I guess." Jessy managed a faint smile. "I bet he takes in a lot of strays, huh?"

Libby smiled slightly. "Usually he restrains himself to cats and dogs, but I guess he figured you were already housebroken."

Sharp, Jessy thought as she laughed. The kid's got a good sense of humor. Maybe she'd be okay after all.

"Mom's just being Mom," Libby said, folding her legs beneath her as she snuggled the teddy bear closer. "She's gorgeous so she thinks I should be too. I think I'm just kind of a disappointment to her. She wanted a cheerleader for a daughter—but she got me instead."

"So what do you do when she says stuff like that?"

"Usually I just come up here and sit by myself for a while."

Libby looked over to the empty potato chip bag and blushed. "And sometimes I eat."

Jessy nodded, remembering her own experiences. "I used to go to my room, crawl into bed with a bunch of comic books, and eat candy until my stomach hurt."

Libby laughed softly. "I've got MTV and potato chips."

They sat in companionable silence for a few minutes. Jessy felt as if they'd reached a turning point; nothing had been said outright, but she was fairly sure that Libby wasn't thinking of her as the enemy anymore. Problem was, she wasn't exactly a friend yet either.

"So do you like my dad?"

Libby's question caught Jessy off guard. "Well—sure. I mean, he's a nice guy."

"But do you *like* him, like him?"

There was no hint of anger or accusation in Libby's tone—only friendliness and genuine curiosity. Jessy was glad that Libby wasn't dwelling on Ann's appalling behavior, but this twist in the conversation wasn't exactly what she was hoping to discuss. She had no idea how she could tell Michael's daughter that yes, she really *liked* her father, and that yes, it was developing into a full-blown crush. She felt like she'd been thrown headfirst into a minefield.

"I—" Jessy took a deep breath and sighed, still smiling. "To be honest, Libby, I don't know what I think right now."

"A lot of women like my dad," Libby said, drawing her knees up to her chin. "They're all the time bugging him for dates and stuff, but he always tells them no. I used to think it was because he was still in love with Mom."

Jessy couldn't quite understand why, but her heart suddenly twisted at the thought. It was one thing to know that Michael had loved Ann *before*—but to think that he might *still* love her, even knowing what she's really like—

"What about now?" Jessy asked, voice soft. "Do you still think that?"

Libby shrugged. "I don't know. Maybe. When I was younger, I used to hope that they'd stop being stupid and get married again. I mean, I love Dad and everything, but I miss having Mom around. Especially now."

A sudden wave of empathy nearly brought tears to Jessy's eyes. She knew all too well what it was like to grow up without a mother, unable to talk to anyone about all the hopes, all the fears, all the questions she'd had when she was Libby's age. But at least Libby still had her mother. And Ann, however flawed, was the only mother Libby would ever have.

Jessy suddenly felt like an unwanted intruder in not just Michael's life, but in Libby's and Ben's and Marie's as well.

"Well," Jessy finally said, hoping to steer the conversation in another direction, "is there anything maybe I could help you with? Anything you want to talk about?"

Libby sighed. "Just Tommy, but he's a jerk. I don't know *why* I even liked him in the first place."

"Have you talked to your dad about this?"

"Yeah, but he just says that boys my age are immature and don't know a good thing when they see it." Libby sighed again, shaking her head. "I think Dad just wants me to feel better. Guys don't like me because I'm too fat."

Jessy studied Libby for a few moments. Already pretty, Libby was well on her way to being beautiful; she had a maturity and intelligence that went far beyond her years. Boys were probably intimidated by her, but Jessy didn't share that opinion with Libby. That's the last thing a ten-year-old girl wanted to hear.

"Sometimes boys can be weird," Jessy finally said, slowly smiling. "They think they have to be cool and have all the right clothes and the right shoes and the right girlfriends. A lot of them are afraid to think for themselves, so they figure it's just easier to do what everybody else does."

Libby nodded, cuddling her teddy bear closer. "Tommy used to talk to me all the time. He liked my jokes. He broke up with his girlfriend last week and I thought for sure he'd ask me to the dance, but—"

"But he asked the other girl instead," Jessy said softly. "It's happened to me, too."

"Does it ever get better?"

Libby looked so sad, so defeated, that Jessy couldn't tell her how she truly felt, that *no*, it didn't get better; if anything guys got even worse as they got older. But a little white lie wouldn't hurt anything—and besides, Libby was too young to be so cynical.

"Yeah," she said and smiled. "It gets better."

"Jessy?" Ben stuck his head into the room. "Miss Purty's ready for you to visit."

"Oh, God," Libby said and groaned. "Ben and his rodent."

"I'll be right there, okay?" Jessy's smile widened as Ben ducked out of the doorway and disappeared into the hallway again. She turned back to Libby. "I'd better go see Miss Purty before she falls asleep," she said and stood. "Are you feeling any better?"

"Yeah, I guess," Libby sighed and nodded as she flopped bonelessly into the pillows. "Boys are just stupid—except for my dad."

Jessy smiled slightly. "Your dad's an exceptional guy."

"Do you have a boyfriend, Jessy?"

Libby's sudden question stopped Jessy short as she headed for the bedroom door. She turned and smiled and hoped that Libby couldn't see through it. "I don't, um—I mean, no—no, I don't."

"Why not?"

"Good question." Jessy laughed quietly, hoping it covered her discomfort. She didn't want to ruin the tentative friendship they'd begun. "Think it'll snow again tonight?"

"You're changing the subject."

"And you're absolutely right." Jessy smiled as she walked toward the open door. "I'll be just down the hall if you want to talk some more, okay?"

Libby nodded. "Okay—and Jessy?"

Jessy paused at the door. "Hmm?"

"Thanks for, you know—talking and stuff. I'm sorry if I gave you a hard time earlier. I didn't really mean it."

"I had a feeling you didn't." Jessy winked and smiled again, closing the door behind her as she headed down the hall toward Ben and Marie's room.

And there was Ann. Waiting to pounce.

Chapter Six

"I'd LIKE A WORD with you," Ann said quietly, taking a step forward as her eyes narrowed. Jessy suddenly felt like a mouse cornered by a huge, hungry cat.

"Fine." Jessy folded her arms across her chest, ready for anything.

"What do you want?"

Jessy couldn't help but to smile with confusion. "Excuse me?"

"You heard me. What do you want? Michael doesn't have any money, so you might as well not even bother."

"I don't want anyone's money, and I don't appreciate your question." Jessy drew herself up taller, fighting to control her rising anger. "Michael invited me to spend Christmas with him and his family. I accepted. That's it."

"And why would he do something like that?" Ann looked Jessy up and down and shook her head. "Obviously he's not doing it to sleep with you."

That's it. Jessy's anger boiled over. "Listen—"

"If he thinks *you're* going to make me jealous—" Ann laughed softly and shook her head.

"I think that's enough." Jessy took a step forward, but Ann blocked her way again.

"Listen, just because you managed to hustle my husband and kids into trusting you, that doesn't mean I buy into your Little Miss Innocent act."

Jessy smiled tightly. "There's pretty much no chance that you and I are going to get along, is there?"

"Just like there's no chance I'm going to let you move in on my family."

"I'm *not* 'moving in' on anybody." Jessy spoke slowly and deliberately, as if explaining to a child. "Michael is helping me—"

Ann snorted. "I'll just bet he is. He just loves his charity work."

Taken aback, Jessy hesitated before speaking, afraid she'd say something she'd later regret if she allowed her mouth free reign. Instead, she bit her tongue and took a deep breath. She wasn't going to take the bait. Absolutely not.

"You should know that Michael and I still have a relationship," Ann said and smiled. "When I come home to see the kids, it's like I never left. The only thing that's changed is our marital status."

"Then why did you divorce him?" The question popped out before Jessy could catch herself.

"That's none of your business."

"I have nothing else to say to you," Jessy finally murmured, turning to walk away. That was one thing Aunt Amelia had taught her well—if you can't keep your temper, leave.

"Well, I have something else to say to you." Ann caught up with Jessy, smug satisfaction in her eyes. "Michael is my husband. He is the father of my children. I might not be here twenty-four hours a day, but when I come home, they are *my* family. Mine."

"You mean when it's convenient for you to be a wife and mother," Jessy said.

"You're not going to ruin this for me."

Jessy studied her for a moment. Ann was unquestionably beautiful, undeniably perfect, but there was a tone of desperation in her voice that she could not hide. She was afraid. The life she had so selfishly crafted to suit her own needs was threatened, and she didn't like it one bit.

"You're right," Jessy finally said, smiling faintly. "I'm not."

With that, Jessy finally stepped around Ann and made it into the guest bedroom, barely managing not to slam the door behind her.

"I LIKE her."

Michael cocked an eyebrow as he turned toward Lyssa and slung a dishtowel over his shoulder. He'd had a feeling his mother was just biding her time before sharing her opinion; he just hadn't expected it to be while they were doing the dishes. "Say again?"

Lyssa glanced up to Michael and smiled as she scrubbed a frying pan. "I said I like her. The kids like her, too."

"Oh, I get it," Michael grinned as he dried another dish and set it into the rack. "You're trying, in your none-too-subtle way, to find out my intentions with Jessy."

"Well," Lyssa's smile slanted. "If you have to put it that way—"

"Okay, okay." Michael dried the last dish and leaned against the counter, folding his arms over his chest. Lyssa rinsed the last pan and then mirrored his posture, leaning against the sink, an eyebrow arching as she waited for him to continue. He cleared his throat and shrugged. "I think Jessy is—great."

"*Great,*" Lyssa said dryly. "My son the poet."

"Well come on, Mom—what do you want me to say?" Michael's smile faltered as he shook his head, keeping his gaze averted as he idly tossed silverware into a drawer. "I like Jessy. I think she's funny and smart and wonderful and—"

"And—?"

"And I like her. I really like her."

"Could this 'like' possibly ever turn into, oh, I don't know—love?"

Michael's eyes widened. "Hello—where'd *that* come from?"

"It's a perfectly legitimate question." Lyssa's eyes twinkled as she studied her son. "I give you my full blessing. I can tell you already that I wouldn't mind Jessy as a daughter-in-law—and I can just imagine the babies you two would have."

"*Mom!* I barely know her."

Lyssa chuckled and strolled up to Michael, reaching up to smooth down his hair. Michael couldn't help but smile back at her. Once again, his mother knew his mind and heart better than he did.

"Okay, okay—I won't push." Lyssa's smile softened as she stroked Michael's cheek, her palm tissue-soft against his skin. "But I will give you one little piece of advice."

Michael nodded, knowing it would do no good to argue. "All right—one *small* piece."

"If you think Jessy is someone you could grow to care about," Lyssa said softly, "then don't let her get away."

"It's more complicated than that, Mom."

"No, it's not. Not if you don't want it to be. I'm not saying you should go upstairs and propose to her right this second. I just want you to—I don't know—just think about it. Think about her."

"Mom, I really do like Jessy, but we barely know each other. *You* barely know her." Michael could feel his cheeks growing warm. "Besides that, I'm not ready to get involved with anybody yet. Not even someone like Jessy."

"Oh, honey. I know Ann hurt you—"

Michael snorted and rolled his eyes. "Hurt" was a polite word for what she did—if one could classify having one's heart ripped out and shredded as being merely "hurt."

"But you have got to stop comparing every woman you meet to Ann," Lyssa grinned. "Not every woman is going to be a selfish harpy hellbent on destroying your life and making you miserable."

Michael had to smile. "I get your point."

"Hmm-hmm." Lyssa raised an eyebrow and nodded, and Michael knew she wasn't in the least bit convinced. "Just think about something for me, will you?"

"Anything."

"Just think about how much better you've felt since you met Jessy. And don't you even try to deny it, Michael. I saw how you were acting tonight at dinner. I don't know when I've seen you smile as much."

Michael fought the urge to smile again. He honestly had no intention of falling in love with her. No. Nope. Absolutely not. He liked her. He thought she was a great friend and a wonderful person—but he wasn't falling for her. No matter how much he smiled when he was with her, no matter how much his kids liked her, he wasn't going to go through that whole song and dance again.

"C'mere, you." Lyssa wrapped her arms around Michael's waist, drawing him in for a hug. Michael closed his eyes and rested his cheek against her soft silver hair, holding her tight. When had she gotten so small? he wondered. It was a frightening thing to see her age, to watch the young woman he remembered grow so lined and weary. She was a walking reminder that nothing stayed the same, that everything had to change. And that time could pass too quickly when you weren't looking.

"You only get one chance," Lyssa whispered. "Don't let this one get away."

Michael smiled and pressed a kiss against his mother's temple. "I love you, Mom."

"I know you do." Lyssa looked up to him and smiled. "Now why don't you go spend some time with our guest."

"Yes, Mom." Michael kissed her cheek once more, feeling more like a kid than a thirty-nine year old man. But his mother was, as always, right. He couldn't keep hiding behind the divorce. It wasn't fair to him or the kids. Ann had moved on—maybe it was time he did, too.

Because if there was any one woman he thought he might be able to trust enough to fall in love with, it was Jessy Monroe.

If he ever decided to fall in love again.

JESSY SAT at her window and watched the snow fall over the fields behind the farmhouse. She'd lit the fireplace and kept the lights off, feeling herself growing drowsy as she gazed at the flicker of the flames. It was better for all involved if she sequestered herself in the bedroom while Ann was there. The kids didn't get that much quality time with their mother as it was; she definitely didn't want to intrude on their holiday.

It amazed her to think that Ann could walk away from this. The house was beautiful, Lyssa was amazing, the kids were adorable, and Michael—well, Michael was Michael and there weren't too many men like him in the world. Now Ann apparently had the best of both worlds: her career in Chicago and her family in Minnesota, when she felt like playing wife and mother.

It didn't seem fair.

"Anti-social much?"

Michael's voice startled her, and Jessy jumped slightly as she turned away from the window. She managed a smile that she didn't feel. "Hey."

"Hey, yourself." Michael sat down beside her on the window seat. "Why are you up here sitting in the dark?"

"I'm being all broody and mysterious."

"Uh-huh."

Jessy sighed. "I thought it'd be best if I kinda—stayed out of sight while Ann's here."

"Best for who?"

"Well, for the kids." Jessy finally managed to meet his eyes again and felt instantly swoony. She didn't know how he did it, but he had a way of looking at her that made her feel as if he could see right into her mind and heart. "And for, you know—you two."

"Me and Ann?"

Jessy nodded. She didn't trust herself to speak.

"Sweetheart, there *is* no 'you two' when it comes to me and Ann. Trust me." Michael's smile quirked slightly as he shook his head. "I try to give her a wide berth when she's here to see the kids. Otherwise the arguing gets pretty ugly."

Jessy couldn't help but wonder how much of that was actually true. Maybe they argued, but from what Ann insinuated, they seemed to enjoy making up, too. The thought made her feel like someone was crushing her heart in their hands.

"And anyway, she's already gone. She got a call and had to rush out of here on some kind of top secret super-important journalist mission." Michael grinned, but Jessy could tell that he'd been hurt by her sudden departures in the past. "I thought I'd see if you wanted to come downstairs and watch a movie with me and the kids before we turn in."

"Sure. I'd like that." Jessy forced herself to push the images of

Ann and Michael out of her mind. She had to remember that they were friends. Yes, she was attracted to him, and yes, she wouldn't mind at all if he were attracted to her, but she knew that wasn't how the real world worked. He might flirt with her. He might touch her hand or make the occasional romantic gesture, but in the end, it meant nothing. He still loved his wife.

"Come on, then. Mom's making popcorn." Michael stood and held out his hand to Jessy. Without thinking twice she took it, relishing the warmth of his skin. Just touching him sent a wave of comfort through her. When she was back in Kentucky, grading papers and watching endless nights of bad TV, she would remember this moment and all the other moments spent with Michael. She would remember how he smelled of woodsmoke and pine and soap, and how his palm felt rough but soft against hers, and how the slightest brush of his body against hers made her feel boneless and dizzy. She would remember how he would study her with eyes so soft and caring that she could fool herself into feeling cherished.

When she was alone, she'd be able to remember all those things about Michael, and a million more little things besides. It wouldn't be nearly enough—

But it was more than she'd had before.

Chapter Seven

THE BED SHIFTED as someone crawled in beside her.

Then the intruders giggled and Jessy felt tiny, clawed feet skitter up her arm. She kept her eyes closed, pretending to be asleep as Ben scooted closer, herding Miss Purty up Jessy's arm and onto the hollow of her shoulder. He giggled softly under his breath as Marie tried to shush him.

Barely managing to hide her smile, Jessy shifted onto her back and—as she expected—Miss Purty crawled onto her throat and sat there. As theatrically as she could, Jessy smacked her lips and fluttered her eyelids and made a show of slowly waking up, knowing that Ben and Marie were probably about to explode with giggles. The twins had the most infectious laughter Jessy had ever heard, and over the past few days she'd found herself going to outlandish ends to hear it. From what Michael had told her, Ben was the more sensitive of the two, sometimes going through periods of total withdrawal whenever Michael and Ann argued. If keeping him out of one of those periods resulted in her getting hamster cooties, then so be it.

Jessy finally opened her eyes, focused on the ball of fur sitting on her chest, and squawked in feigned surprise, sending Ben and Marie into delighted gales of giggles. Miss Purty was unimpressed, too busy grooming herself to care.

"Good morning, Jessy," Ben said in between giggles, echoed immediately by Marie. Ben took Miss Purty and held her in both hands.

Jessy sat up and ran a hand through her disheveled hair, smiling broadly. She could handle waking up this way, to the sound of children's laughter. "And just what do you think you're doing?" she asked in a playfully prim voice.

"Miss Purty wanted to wake you up," Ben said, smiling innocently even as mischief twinkled in his eyes. He looked like Michael in miniature. "Can you come play in the snow with me and Libby and Marie?"

"Yeah!" Marie grinned and nodded fiercely. "Come play with us. We're gonna make snowmen and everything."

Jessy took a quick inventory of herself; last week's cold had passed, leaving her with only a mildly stuffy nose. All in all, she felt pretty good. And the thought of playing in the snow after close to a week of being stuck indoors made her feel even better.

"I'd love to," she said and smiled, resisting the urge to grab them both up in a hug. To her surprised delight, they hugged her instead, Ben cradling Miss Purty carefully to his chest. Jessy closed her eyes, fighting a hot rush of unexpected tears as they squeezed her with childish exuberance.

"I like you, Jessy," Ben said as he released her. He studied her closely, one hand spanning her cheek as he kept her face tilted up. Jessy smiled back, her emotions firmly under her own control again.

"That's good—'cause I like you, too." Jessy playfully tickled his sides and then turned to tickle Marie. "And you, too." Ben and Marie squirmed and giggled, then jumped down from the bed. "Give me ten minutes to get ready, okay?"

"Okay." Ben said as he and Marie went to the door, hesitating to look at each other quickly before turning to face her again. "Jessy?"

Jessy paused midway through a stretch. "Hmm?"

"We're glad you came home with Daddy." Ben smiled and looked at Marie for backup.

"Yeah," Marie said and nodded enthusiastically, a big grin on her face. "Daddy's happy again."

Jessy's smile softened as she gazed at them, touched but saddened by their words. She couldn't tell them that she'd be leaving after Christmas. She couldn't make them think that she would stay forever—even though she wished she could.

"Thank you," she finally said. She managed another smile as Ben and Marie disappeared down the hallway, running back to their room. Once she was alone, the smile faded.

Why hadn't she thought of this earlier? she wondered. Why didn't she see this coming? The last few days had been the most wonderful time of her life; she and Michael and the kids had decorated the house under Lyssa's observing eye, laughing and drinking hot chocolate and singing all the Christmas carols they could remember. Every morning she'd met Michael after he'd done the chores, talking over coffee and breakfast until it was time to wake the kids. She'd helped Lyssa go through treasured Christmas ornaments in preparation for the Christmas Eve tree-decorating party while Michael went about the daily business of running the dairy farm. For the first time in years, she actually felt as if she were part of a family again.

She should have known she'd get attached to the kids—she always did when she was teaching. And she should have known she'd get attached to Michael, too, no matter how much she tried not to like him. But it was too late now. She was here, the kids were wonderful, and Michael was too good to be true. Now she was well and truly stuck. Now it would be harder than ever to leave them after Christmas.

Jessy sighed and flopped back on the bed. Great.

IN THE BACK FORTY of Michael's farm, the world was nothing but snow and sky. Jessy took a number of snowball hits just because she was too distracted gawking at the scenery, but she couldn't help it—the farm was gorgeous. Once again she wished she could see what it looked like in the spring, when the grass was new and the trees and flowers were in bloom.

Most of the morning passed in a blur of snowmen, snow fights, and snow angels. Libby, at that awkward stage where she wanted to look cool but still be able to play like a kid, had eventually loosened up enough to join Jessy and Ben and Marie in their snow battles. Since the upset with Ann, Jessy had kept an eye on her during meals, making sure she didn't pick at her food or excuse herself the moment the final bite was swallowed. Instead, Libby was eating normally. No signs of bulimia, no hint of anorexia.

One reason for the fairly peaceful mood, Jessy guessed, was the fact that Ann had left for an assignment after the scene she'd caused Thanksgiving night. The kids had calmed down, and Jessy was just glad to see all of them laughing and having a good time; in only a few days, she'd grown fiercely protective of them. Which was crazy, but, she realized, understandable. She *was* thirty-two, after all. Maybe she'd hit snooze on her biological alarm clock one too many times.

"Daddy!" Ben's delighted shout startled Jessy out of her thoughts and she clumsily sat up from the snow bank, ruining her snow angel as she struggled to her feet. As she brushed snow from her back and legs, she glanced up and saw Michael walking from the direction of the barns. For a moment she could only stare at him in his denim jacket and faded jeans and battered black cowboy hat. As he drew closer to where Jessy was standing she could see the dark shadow of stubble on his cheeks and chin. He looked tired, but happy.

She swallowed hard, forcing her racing heart to regain its normal beat. The man *was* good-looking. She could attempt to deny her feelings for him, but she could not deny the fact that he was the most handsome man she'd ever laid eyes on.

Which would make what she had to say to him that much harder. She wasn't looking forward to their inevitable talk, but she had to tell him she was leaving.

"Hey, Benny-boy." Michael picked up Ben and helped him clamber onto his shoulders, smiling as he approached Jessy and Libby and Marie. "Ladies," he said and winked.

"Can I go to the mall today, Dad?" Libby asked. "Kelly and Gina want me to go Christmas shopping with them."

Michael glanced at Jessy again and she could see the smile in his eyes. *Don't be like that,* she thought and sighed. *Don't be so damn irresistible.*

"Well, I *was* hoping you'd help me muck out the horse stalls, but—" Michael sighed melodramatically, smiling even as he spoke. "If you'd rather go *shopping*, then—"

Libby grinned and stood on tiptoes to give him a kiss. "Thanks, Daddy!"

As Libby hurried off, Michael swung Ben off his shoulders and turned his attention to Jessy again. She felt her heart stutter as his smile widened and the corners of his eyes crinkled merrily. It was a good thing he had no idea how much he affected her; she'd never be able to look him in the eye again.

"Play with us, Daddy!" Marie tugged at Michael's sleeve. "I wanna play snowballs."

"Snowballs, huh?" Michael's eyebrows rose as he looked from Jessy to Ben. "The three of us against Jessy?"

"Yeah!" Ben giggled as he scooped up a handful of snow and pelted Jessy with it. Laughing, Jessy darted away, taking only a moment to form a snowball of her own. She let fly with it and hit Michael squarely in the chest. The look of comical confusion on his face made her laugh even harder.

"Uh-oh, woman," he said with mock menace. "You're gonna pay for that one."

"Ooh, I'm shaking in my boots." Jessy laughed again as Marie threw an armful of snow into her face. The war commenced, and Jessy couldn't catch her breath for laughing. Ben's aim was amazingly good for a little boy—which more than made up for Michael's inability to hit the side of a barn with his pitches.

After a while, Michael whistled through his teeth and stopped the fight. Jessy couldn't resist and lobbed one last snowball at him, knocking the hat off his head as it connected with his ear. Michael closed his eyes and smiled, trying to retain his dignity even as snow dripped off the tip of his nose and Ben and Jessy and Marie collapsed into giggles.

"As I was about to say," Michael said and looked at them again, smile widening. "I think it's time for certain six-year-olds to go inside and eat lunch."

Ben looked over to Jessy. "I'm six and a half," he whispered. "How old are *you?*"

"Nope, Benny-boy—I'm talking about you and your sister." Michael picked Ben up in a hug and kissed his cheek, swinging him down and swooping Marie up in one easy gesture. "Go keep your gramma company for a while, 'kay?"

"Oh, all right," Marie sighed and looked over to Jessy. "Do you think she'll stay?" she asked in a loud whisper. Jessy acted as if she didn't hear, studying a distant grove of trees as if they were the most interesting things on Earth.

"I don't know," Michael whispered back. "We'll have to work on her, won't we?"

"Yeah!" After accepting a kiss on the cheek, Marie squirmed out of Michael's arms and ran to Jessy, stopping only long enough to give her a quick hug before zipping back to the house in a race with Ben. Jessy waited until Lyssa greeted the kids at the back door before daring to look at Michael. As she'd suspected, he was watching her.

"You've got great kids," she said, hoping she didn't sound as nervous as she felt.

"Yeah, I'm kinda fond of 'em." Michael hooked his thumbs in the belt loops of his jeans and took a few steps closer to Jessy. She had to fight the instinct to move away, to put some safe space between them.

Michael said nothing for a moment, simply gazing at her for what felt like an eternity. Jessy could only imagine how she must look: no make-up, hair flapping wildly in the wind, a nose red enough to rival Rudolph's. She caught a glimpse of her shadow against the snow, wincing at how short and round it was, and wished she could just disappear. Worst of all, she knew that Michael was seeing these things about her, that she couldn't hide any of her flaws from him.

"What?" she finally asked, uncomfortable with his secretive smile. What flaw was he noticing now? she wondered.

"Just thinking," he said airily.

"New experience for you?" Jessy asked and smiled, taking a few steps backward and trying her best to look casual about it.

"You wound me, Jessy. You really wound me." Michael flattened a hand against his chest and managed to look pained for just a moment before his smile broke through again. He scooped up a huge handful of snow and began shaping it into a massive snowball. "You have until the count of three to arm yourself. *One*—"

Jessy laughed and took a few more stumbling steps backward. "And you're *how* old?" she asked as she stuffed her hands in her pockets. "Thirty-nine going on twelve?"

"I'm not joking around, Jessy." Michael tried his damnedest to look serious, but he couldn't stop smiling long enough to be believable. "I am challenging you to a one-on-one snowball battle royale."

"Uh-huh. Sure. Whatever you say."

"I'm serious." Michael threw the snowball up and caught it, taking a few steps closer to Jessy. "Folks 'round these parts call me the rootin'est, tootin'est snowslinger in town."

"And you're able to brag about that with a straight face," Jessy said and smiled. "I'm impressed."

"Okay—don't say I didn't warn you." He hefted the snowball with mock menace. "*Two*—"

"Now, Michael—" Jessy took another step backward, still smiling as she thickened her Kentucky drawl. "Y'all wouldn't throw a snowball at a defenseless woman, now, would you?"

Hesitating a moment, Michael lowered his arm as a playfully pensive frown creased his brow. His expressive eyebrows rose as he sighed. "You know, now that I think about it—"

Before Jessy could blink the loosely packed snowball was in the air and—a heartbeat later—square in her face. She half-laughed, half-yelped in surprise, wiping snow from her eyes as she lurched clumsily toward Michael, who was bent over double with laughter.

"I can't believe you actually did that!" she shouted, laughing as she awkwardly made her way through the shin-deep drifts, pausing just long enough to gather an armful of snow. Michael, his hands planted on his knees as he kept laughing, never saw her coming. She dumped the snow on his head, making sure that some would spill down the back of his shirt, and jumped away as he shouted in surprise and blindly reached for her.

"Hail, oh mighty Snow King," she said as she laughed.

Michael raised his snow-clumped head to look at her, his eyebrows arching almost devilishly as he smiled. "You will pay dearly for that one, my friend."

Jessy batted her lashes, feeling more alive, more free, than she'd ever felt in her life. She could forget about Charlie, forget about her weight, forget about everything but the snow and the laughter and the wonderful smile on Michael's face as he straightened to his full height again.

I could fall in love with him, she thought suddenly, the realization zinging through her like an electric jolt. For the first time in her life, her feelings for a man had moved well beyond a mere crush, light years beyond friendship. She was falling in love with a man she'd known all of a week, a man with a ready-made family and The Wicked Bitch of the Midwest for an ex-wife.

"I am insane," she muttered. "Totally insane."

"What's that?" Michael shook his head and tilted it to the side. "I got snow in my ears."

"I said I'm freezing." Jessy tried a nonchalant smile, but now that she'd admitted her feelings to herself, she'd screwed everything up. No more acting casual for her. "We should go back in now."

"Not yet. There's something I want to show you first." Michael brushed the last of the snow from his shoulders, but a few flakes still clung to his dark eyelashes. He picked up his black cowboy hat and fitted it on his head again. "Come on." Michael grabbed her hand, his smile widening and crinkling his eyes, and Jessy was lost. Every cell in her body warned her to dig her heels in right now and resist him, but he was too damn charming for his own good. And hers.

They walked in silence, crossing the snowy fields as they headed towards one of the barns. Despite the fact that Michael still held her hand as they walked, despite the smiles he kept flashing in her direction, Jessy's gloom deepened with every step. Why did she have to go and admit her feelings to herself? Now she'd never be able to act normal around him again. Now she would have to act like she only thought of him as a friend—and she'd have to bend over backwards to keep everything in perspective. She knew the drill, had gone through it more times than she liked to admit. She was the Queen of Casual, all-too-skilled at hiding her own emotions in order to keep a friendship intact.

And now she'd have to do it again.

"You're awfully quiet," Michael said and smiled, glancing over to her. "Anything wrong?"

Jessy managed a smile and shook her head. She didn't trust her voice.

At the barn, Michael opened the door and allowed Jessy to enter first. The mingled smell of horses and dried hay was almost overwhelming, but not unpleasantly so. Electric lanterns hung from the walls, casting a warm, cozy light over the stalls. A half-dozen horses of varying sizes and colors placidly chewed straw and snorted at the presence of the humans. Jessy, whose experience with horses had been confined to merry-go-rounds as a kid, felt as if she were in the company of alien creatures. A gray gelding snorted and shook its head as Jessy passed.

"Funny looking cows," she said.

Michael grinned as he headed towards the stalls. "Yeah, you don't want to be here around milking time."

Jessy laughed despite herself. As long as she remained cool, she'd be okay. She just had to stop and think before she spoke. She had to remember that she was only here temporarily, that Michael had a beautiful ex-wife and a family and a life that she would never be a part of. As long as she kept that in mind, she'd be fine.

She hoped.

Chapter Eight

"SO WHAT DID YOU WANT to show me?" she asked quietly. She kept her eyes averted, studying the horses instead of Michael.

Michael picked up a dried apple core and offered it to a mottled gray mare, who nibbled it delicately. "Before I take you up to the loft," he said, and turned his attention back to her again, "you've got to promise me not to laugh."

Jessy instantly smiled despite herself. "Why would I laugh?"

"C'mon—" Michael grabbed her hand again, leading her to a rickety wood ladder. Jessy immediately saw herself snapping the boards in two with her weight, falling and breaking her neck. If she was lucky.

"There's climbing involved? Michael—"

"You'll be fine. Just put one hand over the other and don't look down."

Jessy took a deep breath and balefully looked at the ladder, then over to Michael. She had such a bad feeling about this—but she didn't want to seem like a wimp, even though she was the most craven, yellow-bellied coward in the world. Besides, the curiosity was killing her.

She steeled herself, said a little prayer, and started climbing up the ladder—which, she had to admit, felt a lot sturdier than it looked. Michael was right behind her, and for a moment she was mortified by the thought of her wide bottom jiggling just over his head. Thank God her coat was long enough to cover it.

Her head finally poked through the trap door on the hay-strewn floor of the loft. Sunlight flooded the small attic-like room, where an empty easel and a small, paint-splattered table stood waiting for use. Unframed canvases leaned against the walls, paintings ranging from abstracts to landscapes to portraits of Libby and Ben and Marie. Cartoons drawn on typing paper littered the floor and dotted the walls. For a moment Jessy wasn't sure why he had made such a big deal about showing her his art, but then she understood. It took a lot of courage and even more trust to share something so personal.

Jessy climbed the last few rungs and smiled as she gazed around the room. He was good. Really good. Still smiling, she turned to Michael, who was trying his best not to look too proud or relieved by her reaction. "You did all of these?"

Michael shrugged and nodded, hands shoved into his pockets. "Yeah—it's kinda my hobby."

"A hobby—" Jessy repeated softly, looking around the loft. A half-finished canvas rested on an easel, surrounded by crumpled tubes of oil paint and a well-used palette. Jessy stepped closer for a better look. The painting was a view of the farm from the vantage point of the loft, a beautiful landscape of the land in the spring. It was just as Jessy had imagined it might look.

She looked back to Michael, who seemed to be anticipating her reaction. All she could do was shake her head and smile. "Why aren't you a famous painter by now?"

Michael chuckled, and Jessy could hear the relief in his voice. It touched her that he thought so highly of her opinion. "Most famous painters don't get famous until they're dead. I'll take a rain check on that, thank you."

"This portrait of the kids is beautiful." Jessy stood in front of the larger canvas, smiling almost sadly to herself. The painting had been done years ago, when Ben and Marie were toddlers and Libby was a little girl. The realization that she had missed seeing them grow up hit Jessy much harder than it should have. "You have a gift," she finally whispered, looking back to him again. "Why don't—"

"—I sell my paintings?" he finished for her, smiling as he shrugged. "I don't know—I guess I'm not real sure anybody would actually want one."

Jessy heard the note of uncertainty in his voice. How could he not have confidence in his ability? All anyone had to do was look at his work and see that he was staggeringly talented.

"Is this what you did before you came back to the farm?"

Michael nodded as he sat down on a bale of hay, patting the empty space beside him. Jessy hesitated a moment before sitting down. What if the whole bale collapsed beneath her weight? What if she plopped down and sent Michael flying?

I'm being silly, she told herself as she gingerly sat down beside him. The bale shifted, but didn't collapse. And Michael didn't go flying. Instead his thigh nestled quite comfortably against hers. She could feel his warmth through the thickness of their jeans. All of a sudden the temperature of the loft seemed to shoot up a few hundred degrees.

"When I was a kid," Michael said quietly, completely unaware of her hormonal meltdown beside him, "I thought I could move away from here and be this great artist or something. Not the starving, 'I'm suffering for my art' kind of artist. I just wanted to have a career doing something I loved to do. Cartoons, paintings, sketches, whatever I could get. I wasn't a snob. I just wanted to paint."

Jessy smiled, trying to imagine him standing at the canvas, wielding a brush with the mad intensity of a tortured artist. She couldn't. But she *could* see him hunched over a drawing pad, sketching cartoony animals for Libby and Ben and Marie. Michael just wasn't the tortured type.

"So what happened?" she asked quietly, leaning her elbows on her knees as she bent forward, head angled up to look at him.

Michael kept his gaze fixed on the floor, the wryest of smiles twitching across his expression. "What happened was—I got a big, heaping helping of reality. While I was in school I got a freelance gig illustrating children's books. It didn't pay much, but I liked doing it, and I could support myself. Then I met Ann and—well—everything changed."

Jessy grimaced. She knew what was coming.

"Ann encouraged me to get a 'real' job," Michael said with a faint smile, glancing over to Jessy. "And because I was in love with her, I thought she knew what was best for me. So I stopped painting and got a job with a construction company. I was fairly good with carpentry, so—that became my job. Not my career."

"That's unbelievable," Jessy muttered, sitting up straight again. She couldn't imagine not encouraging someone with Michael's talent. She couldn't imagine denying him something he loved to do just because it didn't make truckloads of money.

"Well, I was young and foolish—and in love." Michael smiled again, but couldn't hide the faint pain in his eyes. "Ann knew exactly what she wanted for her own future, so I thought she knew what would be best for mine. Besides, I couldn't believe somebody like her would ever be interested in somebody like me."

"Excuse me?" Jessy blurted it out before she could catch herself. But what the hell? Might as well go on with it. "What do you mean, 'somebody like me'?"

"Oh, well—I wasn't always the stunning hunk of male perfection you see before you now." Michael's smile slanted sarcastically as he rolled his eyes at himself. "I was a big nerd in college."

"That's hard to believe."

"It's true. Thank God I wasn't there when the whole computer thing hit or else I'd really have been a dork." Michael's smile relaxed slightly. "Ann—well, you've seen her. She was just as gorgeous in college. I couldn't believe she could see anything to love about me."

The wistful tone of his voice was not lost on Jessy. If anything, it sliced through her like a knife. Somehow it didn't seem possible that he could still have feelings for Ann, but he just might. Ann was the mother of his children. They shared a bond that Jessy could not even begin to understand. Michael still loved Ann, despite everything. Just like Libby had hoped.

"I wouldn't think it would be *that* hard," Jessy said quietly. What she would have given to have met someone like Michael when she was in college, someone shy and nice and funny and sweet. Instead she'd spent her days in class and her nights either doing homework or working. Meanwhile someone like Ann was lucky enough to have Michael fall in love with her. Yeah, life was fair.

Her pseudo-confession didn't sink in, and Michael let it pass without comment. Jessy wasn't sure if she was relieved or disappointed. "I didn't start painting again until a few years ago. Mom's got 'em all over the house. I think she rotates them according to the season."

Jessy smiled, remembering the gorgeous floral still life that hung in the guestroom. The painting was so lifelike that she swore she could almost smell the scent of roses and lilacs when she stood close to it. "You really do have a gift."

Michael turned his head to look at her, and for a moment they were close enough to kiss. At least Jessy thought so, and the thought was so devastating that she felt as if her heart might explode with the sudden jolt of adrenaline. Michael's eyes, fringed with those long, sooty lashes, held her gaze so effortlessly that Jessy realized he honestly had no idea how he affected her. Which was a very, very good thing.

"Thank you, Jessy," he finally said, his words little more than a gruff whisper. He leaned closer until his shoulder nudged against hers. Jessy felt a shiver that danced from the top of her head to the tips of her toes. "That means a lot to me."

Jessy managed a smile even as she felt the force of his charm torpedo the very last remnants of her defenses. Whatever she might have deluded herself into believing, she could not deny that in the space of a few days she had somehow managed to fall in love with Michael Forrester and his family. She'd finally found the only man she'd even consider worth the trouble and aggravation of falling in love with, only to learn that he came with kids and an ex who could teach supermodels a thing or two about beauty. Story of her life.

"You're welcome," she said, bumping his shoulder with hers as she smiled up to him. She understood her role here very clearly. Michael was still in love with Ann, so Jessy would have to settle for being the supportive, understanding, completely non-threatening friend. Nothing she could do would ever make him fall for her the way he'd fallen for Ann, and the thought was almost liberating, in a sad, pathetic sort of way. All the pressure was off now. She knew her place.

Michael's gaze remained on Jessy's just long enough to make her feel self-conscious. The way he studied her, his expression so serious and intense, made her feel more than a little awkward. She wasn't wearing a speck of make-up, and the cold had chapped her lips and cheeks, and her hair probably looked like a fright wig after the snowball battle, and—oh, she didn't want to think about the rest.

"What?" she asked with a small smile, unable to stand the scrutiny a moment longer.

"I'm just looking at your face. You have beautiful bone structure." He smiled and spanned a hand over the plane of Jessy's cheek, fitting the length of his thumb just beneath her cheekbone. She could feel her face growing hot beneath his palm, but she couldn't look away from his eyes.

"Yeah, right—I bet you say that to all the girls," she said with forced lightness, hoping to spoil the suddenly overwhelming seriousness of the moment. She tried to smile wryly, but couldn't quite get her face to cooperate. All she could do was stare at him with big eyes, throat dry and heart pounding.

If he heard the playful sarcasm of her voice, he chose to ignore it. Michael's fingers traced along her temple, carefully brushing hair away from her face. For a split-second Jessy didn't know quite how to react; she wanted to just close her eyes and lean into his hand, to let him do whatever he wanted. His touch was so unbelievably gentle, almost reverent. Between the softness of his hands and the warmth of his gaze, Jessy felt almost hypnotized.

"Jessy—" he whispered.

And then he changed everything.

WITHOUT SAYING another word, Michael leaned forward and brushed his lips across Jessy's. The whisper of his breath against her skin, the warmth of his mouth on hers, sent a jolt of electricity through her. The kiss ended almost as soon as it had begun, but the effect was nearly devastating.

Michael rested his forehead against hers, and she was absurdly grateful for the chance to catch her breath, stunned into speechlessness. Of all the things that could have happened to her that day, being kissed by Michael—even such a brief, sweet little kiss—was the last thing she'd ever expected.

Michael raised his head, noticing the look on Jessy's face. His smile faded a little. "Did I do something wrong?"

Jessy managed to shake her head, not quite trusting her voice yet. This was ridiculous; she was old enough to be able to handle a little kiss better than *this*. At least she should be. The only other experience she'd ever had with kissing had been Charlie Wilks's half-hearted attempts.

"No," she whispered. "No—it's fine—"

"Then—would you mind if I did it again?"

Oh, Lord—he's trying to kill me, Jessy thought as she studied him. He wanted to kiss her again? Why? Where on Earth was all this coming from? Ten minutes ago she'd thought they were nothing but friends; now he'd introduced kissing into the equation and she didn't know what to expect next.

Smiling faintly, completely unaware of Jessy's emotional turmoil, Michael eased his arm around her and leaned in for another kiss. He captured her lower lip for a moment, then slid his mouth across hers, his tongue lightly flicking against the corner of her lips.

And suddenly it was all too overwhelming.

Jessy shot to her feet, scurrying over to the window.

"I'm sensing some ambivalence here," Michael said dryly, leaning on one arm as he watched Jessy stare out the window. She turned back to face him, knowing that her face was probably a lovely shade of magenta.

"What's wrong?" Michael asked quietly. "Did I cross some invisible boundary just now? Am I rushing you? Is it my breath?"

Caught off-guard, Jessy couldn't hide her smile, relaxing slightly as she managed to look into his eyes once again. Distance helped her think more clearly—but the sight of him in his tight, well-worn jeans and flannel shirt, hunkered down on a bale of hay, nearly derailed her train of thought.

"It's not you—" Jessy nervously twisted imaginary rings on her fingers, then caught what she was doing and abruptly stopped, folding her arms over her chest instead. "No, it's *definitely* not you. You're fine. More than fine."

"Why, thank you, Miss. Monroe. You're pretty fine your own self." Michael grinned, arching an eyebrow. "And so the problem *is*—?"

Jessy gazed helplessly at him for a moment. This was going to be excruciatingly, humiliatingly, *unimaginably* hard for her to admit—mainly because until this moment, her lack of experience hadn't been an issue. One time with Charlie—one miserable, unsatisfying, regrettable time—was not enough to make her an expert in the art of seduction.

"The problem," she finally said, "is me."

"*You?*"

"Me."

Michael smiled again, more from disbelief than amusement. "And how's that?"

Jessy sighed in resignation and leaned against the wall, folding her arms more tightly across her chest. Somehow she managed to meet his gaze. In the past few days, she'd come to think of Michael as a friend, probably the closest friend she'd ever had. And ever since the night he'd held her when she'd been so sick, she'd grown to somehow trust him. Why he'd kissed her just now was a complete mystery—but she knew she had to be completely truthful with him in case he decided to do it again. Better to get all the embarrassment out of the way at once than to let it drag out indefinitely.

"I don't—uh—I don't really know how to say this—" Jessy covered her face with her hands, desperately trying to fight back the burning blush, to cool her heated skin.

Michael quietly stood, moving towards Jessy with an easy grace. She lowered her hands and watched him move, marveling at how comfortable he was with his own body. It made her feel even more unwieldy and cumbersome. He slowly smiled, his self-confidence falling just short of arrogance as he gazed at her. Jessy felt her mouth suddenly go dry, throat constricting tightly as she forgot everything for a moment.

"You were saying—?" he prompted.

Jessy cleared her throat and composed herself slightly. "I was saying that I, um, I don't—" Jessy closed her eyes for a moment to escape his penetrating gaze. He sidled closer to her, backing her against the wall, his chest almost touching her folded arms. She instantly lowered her arms to her sides, then realized she'd made a mistake; now his chest nearly brushed her breasts with every breath he took.

Damn it—how could she think straight when he looked at her like that? His gaze slid from her eyes to her mouth, lingering there for a few excruciatingly long seconds before returning to her eyes again. She felt the strength sliding out of her, ebbing away with each moment he gazed at her.

"What are you doing?" she asked quietly.

"I'm listening to you." He wore the faintest hint of a self-satisfied smirk on his lips. "Please—go on."

Angry with herself for being so silly and with Michael for being so damned sexy, Jessy momentarily forgot she was supposed to be embarrassed. The words poured out in a self-defensive torrent, her gaze slamming head-on into his.

"This is all new to me, okay?" Her eyes flashed as she spoke, daring him to smile or make fun of her. "I mean, I've kissed before but—it was never so—never like that—"

The barn suddenly became a vacuum of sound, the silence broken only by the occasional flutter of bird's wings and the disgruntled huffs of the horses below. Jessy's mouth closed with an audible snap, her eyes widening as she realized what she'd just admitted. She'd said too much. Way too much.

"Oh, God," she groaned, covering her face with her hands. "I'm too old to be this goofy. Please tell me I didn't say what I think I just said."

The corner of Michael's mouth curled up in a smile. "Honey,

I'm not sure exactly *what* you just said."

Jessy pried open one eye and glared at him. "I'm embarrassed, okay?"

"Okay—but *why* are you embarrassed?"

Jessy sighed again. Might have known Michael wouldn't settle for letting her be merely humiliated. Oh, no—he had to know *why*.

"Because I'm thirty-two years old and I've only kissed one man in my entire life. Well—two, counting you." Jessy kept her tone matter-of-fact; she couldn't quite believe it, but somehow the sting of embarrassment was fast fading. She'd never really talked about this with anyone before, and Michael, if nothing else, was her friend. Besides, it seemed only fair to let him know what he was getting himself into. "It's just embarrassing to be my age and still be so—inexperienced, that's all."

Michael smiled faintly. "What's so bad about that?"

"Nothing—if it's by choice." Jessy cringed as soon as the words were out of her mouth. Great. Now he'd think she was a closet nympho.

Still smiling, Michael took her hand and silently led her back to the hay bale. He settled down on the floor, leaning back against the hay, and motioned for Jessy to join him. Moving with as much grace as she could muster, Jessy sat beside him, shoulder to shoulder, keeping her head down and her gaze fixed on her hands in her lap. She knew that he was watching her, but damned if she could bring herself to look at him now.

"So go on," Michael said softly.

"There's not a whole lot more to say." Jessy shrugged and managed a feeble smile, still staring at her hands as she twisted those invisible rings again. "I'm just completely inexperienced with this kind of thing, and when you kissed me I just—"

Jessy's voice trailed away as Michael picked up her hand and held it loosely in his, tracing the faint outline of veins on the back of her hand with his thumb. Despite the sudden quickening of her heart, Jessy managed to continue.

"When you kissed me—I kinda panicked. I don't exactly know

the territory here." Jessy smiled wryly and glanced up to him again. "I can't believe I'm even talking about this to you."

Michael said nothing, lifting her hand instead to trail soft kisses along the length of each finger. He turned her hand over to press a kiss against the center of her palm, lips lingering for a heartstopping moment. Jessy could do nothing but stare at him.

"Wh—what are you doing?" she whispered.

"I'm kissing your hand," Michael murmured against her skin. His mouth trailed along her inner wrist, the tip of his tongue lightly tracing the meandering line of her veins.

Jessy closed her eyes, taken by surprise by how unbelievably wonderful the warmth of his mouth and tongue felt against her skin. She could almost imagine how it would feel to be kissed in other places—

Her eyes snapped open, the moment shattered by an abrupt slap of reality as she imagined what his reaction would be if he saw her body with all its flaws. She could already anticipate his distaste, his disappointment if they ever became intimate. The thought of possibly facing that kind of pain and humiliation sobered Jessy instantly.

Reluctantly she pulled her hand away from him, keeping her eyes downcast as she wrapped her arms around herself.

"What'd I do now?" Michael asked, a trace of impatience in his voice.

"Why are you doing this?"

"Because I want to," he said simply.

Jessy turned her gaze back to him again, not sure of how to respond to that. For years she'd struggled against allowing her sense of self to be shaped by the negative reactions of the people around her. She'd managed to develop a modicum of self-esteem through her schoolwork and her few friendships with others, but part of her had always felt that she shouldn't ever expect anyone to fall in love with her. After all, it was a big world and there would always be someone better out there.

She'd struggled against that mindset for years, logic giving way to emotion every time. She'd fought dearly for the self-confidence she possessed, trying desperately to make herself believe that she *was* a good person, that she really was deserving of love. Yes, there would always be someone prettier, smarter, thinner, better at math, whatever—but that's life. Unfair as hell in some ways, but better than nothing. She'd accepted that, rising above her insecurities and fears to become a person who had finally learned to like herself, flaws and all.

Now, however, she was beginning to doubt all that. She'd managed to put herself through college and graduate with honors. She'd managed to find a rewarding career that she loved. She'd managed to take care of her elderly aunt and make her last years as comfortable and peaceful as she could. She'd managed to do all those things alone, without a thought to her weight or her lack of a relationship. In a quiet, nontraditional way, she'd been a success in life.

But now she was freaking out just because a handsome man wanted to kiss her. She couldn't just relax and enjoy the moment or the attention. She couldn't just accept the thought that he might possibly be physically attracted to her. For all the pining and whining she'd done in her life, she couldn't believe that a man like Michael might actually see and like the person beneath all the weight.

And it wasn't fair. It wasn't fair to Michael or to herself.

"I'm sorry," she finally whispered, lowering her head. "I've been so—I'm sorry."

"Sorry for what?" he asked softly, the faintest of smiles on his lips. He tipped up her chin, gently lifting her gaze back to his. "Jess—?"

"I'm just—" Jessy's eyes shone with tears. She shrugged, unable to find the right words. "I'm just weird."

Michael couldn't help but chuckle as he gathered Jessy into his arms, holding her close as he smoothed down her hair and gently rubbed her back. He felt her stiffen beneath his hand, as though she didn't want to be touched, but he refused to stop, allowing his hand to roam up and down the length and width of her back. He knew why she was so skittish. Everything, sooner or later, seemed to come back to her weight.

It frustrated him to no end. Her weight was the last thing on his mind, and now that he was finally holding her, he realized that her size had nothing at all to do with the way his body was responding to her. She felt so soft, so comforting and warm as her body seemed to mold itself against his. He pulled her closer, the plushness of her breasts pressing full against his chest, and he felt a rush of desire that nearly blindsided him in its intensity. And if he had understood her correctly, the knowledge that she had no idea how deeply she affected him emotionally as well as physically, made him want her all the more.

But he couldn't take advantage of her innocence. She trusted him enough to be bluntly honest about her lack of experience, risking humiliation just so he wouldn't be disappointed—as if such a thing were possible. She trusted him enough to cry in front of him, to lower her guard enough to weep quietly in his arms. The fact that he could even have such intensely sexual feelings about her at this moment made him feel vaguely guilty. And surprised at himself. Since the divorce, his sex drive had crept along at neutral. He'd had zero interest in dating anyone, zero interest in casual affairs. He liked sex, of course, and had enjoyed it immensely while he was still married—but that was exactly the problem. He couldn't just drift into a "wham-bam-thank you ma'am" kind of one-night stand. He had to be in love with the woman. Maybe that made him a prude, but he couldn't help it and refused to change it. He had been raised to believe that sex was the ultimate gift two people who loved each other could share. It was a serious commitment with serious consequences, and it was something he refused to enter into lightly.

But here he was, comforting a woman he'd come to care deeply for as a friend, a woman he might not have even noticed had the situation been different, and he was so aroused by her that he didn't dare to even move. Years of a monk-like existence had come screeching to a halt—and all because of this shy, unassuming woman who had only kissed two men in her life.

"You okay?" he whispered, sliding his chin along the silkiness of her hair. She sighed deeply, and the hot rush of breath against his throat was nearly his undoing.

"I'm fine." Jessy raised her head from his shoulder, sniffing as she wiped at her eyes and shakily smiled. "Sorry about that."

"Don't you dare apologize." Michael smiled and drew the backs of his fingers along her wet cheek. "Besides, you look pretty when you cry."

Jessy laughed self-consciously and playfully slapped at his arm. "Liar."

"I'd prefer the term 'sweet-talker,' thank you."

"Do you always know the exact right thing to say?"

Michael studied her for a moment. If that were true, then he would have already told her how he felt about her—and she might have already bolted.

"No," he finally said, smile fading slightly. "Not always."

He couldn't stop staring at her mouth, the perfectly sculpted shape of her lips, the faint blush of color that no lipstick could ever duplicate. In that brief kiss they'd shared earlier, he'd discovered that her lips were almost unbelievably soft and pliant. Her kisses alone could bring a man to his knees.

But not just any man. He didn't want to think of Jessy with anyone else. Damn it, he felt territorial now.

"I need to ask you something," Michael said softly.

Jessy smiled almost nervously. "Okay—"

"Would you mind if I kissed you again?"

"What?"

"Would you mind if I kissed you again," Michael repeated quietly, reaching up to smooth back an unruly wave of hair from Jessy's cheek. She had the softest skin he'd ever touched. "A real kiss this time."

"But I don't—"

"Just follow my lead," he whispered as he gently lowered his lips to hers again, kissing her with the slow tenderness he sensed that she needed. She shyly responded, tentatively returning his kiss, her hands fluttering lightly against his chest. He felt her relax against him, sensing that she was slowly growing more comfortable with his touch, more confident of her own ability. He felt as if he could kiss her for hours, that despite his earlier desire for more, he could be perfectly happy just holding her, touching her—

But first he had to tell her how he was beginning to feel about her. No matter what the consequences.

He broke away from the kiss, reluctantly lifting his head so that he could see her face, gauge her reaction. She gazed up at him with the most innocent, most trusting eyes he had ever seen, so completely different than—

"Ann," he muttered aloud, wincing as he fell back against the hay bale. He laced his fingers behind his neck, leaning forward to prop his elbows on his upraised knees. "Oh, my God—"

If ever a moment could be shattered—

"*Ann?*" Jessy said quietly. Michael's distracted gaze snapped back to hers.

"If she knew about this—with us—" Michael closed his eyes again, scrubbing at his face as he sighed deeply.

Jessy went cold, thinking of the conversation she'd had with Ann on Thanksgiving. "What do you mean?"

Michael shrugged helplessly. "My relationship with her is—complicated."

"Complicated," Jessy said tonelessly. "Okay."

"When we divorced, she didn't contest custody of the kids. She wanted to work in Chicago and the kids didn't fit into that." Michael looked at Jessy again. "We've had a pretty peaceful agreement about the kids, at least. She knows they're happy here, and she's welcome to visit anytime she wants."

"That's—civil of you both." Jessy thought of Ann's words. They still had a relationship. For all intents and purposes, they were still together.

"It's for the kids' sake, more than anything else." Michael took Jessy's hands in his, thumbs lightly stroking across her knuckles, his voice as soft as his touch. Jessy had to fight the urge to pull her hands away from him. It felt wrong.

"I have to ask you this—" The words bubbled up and out before Jessy could stop them. "Do you still have feelings for Ann?"

Michael said nothing for a moment, and to Jessy, that said it all. He looked away from her, let her hands slip out of his.

"Honestly? Yeah—I did. For a long time, I did."

Jessy felt her heart shatter. She should have known. She should have seen this coming. Why she ever thought for a moment things could have turned out differently—

"Okay," she managed to say, struggling to paste a smile on her face. "I understand."

"No, I don't think you do." Michael took her hand again, lacing his fingers with hers. "Things changed."

"They don't change just like *that.*" Jessy pulled away from him and stood up. She had to put some distance between them.

"What's going on, Jess?"

"What about Ann?" she asked quietly, forcing herself to keep his gaze.

"Ann's always going to be a part of my life because of the kids, but—"

"But you haven't let her go, have you?" Jessy saw a shadow of guilt drift across Michael's face.

"Jessy—"

"No—don't tell me. It's none of my business." Jessy looked away from him, swallowing hard as she stared at her hands, feeling silly and stupid and hurt and irrationally betrayed.

"We were married for a long time—"

"Michael, please—don't." Jessy could actually feel herself hollowing out inside, could feel her heart tightening, aching. It felt as if everything was ending before it even had a chance to begin. "So—what happens now?"

"What do you want to happen?"

"I want you to keep your kids."

"What about us?"

"All we did was kiss," Jessy said, sighing as she looked back to him again. "We can leave it at that and walk away."

Michael remained silent, his gaze so penetrating that Jessy almost couldn't speak. She swallowed hard, thinking of a thousand reasons to just allow herself to be swept up in a relationship that had the potential to be everything she'd ever dreamed. But every one of those reasons seemed to be rooted in selfishness. No matter how much she cared for Michael, no matter how lonely she had been before she met him, she could not—*would* not—put her own needs ahead of the kids'. They needed a father. And Michael needed them.

"*Can* you walk away?" Michael asked quietly. A muscle in his jaw jumped as he ground his teeth, his eyes so dark they seemed almost black.

"I think we have to."

Michael slowly nodded his head, biting at his lower lip. "So—is that how it's going to be then? We just walk away from it now, stay friendly, and then you leave us after Christmas?"

The pain in his voice was masked by a low, sarcastic anger. But Jessy wouldn't be swayed. It would be better this way, ending it now before it could begin.

"I'm sorry, Michael—"

"Yeah," Michael said roughly, abruptly getting to his feet. "Me, too."

He crossed the room without another word, climbing down the ladder without looking back. Jessy watched him go, wishing with all her heart that everything could have been different.

But it wasn't. And the sooner she accepted that, the better.

Chapter Nine

JESSY WATCHED THE SUNRISE from her bedroom window. A fresh layer of snow blanketed the rolling hills, marred only by the line of footprints Michael had made on his way out to the barn. Every day since he'd brought her home she had gotten up to have coffee with him after he finished the chores. She'd loved those hours they spent together in the mornings. By dawn they'd be on their third cup of coffee, comfortable in their friendship, their easy companionship.

It had been a long night. She'd managed to avoid him after that kiss in the barn yesterday, and he seemed to be staying out of her way as well. It was just so hard to face him now. Knowing what she knew, she couldn't act like nothing was wrong, like the thought of Michael and Ann together didn't give her heart a vicious twist.

But they needed to be together. The sad thing was that Jessy had ever thought for a moment that she might have had a chance.

She turned away from the window and caught a glimpse of her reflection in the dresser mirror. Usually she could almost forget how big she really was, pushing the reality of her weight into an abstract concern. Even though her size influenced every aspect of her life from the clothes she wore to the way she sat down, she could usually manage to deny that she was as big as she really was.

But not now. Now she felt every ounce of her weight, saw every flaw. She looked wide and bulging in her flannel nightgown. And to think that once upon a time she'd believed that maybe one day she would meet someone who would see her good qualities before he saw her flaws.

The one night she had spent with Charlie, he'd had to get drunk before he could bear to make love to her. And she couldn't call what they'd done making love. She'd been a virgin, scared to death, sick with fear that he'd look at her and be disgusted. And he'd been so drunk that she could have been anyone. To say it was perfunctory would be generous to Charlie. For her, it was painful in every way possible.

But the next morning, when Charlie had woken up, he had looked at her and been horrified. Even though he had tried to hide it, she saw the truth in his eyes. She would never be anybody's idea of beautiful or desirable or sexy. He got away from her as fast as he could, apologizing profusely without looking her in the eyes, and they'd never discussed that night again. He seemed to forget about it by the next day.

But Jessy thought of it every time she looked at her body. How must she have looked to him? How must she look to Michael?

A knock startled her out of her thoughts. Michael opened the door before she could jump back into bed or grab a robe, and for a moment all she could do was stand there in mortified silence as they stared at each other.

"Sorry," Michael muttered, looking away as Jessy snatched up a heavy chenille robe and slipped it on, embarrassment reddening her cheeks.

"What do you want?" The words came out wrong, sounding far more abrupt than intended, but she didn't apologize. She pushed her hair over her shoulders and tried not to look as awkward as she felt.

"I couldn't sleep last night." Michael looked at her again. His eyes were dark-ringed, his cheeks unshaven, his dark hair dusted with melting snowflakes. "I couldn't stop thinking about—everything."

Jessy needed something to do, something to keep her busy so she wouldn't have to face Michael directly. Without a word she began to make up the bed, hoping that he didn't notice how she had also tossed and turned and messed up the covers. She hadn't been able to sleep, either; every time she closed her eyes, she saw Michael and Ann together, talking—laughing—making love.

Michael sat down at the windowseat, silent as he watched Jessy make up the bed. Jessy didn't look at him, but she knew all too well that he was staring at her. She knew how thick her waist must look to him as she kept her back to him, how broad her hips were as she leaned over the bed. For an instant she wanted to scream at him to stop looking at her, stop comparing her to Ann.

"What happened with us?" he finally asked, his voice a rough whisper.

"First of all, there *is* no 'us.'" Jessy fluffed up a pillow and tossed it onto the bed, anything to keep from looking at him. "It was all just a mistake. Bad decisions."

"What's that supposed to mean?"

Jessy stiffened and finally turned to face him again. "It means that I shouldn't have come here. You shouldn't have kissed me. It means you're still in love with Ann—and that unless you get your act together and remarry her, you're going to lose your children."

Michael slowly frowned. "*What*—? How in the hell did you come up with that?"

"That's not important—"

"I think it is."

"What's important here is the fact that unless you do something, you are going to lose custody of your children."

"And by 'do something,' you mean get back together with Ann."

"*Yes!*" Jessy couldn't hide her exasperation. "You still love her, and it's obvious that she still loves you—"

"So we should get back together for the kids' sakes." Michael's disbelieving smile twisted. "You've been here exactly a week, Jessy. What makes you think you know how I feel about Ann? Or about you, for that matter?"

"I'm just a friend," Jessy murmured, needlessly smoothing down the quilt and arranging pillows.

"What?"

"I said, I'm just a friend." Jessy straightened and faced him full on. This entire conversation was becoming surreal. "Like you said, I've been here all of a week. You've known me for six, maybe seven days. *Days,* Michael. I feel like I'm pushing it by calling myself a friend."

"But we've spent every one of those days together." Michael ran a hand through his snow-dampened hair, forehead furrowed.

"Being friends with someone isn't the same as—"

"Who said I just wanted to be friends?"

Jessy would have done a double take at that moment had she been able to move. Or breathe. Or react in any way but to stare dumbly at him in shock. The conversation had moved from surreal to completely absurd. She couldn't begin to comprehend even the possibility of what he could mean by that remark. She couldn't accept it.

"I shouldn't have said that." Michael shoved his hands in his pockets, then changed his mind and folded his arms over his chest, trying to look more casual than he felt. "I'm sorry."

"Sorry for what?" Jessy asked quietly.

"For everything." Michael took a deep breath and sighed. "I'm not doing this right at all. I don't know how to say things like this. Never have."

"Say things like what?"

"That I—" Another deep breath and time-buying sigh. "I—have feelings for you."

"Feelings?" Jessy sat down on the edge of the bed, utterly baffled by the entire situation. "Michael, I don't think you know *how* you feel. Especially about me."

Michael laughed grimly. "And I suppose you do."

"I know that I'm not the kind of woman who inspires love at first sight," Jessy said quietly. "And I know that if we hadn't been forced to share that motel room, you would have never even given me a second glance. Right?"

Jessy knew by the look of shamed surprise in Michael's eyes that she was absolutely right. A sudden swell of disappointment and hurt choked her for a moment, but she willed it away. If nothing else, the pain would make it easier for her to let go.

"I may not know you very well," Jessy continued, voice softening, "but I saw something in the way you looked at Ann that—well, maybe you weren't even aware of it, but it was there. And I saw it in the way Ann looked at you."

"And you don't see it when I look at *you?*" Michael walked over to the bed, towering over Jessy. She raised her head, even though she didn't know how in the world she was going to be able to meet his eyes. "Jessy—I don't know any other way to tell you that I like you—"

"Of course you *like* me," Jessy said quietly, lowering her head again. "It doesn't take a whole lot of effort to *like* somebody—"

"Would you please, for once, stop feeling so damn sorry for yourself?" Michael snapped, losing his patience.

Jessy froze, stunned as she managed to meet Michael's eyes again. For a moment the silence in the room felt like a tangible thing. Michael's face paled as he abruptly turned away from her, looking out the window to the rising sun.

"*What?*" Jessy couldn't hide the sharp edge of anger in her voice.

"You heard me." Michael faced her again, meeting her glare dead-on. "Every other word out of your mouth is some kind of self-deprecating remark and I'm getting just a little damn tired of it."

"Oh, okay—so is this the standard 'How do you expect anyone to love you if you can't love yourself' speech?" Jessy could feel rage thrumming through her entire body, could hear it trembling in her voice. "If it is, then spare me, Michael. Because I've heard just about every variation of it that there is."

"Then why hasn't it sunken in yet?"

"For God's sake—" Jessy muttered, turning away from him as she strode towards the door. She opened it wider, an unmistakable gesture that Michael ignored.

"I'm just trying to help you, Jess—"

"Help me? How is this helping me?" Jessy caught herself and looked away for a moment. "Please leave me alone."

"Why are you doing this?"

Jessy gritted her teeth. "What do you expect me to do, Michael?"

"I don't *expect* you to do *anything.*" The sharpness of his tone inflamed Jessy's rage even further. His anger easily matched hers. "Damn it, Jessy—if you can't even accept how I feel about you—"

"You haven't heard anything I've said, have you?" Jessy stood, braced for battle. "Michael, you don't have 'feelings' for someone you've only known for a week. And you've got to think about the kids—"

"The kids love you."

"I don't mean that." Jessy pushed a hank of hair away from her eyes and paced the length of the room. "Have you even stopped to think of what Ann might do if she found out about this? You were the one who said she'd try to take the kids away from you."

Michael remained stubbornly silent, eyes hard as he stared at Jessy.

"You were married to Ann for a long time. You built a life and family with her. As you said, you'll always love her because of the kids." Jessy took a deep breath and sighed. "I know you like me, Michael, but it's just because I'm a distraction from what's worrying you. It's not love or anything else. This isn't some kind of silly fairy tale."

Michael's jaw twitched as he ground his teeth, looking away from Jessy for a moment as he shook his head.

"So what are you saying?" he asked quietly. "That Ann and I should get back together for the kids' sake?" Michael's gaze met hers again, a bitter smile twisting on his lips. "That's pretty damn noble of you, Jess."

"I'm not trying to be noble, Michael." Jessy's voice was little more than a whisper as she looked into his eyes again, hoping to make him understand. "I'm trying to keep those kids from getting hurt."

"Do you think that I *want* them to be hurt?" Michael's brows drew together in a fierce scowl. "Do you think I want her to take them away from me?"

"Of course not." Jessy stared him down, unblinking as she returned his glare. "I just don't think you're considering your other options."

"And those would be——?"

Jessy couldn't speak for a moment, too exasperated, too frustrated, to think clearly. She wasn't doing this right. She didn't have enough practical experience with these matters to know what to do or say. What if she *did* have a relationship with Michael? Would Ann be spiteful and try to use that against him in order to win custody? What would losing the kids do to Michael and Lyssa? It all seemed like too much to risk for a so-called relationship that wouldn't last past Christmas. There was just far too much at stake.

"Michael," she said softly, "I think you know in your heart what you should do."

"In my heart," Michael repeated dully, nodding as he slowly walked to Jessy. "In my heart, I know that my feelings for you are more than——"

"Don't," Jessy whispered. Part of her wanted desperately to hear him out. But for the kids' sake—for her *own* sake—she couldn't let Michael delude himself into thinking that his feelings for her went any farther than friendship. The silence that settled between them chilled her to the soul.

"Michael," she finally said, "you don't know me. Not really. And I don't know *you*. All we really know about each other is that we're both lonely—and that we met at a time when we both needed a friend."

"This is ridiculous," Michael muttered. "We've had this argument before——"

"And we'll keep having it until you realize the truth."

"And what *is* the truth, Jessy?" Anger made his tone brittle. The lines in his brow, between his eyes, deepened. "Come on—I'm listening. What is this mysterious truth that you and *only* you know?"

Jessy hesitated a moment before speaking. The reasoning that sounded so good to her own mind suddenly seemed pathetic. Regardless, she forced herself to keep Michael's steady gaze, forced her voice to remain calm and controlled.

"I don't belong here, Michael." Jessy swallowed hard, pausing a moment as Michael angrily rolled his eyes and turned away. Jessy continued, raising her voice slightly, forcing him to hear her words. "You want someone in your life, someone to share your family with, but it's not me. I can't step into Ann's role when she—when she's never really left it."

Michael slowly turned to face her again, stunned. "So—you could walk away from this. You could walk away from us."

"I don't want to, Michael—but if you'd just stop and think about it—" Jessy shook her head, voice dropping almost to a whisper. "I don't really have any choice."

"You don't have a choice," he repeated, the slightest undercurrent of mockery in his voice. "After everything—"

"What *everything*, Michael? We've only known each other a week." She caught herself, taking a deep breath before continuing. "You're getting pity and loneliness and infatuation all mixed up. It's not *me* you feel anything for, Michael. It's the *idea* of having someone. That's all."

Mouth set in a tight line, Michael nodded his head, rubbing at the back of his neck as he took a deep breath and then slowly, deliberately released it. He looked away from Jessy for a moment, swallowing hard when he finally glanced back to her again.

"I—uh—" He shrugged, as if struggling to retain his composure. "I don't know what else to say. I guess you've just got it all figured out. You obviously know what's best for me and my kids, so—I don't suppose there's any use in arguing with you, is there?"

Jessy's gaze was unwavering as she looked back at him. "You know that's not what I'm saying."

Before Michael could reply, Ben opened the door and poked his head into the room. "Daddy? Can we ride horses today?"

Michael turned to face him, plastering a makeshift smile on his face as he lightened his tone. "Sure, Benny-boy—go on downstairs and eat breakfast first."

Ben grinned and disappeared again, footsteps thundering down the hall. Michael turned back to Jessy again, smile gone.

"I know you're self-conscious about your weight, Jessy. I've seen the way you try to hide yourself, the way you avoid mirrors. If that's the reason why you can't believe what I'm telling you—"

"My reasons are none of your business," Jessy said sharply.

It was as though she had slapped his face. Michael said nothing for a moment, studying Jessy with an intensity that made her feel foolish and mean. Neither of them spoke; neither of them looked away. It was a war of wills that would have no winners.

"Fine," Michael finally said, his tone clipped and cold. "If you've decreed that this is the way it's going to be, then I guess you're right. It's none of my business."

He strode past Jessy, taking particular care not to touch her. Somehow that was worse than anything he could have possibly said. She felt suddenly repugnant, acutely self-conscious. Michael paused at the doorway, half-turning to face her again, keeping his eyes averted as he spoke.

"I don't understand why you're doing this, Jessy. I know you've got your reasons. I know they're none of my business, but—" He shook his head and finally met her eyes again. "But if you think I can't have feelings for you—or God forbid, maybe even fall in love with you—because of something so unimportant as your weight, then—"

His voice trailed away as he held her gaze for a few long moments, his eyes darkened by either rage or regret—Jessy couldn't tell the difference anymore. Without another word he walked out of the room, closing the door behind him.

Jessy sank down on the bed, staring at the reflection of herself in the dresser mirror, looking at her protruding stomach, her drooping breasts, her double chin. Even with all the good qualities she knew she possessed, she could never get past this, the unlovely exterior. And if she couldn't accept it, how could she ever expect someone like Michael to accept it?

Wrenching her gaze away from the mirror, she looked at the door again, wondering just what she had done.

"**Hold on, hon**—don't wiggle around the saddle." Michael held onto Ben as he led the pony along the edge of the corral. Marie and Libby sat on the fence, watching and waiting their turn. The three of them were unusually quiet this morning, acutely aware of Jessy's absence. They hadn't asked Michael yet why she wasn't with them, but he knew it would just be a matter of time. And then the fun would begin.

"Daddy, look!" Marie jumped down from the fence. "Here comes Mommy!"

Michael stopped and turned around, his already thin smile fading when he saw Ann's car coming up the driveway. He'd forgotten all about her day with the kids. He helped Ben scoot down from the pony, remaining inside the corral as the kids ran to meet her. Maybe he could get away with avoiding her completely—

Ann saw him and waved, immediately making her way over to him.

Michael took a deep breath and sighed, feeling as if he were girding himself for battle.

"Hey there, cowboy," she said and smiled. As always, she looked absolutely stunning, with her hair teased and styled to perfection, her make-up exquisitely applied. And he noticed that under her long coat she wore the outfit he'd once told her he liked best: tight jeans, red silk blouse, and knee-high black boots.

"Good morning, Ann," he said evenly. He leaned on the fence, feeling more at ease with something standing between them.

Ann smiled brilliantly. "What? No kiss hello? No 'happy to see you'?"

Michael said nothing. Right now, Ann was the last person in the world he was happy to see.

"Grinch." She leaned against the fence from the other side, folding her arms over the top slat. The movement lifted her breasts, widening the gap in her open collar. Michael noticed, then quickly looked away. "Listen, babe—what I said the other night about missing you—I meant it."

"Ann, we've gone over this before—"

"Honey, I know why you brought that woman home. You felt sorry for her. And I think that's so sweet of you." Ann reached out and covered his hand with hers. Her palm felt cold against his skin. "I know I acted badly the other night, but it's just because I still love you."

Michael slid his hand away from hers. "Annie, don't—"

"Don't what? Don't tell my husband that I love him?"

"I'm not your husband, Ann. How many times do I have to remind you of that?" Michael caught himself, lowering his voice so the kids couldn't hear. "You walked out on me. On us."

"I made a mistake."

"Yes, you did." Michael looked around, feeling absurdly guilty, and lowered his voice. "We're not together anymore, Ann. It's over. *Everything* between us is over."

"You weren't complaining the last time I came home—"

"That was six months ago. And *that* was a mistake, too."

"I want to come back." Ann took his hands again, this time holding them tightly. "Baby, I still love you. I've always loved you. And I miss you so much. I want us to be a family again. The five of us. Together."

Michael studied Ann for a few long moments. How many times after the divorce had he dreamed of hearing her say those words? How many nights had he dreamed of this instant? Every time they'd slept together after the divorce, he'd hoped she would realize what she was giving up and come back to him. And every time she left to go back to Chicago, it was just as painful as the first time she'd walked away.

"Ann—I can't do this—"

"Shhh, baby—I know it's a lot to think about all at once." Ann smiled and cradled his cheek in her hand, stroking her thumb along his cheekbone. The gesture slammed into Michael with unexpected force, bringing back a flood of memories of better days. "But we can work this out. I know we can."

And with that Ann leaned over the fence, capturing Michael's lips in a soft, familiar kiss. It caught him off-guard, shocking him with its unexpected warmth.

"You think about it today," Ann whispered, nuzzling his nose with hers. "We can talk about all this tonight, when we come home. I know we can work this out, baby."

Michael couldn't speak. He managed a faint nod, feeling disembodied as he watched Ann pull away. There seemed to be something like triumph shining in her eyes.

"We'll be back by eight!" she said, waving cheerily as she headed back to the car. "Bye, babe!"

Michael remained at the fence, frozen there. For the first time in his life, after all of Ann's sweet talk, after all of her touches and kisses and smiles, he felt absolutely nothing for her.

Because all he could think about was how much he wished it had been Jessy saying those words.

Chapter Ten

MICHAEL STUDIED the scattered pieces of a build-it-yourself bicycle and groaned, leaning against the wall as he stretched his legs out before him and tossed the instructions to the side. No use trying to concentrate. His mind kept wandering back to Ann's visit that morning. And to the argument with Jessy.

After thinking about it all day, he could finally begin to understand her reasons. He'd come on way too strong, said too much too soon. He didn't even stop to think about the relationship she'd been running from. Maybe she was still in love with the creep.

But he didn't like to think about that. Something in what remained of the caveman portion of his brain couldn't stand the thought of Jessy with another man.

Which is probably exactly how Jessy felt about the thought of him and Ann. The realization hit him hard, and he winced at how dumb he had been about the whole situation.

"Michael—?"

Jessy's voice was so soft that for a moment Michael thought he might have imagined it. He looked up, saw Jessy in the doorway of the garage, and felt his heart go out to her. She had been crying, her eyes red and slightly puffy.

"I think I—*we*—need to talk."

"Uh, sure." He fought the urge to apologize for what he'd said that morning. Every word he'd said about the way he felt was true. He saw no need to make excuses. Unfortunately, he also saw no way to make her believe him. Maybe he didn't know her inside out, but he knew her well enough to sense that once she'd made up her mind about something, nothing less than an act of God could change it.

"So where do we start?" he asked quietly, resting his elbows on his upraised knees. He watched Jessy carefully perch on the edge of a trunk, aware that she purposely kept a good ten feet between them. She wouldn't meet his gaze, keeping her eyes downcast as she clasped her hands on her lap, tightly lacing her fingers.

"I've been thinking about this morning," she finally said, her voice an unreadable monotone. She looked up, gaze pinning his with remarkable strength. What he had believed to be reticence was actually caution, wariness masquerading as fear. Once again, he wondered exactly what she had gone through in her life, what kind of pain could give someone so young such a world-weary strength.

"And?"

"You were right," she said.

"About what?"

"About all of it."

Neither of them spoke for a few moments. Jessy picked up one of the bicycle pedals and absently studied it. Michael sensed that she was gathering courage, choosing her words carefully so this fragile understanding would not be shattered.

"Can you understand why it's so hard for me to believe you?" she finally said, turning the force of those eyes back to him again.

"Honestly?" Michael smiled faintly, sadly. "No. I can't."

The faintest ghost of a smile flickered across Jessy's lips even as her eyes darkened with sadness. Michael wanted to go to her, to hold her until that sadness went away, but knew he needed to keep his distance. For the moment, at least.

"I don't mean for this to sound melodramatic," Jessy said quietly, "but I don't know how to do this."

"Do what?"

Jessy hesitated before she spoke, her gaze dipping away from Michael's.

"I've never really been a *part* of something. Family. Couple. Whatever. I've been a self-contained unit for a long, long time now." She looked back to Michael again, a faintly sardonic smile on her lips. "And I've never had anyone say that they've had any so-called 'feelings' for me before. To be completely honest, it scares me."

"What about—" Michael caught himself before he could finish. Even though he burned to know more about Jessy's relationship with the mystery man in Kentucky, he knew he didn't dare push. He had to wait for her to trust him enough to tell him. That's the way it had to be.

"What?" Jessy looked at him, expectant. "What were you going to say?"

"I was going to ask you about—" Michael sighed in resignation, dreading the answer almost as much as he anticipated it. "I was going to ask about the guy in Kentucky. What about him? Do you still love him?"

The question seemed to hang in the abrupt silence, and Michael wished fiercely that he'd kept his mouth shut. Jessy's cheeks reddened and she looked away from him, staring down at the floor.

"I guess I would have had to tell you sooner or later." Jessy took a deep breath and slowly released it, raising her gaze to Michael's again. "Until last year, I'd never dated in my life. Nobody asked me out. Simple as that. And I was okay with it. I know that I'm not the kind of woman men ask out, so I accepted it. I went to school and worked and read and only felt lonely once in a while. It wasn't that bad." Michael remained silent, hearing the pain that Jessy was so desperately trying to disguise.

"My Aunt Amelia was in her eighties when she died," Jessy continued, voice softer than a whisper. "I took care of her for a long time. It seemed like the house got twice as big and ten times as empty once she was gone. I thought I'd been lonely before, but— this was almost suffocating."

Jessy fell silent for a moment, staring at her folded hands. Michael noticed that her nails were short, almost gnawed to the quick. He moved over to the trunk to sit beside her.

"Charlie Wilks was a guy I'd gone to high school with," she continued. "He moved back to town and started teaching gym at my school, so we would have lunch together and talk. He was the first guy who ever seemed interested in me. So when he asked me out to grab some dinner, I went. And it just kind of grew from there. We'd hang out together, watch videos during the week. Anything to keep that house from being so quiet and empty. And that led me to make some bad decisions that I still regret."

Michael brushed a tendril of hair away from her eyes, allowing his fingertips to linger along her cheek. If she noticed his touch, she didn't react to it.

"To make a long, ugly story short," Jessy said, smiling sourly as she looked up from her hands, "things didn't work out. He moved to Minneapolis a little while back and we kept in touch. I thought I was in love with him, and I missed him like crazy, and so one night when he called me and said all these wonderful things to me about how much he missed me and how much he loved me and how he wished I would come up to live with him—I believed him. The fact that he was drunk when he called never crossed my mind. I wanted to believe that he loved me, so—"

Jessy's voice faded away as she closed her eyes and leaned her head back against the wall. The sardonic smile remained on her lips, but a tear escaped her eye. At that moment, Michael had never felt so helpless, so distanced from someone.

"I'd just lost my job at the school," Jessy said, voice soft. "Budget cuts. So I was out of work and living in that quiet old house alone and when Charlie finally said he wanted to be with me—I went. I left everything behind in Kentucky to go to him. Like an idiot." Jessy opened her eyes and looked at Michael again. "And when I got there, I met his fiancée, a very pretty girl named Kirsten. Charlie hadn't told me about her because he didn't want to hurt my feelings. He didn't even remember calling me that night, much less anything he'd said."

Michael forced himself to keep breathing evenly, to tamp down the sudden flare of anger he felt for the son of a bitch who'd hurt Jessy. For a few moments, he couldn't speak. He mimicked Jessy's pose and leaned his head against the wall, staring at the ceiling. She took a deep breath and sighed, and he did the same.

"Jess—"

"I know."

"I had no idea."

Jessy rolled her head to look at him. "Well it's not exactly the kind of thing a person feels like chatting about. I'd prefer that the world not know how big of an idiot I am. Was. Will inevitably be again."

Her droll tone and slow smile was enough to momentarily distract him from his anger. Without even being aware of it, he smiled back.

"So what happens now?" Jessy asked.

Michael reached over and took her hand, entwining his fingers with hers. "What do you *want* to happen?"

Jessy gazed at him for a few long moments. "To be honest—I don't know."

"Mind a suggestion?"

"I'd welcome one right about now."

"How about this—" Michael's gaze caught on hers, holding it for a long moment. "You stay with us for as long as you want—as long as you need. No pressure. No expectations. And whatever happens can just—happen."

"What if it doesn't—"

Michael shook his head. "Nope—I don't want to hear that."

"You're going to be stubborn about this, aren't you?" Jessy grudgingly smiled, lowering her gaze to their joined hands. Her smile slowly faded as she kept her eyes downcast. "But what about Ann?"

"Ann—" Michael took a deep breath and slowly released it. "Ann will just have to deal with it. Whether she likes it or not."

"What if she tries to take the kids? I don't want to be responsible for that—"

Michael slipped his finger under Jessy's chin and tipped her gaze up to his again. "She won't. I know her. She'll do what's best for the kids."

"What about you?" Jessy didn't look away from his eyes. "Is it really over between you?"

Michael nodded, remembering how hollow her touch had made him feel earlier that day. Six months ago he would have been on top of the world if Ann had said she wanted to come home again. Now he realized that they had only been using each other.

"Yeah," he said quietly. "It really is."

Jessy said nothing, and Michael knew that she was struggling to believe him.

"Everything will work out," he said quietly, trying to make himself believe it too. "It'll be okay—trust me."

The corner of Jessy's mouth quirked up in a half smile. "Trust me, he says—"

"Yes, I says," Michael said as he smiled back to her. Amazing how easily smiling came to him when he was with Jessy. "So—now that we've got this cleared up, I have a favor to ask you."

"Anything."

Without saying another word, Michael leaned closer and brushed his lips against hers, cradling her face in his hands, stroking his fingertips against her soft cheek. She caught her breath in surprise, then sighed into his mouth, her lips opening to him. Michael closed his eyes and allowed himself to react instinctively to the tentative strokes of her tongue against his, deepening the kiss by slow, gentle measures. Her hands moved to his throat, palms flattening against the throb of his pulse, then sliding down to cup his shoulders. He could feel her need to touch, to be touched. But she was holding back—

He pulled away from her for a moment, keeping his face so close to hers that she was all he could see, all he wanted to see.

"Jessy—don't be afraid of me."

"I'm not—"

"I won't hurt you like he did. You don't have to be afraid—ever."

He saw the tears well unexpectedly in her eyes and felt his heart breaking for her. In that moment, any doubts he might have had vanished. If what he felt for her wasn't love, then that emotion simply did not exist.

"I don't know—I mean—" Jessy's voice caught, eyes closing for a moment as tears trickled over her cheeks. "I don't know if I can do that—"

Michael kissed her closed eyes, tasting her tears. He gathered her into his arms, holding her tightly. "It's okay," he murmured, kissing her hair, her brow, then closing his eyes as he rested his cheek against the crown of her head. "We've got time. I'll give you all the time you need."

THIS IS NOT a promising start to a relationship, Jessy thought as she sipped at her water and listened to the tick tock of the grandfather clock in the hall.

They had planned to take advantage of the empty house by having their first "date"—dinner by candlelight. With Michael forbidding Jessy to do anything but sit in the kitchen and keep him company, he had broiled steaks and baked potatoes, stealing quick kisses from her whenever he had the chance. Each kiss had made her feel more comfortable, and each touch had made her realize that maybe something good could grow between them. Because there *was* something between them. She didn't know exactly what it was, or how it had developed, but a wonderful tension was building with each moment they spent together.

They had the house to themselves, with Lyssa away with a group of friends from her church and the kids still shopping with Ann. Until eight that night, they would be able to talk and kiss and behave like two adults on the cusp of a relationship. For the first time since that first night in the motel room, they were completely alone.

Unsupervised. Unchaperoned.

And miserable.

Jessy leaned back in her seat, her appetite gone. Michael picked at his dessert and kept his head down, looking up only to glance at the clock on the wall. Everything had been wonderful until the grandfather clock had struck eight. After that, every attempt at conversation had fallen flat. Jessy had finally lapsed into silence.

She knew what was preoccupying Michael's thoughts.

Ann. She still had the kids and she hadn't called to say she'd be late. Jessy knew by Michael's growing distraction that he was imagining a million scenarios, all of them bad.

"What time were they supposed to be home?" she asked quietly.

Michael glanced at his watch again. "An hour ago."

"Does she usually keep them later than—?"

"No."

The terseness of his reply caught Jessy off-guard. "Did you have another argument with Ann or something?"

He said nothing, looking back to his plate again.

Jessy knew a guilty conscience when she saw one. She also knew that she should just let it go, that she should change the subject and try to distract him from his worry. But she couldn't.

"Are you not telling me something?"

Michael's head snapped up. "What?"

"You're acting like there's something else bothering you."

"I'm not—" Michael caught himself and took a deep breath. "Okay. This meant nothing to me, but—this morning, when Ann came by to pick up the kids, she kissed me."

For just an instant the world went totally silent for Jessy, her entire body going cold. She could not believe Michael had kept that bit of information to himself all day long. Even as she cried on his shoulder. Even as they'd kissed in the garage. He had been with Ann that morning.

Jessy couldn't help but wonder what else Michael hadn't told her. "She what?"

"We were talking and actually getting along for once and—"

"She kissed you," Jessy said, voice flat. "Well—"

"It didn't mean anything to me."

Jessy looked him in the eye. "That's pretty cavalier of you."

"What do you want me to say?"

Jessy abruptly stood up, picking up her plate and silverware. "I don't think I can have this argument with you again."

"What argument?" Michael stood and followed her into the

kitchen. "Would you please tell me what's going on here, because I haven't got a clue."

Jessy kept her back to him as she busied herself at the sink, not trusting herself to look him in the eye. "This is exactly what we talked about this morning—you and Ann."

"Jessy, nothing happened."

"Except you kissed her." Jessy finally faced him again. "You kissed her and didn't even mention it to me today. I don't consider that 'nothing.'"

"I don't believe this." Michael leaned against the countertop, exasperated. "We talked. She kissed me. It meant nothing!"

Before Jessy could speak, the front door opened and the house exploded with life again. Ben and Marie thundered through the house, followed by Ann's cheery voice. "Hello? Anybody home? Mike?"

Michael turned towards the doorway, his relief so obvious that Jessy didn't have the heart to keep the argument going.

"I'll get the dishes done," Jessy said quietly, knowing that his attention was already wandering. "It would be better if I don't have to talk to Ann."

Michael looked to her again. "This conversation isn't finished."

Jessy said nothing, focusing on the soapy water and dirty dishes. Without another word, Michael walked out of the kitchen. To Ann and their children.

To his family.

It took only a few minutes to wash the dishes. Dimly aware of the sound of their conversation in the living room, Jessy tried to stall, to divert her attention by keeping busy, but finally ran out of things to do. She'd have to face them if she wanted to go upstairs. She had to square her shoulders, take a deep breath, and walk through the living room like it didn't kill her to see Ann and Michael together.

This was going to be hard. But she refused to hide.

Before she could change her mind, Jessy tucked a few errant strands of hair behind her ears and walked out of the kitchen, through the dining room, pausing just outside the living room entryway as her courage stuttered and faded away.

"Now you just try to tell me that our little girl isn't going to look like an angel in this!" Ann's voice sounded warmer, more loving than usual, and Jessy peeked around the edge of the door to the living room, hesitant to intrude.

Ann stood behind a beaming Libby, one arm around the girl's shoulders as she held up a gorgeous white dress. They looked as if they'd never had a cross word, as if Ann had never said one hurtful thing to her daughter. Libby gazed at Ann adoringly, almost starstruck, giddy with the joy of being the focus of her beautiful mother's attention.

For a moment Jessy didn't know whom she envied more: Ann or Libby.

"We practiced singing all the way home," Libby said, laughing. "Mom made me sing all the high notes because she said she'd crack the windows."

"Now *that* I believe." Michael grinned. "One time she tried singing 'The Star Spangled Banner' at a ballgame and ended up shattering every pair of sunglasses in the stands."

"Not fair!" Ann said, laughing with mock indignation as she playfully swatted Michael's arm. "I can't help it if our children inherited my good looks and your singing ability."

"Well, at least we got lucky with that, didn't we?"

Ann's smile mellowed, gaze softening as she studied Michael. "Yeah, we did."

As Jessy hid in the doorway, she watched as Michael and Ann gazed at each other, something silent and momentous passing between them. Something intimate. Something loving.

Something she had no right to interfere with.

"I'm going to go try on my dress again," Libby said, also sensing the change of atmosphere in the room. "Mom—will you come up and help me fix my hair?"

Ann reluctantly dragged her gaze away from Michael's. "Sure, baby—I'll be up there in a few minutes. I need to talk to your dad first."

Libby smiled and rose up on tiptoes to kiss Ann's cheek. "Thanks,

Mom. I love you."

"I love you, too." Ann hugged Libby extra hard and then let her go. "Maybe we'll even experiment with some makeup—how's that sound?"

"Cool!" With another huge smile Libby turned to leave the room, passing by the doorway as she crossed to the stairs. Horrified by the thought of being caught eavesdropping, Jessy scrambled away from the door frame, racing back to the kitchen. She hurried to the sink and plunged her hands into the lukewarm dishwater, her heart hammering as she simply stood there for a few moments. She heard Libby's footsteps on the stairs. Michael and Ann were finally left alone.

And the thought brought a sudden, unexpected wave of nausea. She had seen the tenderness that had passed between them. She had seen the way their marriage must have been once. The way it could be again.

Jessy gripped the edge of the sink. She could hear the faint whisper of their voices in the other room. The urge to go back to the door, to listen, nearly overwhelmed her. It would be wrong to eavesdrop. It would be wrong and hurtful and—

And impossible to resist.

Jessy dried her hands again and edged to the kitchen doorway, her heart beating almost painfully, a stomach-twisting sense of dread building with each moment that passed. She didn't want to hear what they were saying to each other, didn't want to know.

But she did. She had to know. For better or worse, no matter how awful the truth might be, she had to know.

She moved closer to the living room, ears pricked, listening. The whisper of their voices had stopped. They weren't speaking at all.

Jessy knew what she would see before she even reached the door.

She didn't even bother to hide. Michael and Ann were unaware of anything but each other, kissing with a passion and urgency that seemed forever out of Jessy's reach. Ann luxuriated in his kiss, her arms entwined around his neck, her hands dug into his soft, thick hair. Their bodies seemed to fit together perfectly—Michael's hard muscles and Ann's perfect curves molding themselves against each other so intimately that they looked as though they had been made for each other.

Jessy felt oddly detached from the moment. She felt as if she were being anesthetized, aware of the blurry edges of the pain descending upon her, but not yet feeling the full impact. That would come later. Right now there was just the sight of Michael's hands on Ann's slender waist, his mouth against her lips, his body pressed tightly against hers—and Jessy knew that every time she closed her eyes she would relive this moment.

The dishcloth fell from her hands as she forced herself to turn away, forced herself to move and walk away from the doorway, away from Michael and Ann and their rediscovered intimacy. She had known it was too good to be true. She had known it deep down in her heart and yet she had ignored those doubts, so desperate to be with Michael that she was willing to make a pathetic fool of herself.

But no more. Michael had made his decision, whether he was aware of it or not. And so had she.

An unnatural calmness settled over Jessy as she picked up the phone in the kitchen and called information. Then, without hesitation, she dialed the number of the only hotel in town. That would do until the next bus ran.

She had stayed long past her welcome.

Chapter Eleven

MICHAEL MANAGED to push Ann back a step, breaking away from her kiss with a gasp of breath. "Ann—stop it!"

Ann gazed up at him with a voluptuous smile on her lips, her eyes filled with invitation. She sidled up against him again, pressing her hips against his, rubbing against him as she flattened her hands against his shoulders. "Your heart's racing," she said, pressing her lips against the center of his chest. "You liked that, didn't you?"

Michael gently but firmly pushed her away. "Ann, I've told you—"

"And I don't believe you." Undeterred, Ann slithered against him again, nuzzling his neck through the open collar of his shirt. "I think you want this just as badly as I do."

"No—"

"That'd sound more convincing if you weren't so obviously enjoying this." Ann's gaze dipped down between their bodies, then back to Michael's eyes again. "I want you, Michael."

Michael shook his head. "It's not going to work, Ann."

Anger flared in Ann's eyes. "Why not?"

"I don't love you anymore."

"I find that hard to believe." Ann's lips slanted in a sardonic smile. "I know you, Michael. You're not the kind of man who can just fall out of love—especially with me."

"And why do you say that?" Michael asked, almost amused by

her vanity.

"Because I'm your wife," Ann said quietly. "I'm the mother of your children."

Michael said nothing for a moment, studying the smug perfection of Ann's smile. She was so assured, so certain of herself. She had never had one moment of doubt or self-consciousness in her life. Once upon a time, that had been one of the things he'd loved about her.

"What about Jessy?" he finally said, voice soft.

Ann laughed at that, dismissing him with a flap of her hand as she collapsed onto the couch and carelessly crossed her long legs. "Jessy? You mean the Jessy who is staying here? With you?"

"Yes." Michael kept his voice carefully monotone, his face neutral.

"Oh, honey—please." Ann laughed again, shaking her head. "You do *not* want to be seen with her. Can you imagine what the people in town would think?"

"Maybe I don't care what they'd think."

Ann's smile abruptly died. "Well, maybe I would."

"Why? You don't even live here anymore."

"The people in town know we were married. And they know that our divorce is just temporary."

Michael's eyes widened. "Just *what?*"

"We married too young, Mike. You knew that I wanted to do more than just live on a farm. I needed to experience life—and I couldn't get that by staying married to you." Ann shrugged, as if divorcing Michael, tearing his heart out by rejecting his love, hadn't mattered to her. "I'd always planned to come back when I was settled—so here I am."

"No." Michael shook his head, suddenly so furious that he couldn't stay still. He stalked over to the fireplace, gripping the mantel with both hands and squeezing so tightly his knuckles whitened. All those nights of sleeping alone in their bed. All those tearful talks with the kids about why their mother forgot their birthday or didn't visit. All those memories that had haunted him during the empty early days of their divorce—

"I thought about you all day today," Ann said as she rose from the couch. She wrapped her arms around Michael's waist, pressing her breasts against his back as she kissed the hollow between his shoulderblades. "I kept thinking about making love to you. The way you used to kiss me. The things you used to do to me—"

Michael squeezed his eyes tightly shut. He remembered all those things, too. Remembered them with such graphic detail that he couldn't control the rush of heat that flared through his blood. Making love to Ann had always been good. That was the one thing in their marriage that had been perfect. Even when everything else had gone to hell.

Her hands snaked around his waist to his stomach, flattening there for a moment, temptingly hovering just above his belt. Ann stood on tiptoes and nuzzled his neck, kissing just below his ear, knowing full well the effect it would have on him.

"Let's make love, Michael," Ann whispered. "I haven't been with anyone in so long—nobody has ever made me feel the way you do."

Michael turned to face Ann. She had that look in her eye, the one he'd dreamed about for so many years after the divorce, the one he'd remembered so well from all their years together. She wanted him, wanted him now, and would do anything he asked. Once upon a time, that alone would have ignited a passion that couldn't be satisfied until he'd buried himself inside her.

Now it did nothing for him. Nothing at all.

"Ann—" His voice trailed away as he caught a glimpse of movement in the doorway. Jessy. Looking at him as if he'd driven a dagger into her heart.

How much had she heard? What had she seen?

Ann turned her head, her smile turning into a smirk at the sight of Jessy. "Well, well—I suppose no one ever taught you not to eavesdrop, did they?"

"Hello, Ann." Jessy said tightly.

"It's Mrs. Forrester, please." Ann's smile quirked.

Michael disengaged himself from Ann's clutching embrace. "Jess—this isn't—"

"I'm just going upstairs," Jessy said as she entered the room, carefully avoiding his gaze. "Please don't let me interrupt."

"Jessy—"

"Let her go, Mike." Ann smiled coolly. "At least she realizes when she's worn out her welcome."

Michael lunged forward, fingertips brushing against Jessy's arm, the contact just galvanizing enough to stop her in her tracks. It took every ounce of courage, every bit of control, to keep her expression impassive as she turned to look at him.

"You heard her, Michael," Jessy said quietly. "Let me go."

"Yes, Mikey. Let her go back upstairs." Ann's smile grew venomous as she looked at Jessy. "You interrupted a very important conversation between my husband and I."

"My husband and *me*," Jessy muttered.

Ann's eyebrows arched. "Excuse me?"

"If you're trying to fake intelligence, at least get the grammar right." Jessy returned Ann's stare just long enough to see the anger flashing in her eyes, then glanced to Michael again. "I've called a taxi. I need to go upstairs and pack."

Michael blinked, stunned. "You've what? Jessy—"

"Excuse me, Michael." Jessy stepped past him, but he captured her arm again.

"You're not leaving."

"Yes, I am."

"Well, how about this?" Ann laughed, the sound ugly and harsh in the silence. "She actually has enough brains in her head to realize when the game's over. Good for you, Jessy."

"This has never been a game to me," Jessy said quietly, trying to control the quaver in her voice. "I don't play games with people's emotions the way you do, Ann. I don't use people until I get tired of them."

Michael moved toward Jessy, who would not look away from Ann's icy gaze. "Jess—"

"Oh, that's right, Michael," Ann sneered. "Go running to her. Make sure your little fat friend's feelings aren't hurt. Where was all this concern this morning out at the corral?"

"That's enough, Ann!" Michael's voice tightened with anger as he turned to face Ann.

"What's wrong, Michael? You don't want her to know you and I were together this morning?" Ann glanced at Jessy and smiled spitefully. "Lovely time. Have you had the chance to kiss my husband yet? It's delicious."

Jessy winced but was damned if she'd let Ann see how deeply her words cut. "I can't believe you're being this way after what happened this morning, Mikey," Ann continued, focusing all her attention on Michael now. "After what we discussed—what we did—"

"What we did meant nothing to me, Ann."

"Michael," Ann said softly, "I'm just trying to make you see before it's too late,"

"Too late for what?"

"She's using the kids to get to you. I can't believe you don't see through her little act."

"That's ridiculous," Jessy said, barely able to control her outrage. "You're the one using the children to get back at Michael. You don't even realize how much you're hurting them."

"Oh, really?" Ann took a step closer, almost cocky as she flicked her gaze over Jessy. "Tell me—how on Earth could you even imagine that Michael would possibly fall in love with somebody like you?"

"Somebody like me?" Jessy repeated quietly.

"Stop it, Ann," Michael said, slipping his arm around Jessy's shoulders. She cringed to think of how huge she must seem beside him.

"Look at yourself," Ann continued, eyes gleaming with malicious delight. "It's not like you're going to have too many offers, as fat as you are. When an easy touch like Michael comes along, you're going to take advantage of it. And all Michael feels for you is pity. Not love. Certainly not sexual attraction. Just plain old pity—he felt sorry for the lonely fat girl."

For a moment Jessy couldn't speak, so choked with anger that she could actually taste the rising bile. Somehow, with the intuition of the truly cruel, Ann had known exactly what to say to inflict maximum pain.

"Really, Michael," Ann said with a suddenly brilliant smile. "Is this the *best* you can do? I'm disappointed in you."

"Jessy is a wonderful woman—"

Ann cut him off with a disdainful laugh. "Oh, right—a 'wonderful woman.' And I'll bet she has a great personality and a helluva sense of humor, too. Right?" Ann's smile faded as she looked back to Jessy again. "Did you really think Michael could fall in love with you? Were you *that* deluded to think he could actually love somebody like *you?*"

Jessy couldn't bring herself to respond to that. Every fear, every doubt—Ann had magically magnified them a thousand times over.

"How can you stand there and say that?" Michael asked, voice dropping to little more than a whisper. His eyes blazed with anger. "How can you *say* that?"

"I thought we'd discussed everything this morning, Michael. I thought we'd worked everything out." Ann's eyes cut to Jessy's. "We're getting back together."

"You're what?" Jessy hated the quaver in her voice but couldn't hide it, couldn't control it. She looked to Michael, saw the sudden guilt in his eyes. "Is this true?"

Ann's smile widened. "Of course it is, hon. Don't tell me Michael didn't mention it to you, as 'close' as you two are."

Jessy studied Ann for a moment. There was something in the woman's eyes that no amount of cruelty or anger could hide. She still loved Michael. And she still wanted him. Whether she wanted him because she loved him or because she didn't want anyone else to have him was still in question.

Jessy turned to Michael again. "Is that true?"

Michael shook his head. "No—"

"You don't know what you're saying, Michael. You never do." Ann took a deep breath and fixed her gaze on Michael, stubbornly refusing to acknowledge Jessy's presence. "It comes down to this, babe. Either *she* leaves, or I do—and you know I'll take the kids with me."

"You can't do that! I have custody—"

"That can be changed."

For an eternally long moment they stood locked in silence, Ann's smile twisting smugly.

"You wouldn't do that," Michael whispered.

"Oh, yes." Ann's eyes were as cold as the wind that rattled through the rafters of the house. "Yes, I would. In a heartbeat. I want my family back, Michael."

Jessy suddenly couldn't breathe. She took a step back, feeling as if someone had punched her in the gut. She had to leave. She had to go right now. Even though she knew she was leaving Michael to Ann's manipulations, she couldn't bear the thought of Michael losing custody of his children because of her.

Suddenly any pretense of strength, of courage, fled. Without a word she walked out of the room.

JESSY CAREFULLY FOLDED the last blouse and tucked it into her suitcase, hesitating for a moment as she realized how final everything suddenly seemed. She was actually going to leave. It didn't seem real.

But she had to go.

She heard footsteps in the hall and stiffened, listening. The sounds stopped at her doorway, and Jessy could almost see Michael hesitating on the other side, one hand raised and ready to rap against the door.

A half-second later, he knocked.

"It's open," she said quietly, almost unable to work up the energy to speak. She felt wrung out, exhausted after the highs and lows of what had seemed to be an unending day.

The door opened and Michael stepped into the room, frowning at the sight of the open suitcase. "What are you doing?"

"What I should have done before," she said softly, the snap of the suitcase latches punctuating her words.

"You're actually leaving?"

Jessy met his gaze, her eyes unwavering. "Yes."

"If it's because of what Ann said—"

"It's not just that. It's—" Jessy caught herself before her emotions got the best of her, closing her eyes for a moment as she calmed down. "I think it would be best for everyone involved if I just—go."

"Of all the—" Michael smiled faintly, shaking his head in disbelief. His smile quickly faded when he saw the tenseness drawing down the corners of Jessy's mouth, the sadness in her eyes. "You're really going, aren't you?"

Jessy nodded, but said nothing. Her eyes stung, her throat burned, as she fought back useless tears.

"I thought we worked everything out—"

"Nothing's worked out," Jessy said bitterly.

"Is this what you really want, Jess?"

"Of course not!" Jessy's voice rose slightly, shaky with an anger that felt directionless, helpless.

"Then why do you think you have to leave?"

Jessy's gaze faltered a moment. She looked away from his eyes, lowering her head as she took a deep breath and sighed.

"I am not going to be the reason those kids are taken away from everything they love," she said quietly, meeting his eyes once more. "I don't want you to lose them."

"We had this discussion before—"

"And that was before Ann started flinging threats around."

"She doesn't mean anything by it."

"It didn't sound that way to me. I believed her—and I think you did too. Didn't you?"

Michael fell silent for a moment, shaking his head as he turned back to the door. He took a step, hesitated, and then looked to Jessy once again.

"Ann realizes that the kids are better off with me," he finally said, his voice low and controlled.

"*This* week," Jessy said and smiled bitterly. "What about the next time? She wants you back, Michael."

"I know that."

Jessy faltered, taken aback by the quiet acceptance in his voice.

That familiar emptiness reopened inside her. "I have to go," she said softly, forcing false strength into her words.

"No, you don't." Michael edged closer to her, not quite daring to reach out to her just yet. "Please, Jess—stay. Until Christmas, at least."

Jessy slowly shook her head. "I can't."

The pain in her whispery voice made Michael's heart catch. He cupped her cheek, gently urging her to look at him again. "Please," he whispered. "For the kids. For me."

Jessy gazed into his eyes for a few long moments, longing to give into him and stay. She didn't want to leave, couldn't bear to imagine the rest of her life spent without Michael and his family.

But she would have to bear it. Ann had drawn blood with her ugly words. How could Jessy expect Michael to fall in love with someone like her? It was a wonderful fantasy, but that's all it would ever be: a fairy tale. A fairy tale with an unhappy ending.

"No," she finally whispered, shaking her head as she lowered her head and slowly pulled away from his touch. "I have to go."

Michael's eyes darkened, brows knitting as he looked at her with a directness that made her uneasy. "Are you sure this is what you want?" he asked softly.

"It's never been a question of what I want."

Until that moment, Michael hadn't realized that it was actually possible for a man to feel his heart break, but right then his heart ached for Jessy. He wanted so badly to be able to take her grief away, to make up for all the cruel words she'd heard, to take away all the pain.

But in the end, he couldn't. In the end, he had to love her enough to respect her decision, no matter how much it hurt.

"Okay," he finally said, nodding as he reached out to touch Jessy's face again, gently trailing the tip of his thumb over her cheek. "What do you need me to do for you?"

Jessy couldn't hide the relief in her eyes, and Michael felt a fresh stab of pain at the thought of letting her go. "Nothing. I've got a room in town tonight. My bus leaves at noon—"

"So soon?" Michael caught himself before he could say anything more and forced himself to nod again, as if the thought of never seeing her again didn't rip a hole in his heart and soul. "Okay, then," he said, managing a faint, tight smile. "Tomorrow it is."

And then, without thinking about the repercussions, he leaned forward and pressed a soft kiss against her forehead, lingering only a moment before pulling away and turning toward the door. Every step away from her seemed to resonate in his heart.

"Michael—?"

He turned as he reached the door, almost hopeful as he looked at her again.

Jessy folded her arms tightly over her chest, looking as if she were trying to hold herself together. "You understand why I have to do this, don't you?"

Michael studied her for a few moments, slowly shaking his head. "No," he finally said, voice little more than a whisper. "But it's your choice to make. You know how I feel."

Jessy half-smiled at that, the gesture completely humorless. "That's part of the problem, isn't it?"

Michael took a deep breath, one hand gripping the doorknob. He wasn't quite able to make himself leave just yet. Not without one last gambit.

"The kids are going to miss the hell out of you," he said quietly.

"I'll miss them, too." Jessy felt her eyes burning again and looked up to the ceiling, fighting the tears away. "Don't do this, Michael."

"Do what?"

"Don't try to use the kids."

"I'm not—" Michael caught the frustration in his voice and stopped himself. "What am I supposed to tell them tomorrow?" he asked in a more tempered tone. "What do I tell them when they ask where you're going—or *why* you're going?"

Jessy shook her head, digging a hand through her hair as she turned away from him. "I don't know."

"It's almost time to put them to bed," Michael said quietly, opening the door again. "If you want to cancel your cab, I'll drive you out to town tonight. You might want to spend a little time with the kids—since tomorrow—"

Michael's voice trailed away when he realized that Jessy wasn't going to turn back to him again. With a faint nod he ducked out of the room, closing the door quietly.

Jessy waited until she heard the click of the latch before she finally allowed herself to cry.

Chapter Twelve

JESSY HELD OUT as long as she could. Then the sounds of Ben and Marie's laughter got the best of her and she peeked out into the hallway, towards the bathroom. Michael stood in the doorway, a towel slung over his shoulder as he refereed a waterfight between Ben and Marie. He smiled, but Jessy could see that it was forced. If he felt half as bad as she felt, smiling was the last thing he felt like doing.

"Okay," Michael said and stepped into the bathroom. His voice carried into the hallway. "Now how about trying this again—and using some toothpaste this time?"

Jessy stepped out of her bedroom, regretting each step she took but helpless to stop herself. Rationally, she knew that helping Michael put the kids to bed would only make things harder for herself. She'd feel like she was being drawn into the family, accepted into their lives, and then tomorrow morning would come and she'd climb onto that bus and feel like she was leaving her heart behind. Time spent with Michael and the kids would only end up hurting her in the long run.

But she wasn't listening to rationality. She was listening to the sound of Ben and Marie splashing water at each other as Michael struggled to see that they brushed their teeth. She was listening to the sound of Libby's muffled laughter as she huddled in her room with the phone. She was listening to the sound of Lyssa's voice as she sang Christmas songs off-tune and rustled wrapping paper downstairs.

She was listening to all the things she knew she'd miss once she was on her own again. Was it so wrong for her to want to enjoy them just a little longer?

Jessy leaned against the door frame, smiling despite herself as she watched Michael kneel down beside Ben and gently wipe toothpaste foam from the boy's mouth. He did the same for Marie, who immediately burbled out another chinful as she giggled. Laughing, Michael covered her face with the towel and pulled her into a bearhug.

"You guys have the hygiene of piglets," he said as he pulled Ben into the embrace, lifting him under one arm and Marie under the other. They immediately began oinking. Jessy laughed and quickly covered her mouth with her hand. She'd hoped to sneak away unnoticed.

Too late.

"Hey," Michael said, grinning as he hefted the kids under his arms and got them giggling again. For a moment, it was as though nothing had happened between them. Jessy was more than willing to leave it at that.

"Hi," she said softly, still smiling. "You look like you could use some help."

"Always." He tipped her a quick wink and then looked to Ben and Marie. "You two rugrats ready for bed?"

"No!" They yelled in unison.

Michael grinned at Jessy again. "Told you. I need help."

"Then maybe I'd better stick around for a while."

The words carried more meaning than she'd intended, but Michael let it pass. His smile slanted slightly as he nodded. "Yeah—maybe you'd better."

Without saying anything more, Michael turned his attention back to the kids, carrying them down the hall to their bedroom as Jessy followed. Ben and Marie giggled almost deliriously as Michael pretended to lose his grip and drop them.

"Okay, munchkins—end of the road," Michael said as he entered their bedroom, depositing Ben on his bed with a bounce.

He gave Marie an extra swooping dive before dropping her onto the mattress. "Bedtime. Get under the covers so your toes won't freeze."

"Can I brush your hair?" Marie asked, grabbing a pink plastic brush from her nightstand. "Please, Daddy?"

Michael glanced to Jessy—who arched an eyebrow and smiled faintly—and then nodded, grinning, to Marie. "Okay, sweetpea. Scooch down."

Marie did as told, tucking her feet beneath her flannel gown as Michael sat cross-legged in front of her. She began to gently brush his thick black hair, careful not to pull or tangle. She carefully clipped plastic pink bow-shaped barrettes into his hair, making tiny ponytails that stood at end all over his head. Jessy covered her smile with her hand as Michael patiently endured.

"Might as well come on in," Michael said and smiled at Jessy. "You're making me nervous standing there in the doorway."

Jessy's own smile slid away as she cleared her throat. "I, uh—I really should be getting to bed. I just wanted to say goodnight—"

"Will you stay and tell us a story?" Ben asked.

Michael saw the indecision in Jessy's eyes. She wavered for a moment, then stepped into the bedroom, moving awkwardly as she sat on the edge of Ben's bed. Ben was immediately hanging onto her shoulders, arms wrapped around her neck.

"What's the matter, Jessy?" Marie asked, frowning faintly. "You look sad."

Jessy helplessly glanced to Michael, who raised his eyebrows but remained silent. No help there, although it was hard to take him seriously with so many pink bows in his hair.

"I'm not—sad," she said, trying an unconvincing smile. "I'm just sleepy. It's past my bedtime."

Ben swung around her shoulders and plopped into her lap. "Do you want Daddy to tell you a bedtime story, too? He's real good at it."

Jessy's smile softened as she gazed at Ben, and then to Michael and Marie. "I'm sure he is."

"Or he can sing to you," Marie said, leaning against Michael's back. He reached back to wrap his arms around her and lifted her over his head and onto his legs as she giggled.

"He sings, too?" Jessy's gaze held Michael's a moment longer, her smile growing a little stronger.

"Yeah," Marie said and nodded. "But he doesn't sing real good."

"Thanks a lot, chatterbox." Michael growled and planted a sloppy kiss against Marie's neck, grinning as she laughed. "Now help me get these bows out of my hair before I get to feeling too pretty."

"Are you going to write to Santa Claus?" Ben asked, drawing her attention away from Michael as he and Marie began taking out the barrettes. "Daddy says that if we write a letter to Santa, he might come see us before Christmas."

"Wow." Jessy smiled and widened her eyes. "What are you going to ask Santa to bring you?"

Ben's eyes grew solemn. "It's a secret," he said quietly, glancing over to Marie, whose expression mirrored her brother's.

"But you're going to tell Santa in your letters, aren't you?" Jessy asked, quickly smiling at Michael. He ruffled a hand through his previously styled hair and shrugged.

"Uh-huh—but he can't tell *anybody*."

"Ah—I see," Jessy nodded sagely. "What about Rudolph? Can Santa tell him?"

Ben considered it a moment and then grinned. "Yeah, but only because Rudolph can't talk and tell anybody else."

"Okay, guys," Michael said, scooting back to lean against the headboard of Marie's bed. Marie immediately curled up beside him. "Story time. What's it going to be tonight? Book or made-up?"

"Made-up!" Marie said and looked up at Jessy. "Come on, Jessy. Sit with me."

Ben leapt off Jessy's lap and crawled up to nestle beside Michael, so Jessy rose and sat at the foot of Marie's bed.

"No," Marie said impatiently. "Up *here.*"

Jessy sighed in mock exasperation, drawing a few giggles from them, and moved to Marie's side of the bed. "I don't think there's enough room for me."

"Sure there is," Michael said, scooping both Ben and Marie onto his outstretched legs. "That's what laps were invented for."

Jessy smiled reluctantly and stretched out beside Michael, their legs touching from hip to ankle. Marie settled comfortably atop their legs as Michael slipped one arm around Ben and the other around Marie and Jessy.

"No fair," Jessy murmured.

Michael grinned. "Who said we were playing fair?"

Marie twisted to look up at Michael. "Can I play?"

"No, sweetie." Michael glanced to Jessy over Marie's blonde head, his smile quirking slightly. "This is a grown-up game."

Ben tugged at Michael's flannel shirt. "The *story*, Daddy!"

"Huh? Oh, right—the story." Michael smiled to Jessy once more, then gave his attention to the kids again. "Let's see—once upon a time, in a far-away land, there lived a beautiful girl—"

"But she was really a princess," Marie said, smiling dreamily. "A beautiful princess."

"But she didn't know she was a princess," Michael continued. "She lived in a huge stone castle with her guardian, all alone except for—" His voice trailed away, waiting for Ben or Marie to interject their ideas.

"A pet dragon," Ben said, smiling shyly at Jessy. "A baby dragon with wings and feathers."

Michael chuckled. "Okay—a baby dragon it is. One day she was sitting at the window of her room and she saw an evil ogre running towards the castle. The ogre liked to frighten her, so before he could scare her again, the princess escaped by braiding her long, long hair and climbing down the castle wall."

Marie frowned faintly. "Daddy, that's from Rapunzel."

"Rapunzel was the princess's cousin," Jessy said, smiling as she glanced at Michael and then to Marie. "Taught her everything she knows about hair climbing."

"So the princess and her dragon escaped," Michael said. "They ran into the huge forest that surrounded the castle, and even though the princess was afraid of the evil ogre, she was very brave. She kept going until one night a storm made her take shelter."

Startled by the story's suddenly all too familiar turn, Jessy looked at Michael. Ben and Marie's heads were nestled against his chest, and as he raised his gaze to hers, she felt a sudden flood of sadness. She didn't want to go. She wanted to stay with Michael and his children more than anything in the world.

But she couldn't. This was exactly the reason why she *had* to go. She couldn't take this away from Michael and his kids.

"Then what happened?" Marie murmured sleepily.

"Well—" Michael kept gazing at Jessy, never looking away as he spoke. "The princess met a lonely old man who had room in his cottage. She was afraid to stop running, just in case the evil ogre found her, but she was so very tired and lonely that she decided to wait out the storm with the old man."

Ben raised his head. "But was the old man really the evil ogre in disguise and she had to karate chop his neck?"

Michael laughed as he shook his head. "No—but that was what the princess was afraid of. She was afraid that everyone was like the evil ogre—and so she was afraid to trust anyone."

"Except for Al," Marie said and smiled.

"Al?" Michael asked. "Who's Al?"

"The baby dragon."

"Ah." Michael pressed a quick kiss to her forehead and continued the story. "So the princess stayed with the old man for a few days, and when the storm finally passed, he told her that he knew of an enchanted land where she could hide from the ogre and live without being afraid. It took some talking into, but the princess finally agreed to go—but only for a few days. She would stay until the full moon, but then she had to leave."

"Or she'd turn into a pumpkin!" Ben said and giggled.

Laughing, Michael kissed the top of Ben's head. "That's another story, Benny-boy."

"So what happened?" Marie asked, then yawned ferociously. "Did she go with him?"

"Yes, she did," Michael said softly, looking to Jessy again. "And she found that she was very happy in that enchanted place. The old man became her very best friend in the whole world, and she never wanted to leave."

"Was she in love with him?" Marie asked quietly.

Michael hesitated, half-smiling at Jessy. "Maybe—but the princess didn't believe in true love. Even though she had bushels and bushels of love to give, she didn't believe that anyone could love her."

Jessy shifted uncomfortably. "Michael—"

"But the old man did," Marie said. "He fell in love with the princess because she was beautiful and nice and kind."

"And when the evil ogre tried to kidnap the princess," Ben added, "the old man turned into a monster!"

"No, silly," Marie shook her head impatiently. "The princess kissed the old man and he turned into a prince."

Ben pouted. "I like monsters better than that old mushy stuff."

Michael laughed, giving them both kisses, and then smiled to Jessy again. She could hardly bear to see the tenderness, the affection, in his eyes. It made her all too aware of what she was leaving behind.

"How does the story end, Daddy?" Marie asked, tilting her head back to look up to Michael. "Do they live happily ever after and have lots of babies and stuff?"

"Lots of babies?" Michael's smile curled in surprise. "Where did you get *that?*"

Marie smiled. "I dunno. Do they?"

Michael took a deep breath and slowly released it, looking from Marie to Jessy again. "I don't know," he said quietly, raising his brows questioningly to Jessy. *"Do they?"*

Jessy felt her heart catch between beats. *Don't do this to me,* she thought, closing her eyes so the kids wouldn't see her sudden tears. She swallowed hard, unable to speak without betraying herself.

Michael, thankfully, let it go.

"Okay, guys," he said, smiling again. "Let's finish the story tomorrow night."

"Will you tell the story tomorrow, Jessy?" Ben asked, rubbing his eyes with his knuckles. "Tell us about your pet dinosaur?"

Jessy managed a wan smile. Who knew where she'd be tomorrow night at this time? "We'll see, Ben."

Ben frowned, sensing her sadness, but before he could speak, Michael gave him a squeeze. "Jump back in bed, Benny-boy, and I'll tuck you in."

"Sing us a song, Daddy," Marie said, smiling up to Michael in a way that Jessy knew he would not be able to resist. "Please!"

Michael studied Jessy for a moment, trying to read her thoughts, all too aware of the pain in her eyes. He hated hurting her like this, but it was the only way he could make her want to stay. Until she believed him when he said there was no reason for her to go, he would have to show her everything she would miss.

Even though seeing her struggle to hide her tears tore him up inside.

"Okay," Michael finally said, managing to smile back at Marie. "If Ben will get the guitar—"

Ben was off his lap in an instant, darting across the room to the closet. He returned with the guitar and Michael crawled to the foot of the bed, leaving Marie and Ben to curl up beside Jessy. She hesitated only a fraction of an instant before slipping her arms around them, resting her cheek against Marie's soft curls.

Michael strummed the guitar, then sang "Do-Re-Mi" in a purposely awful voice. Ben and Marie laughed as he cracked and yodeled and chortled. Jessy smiled faintly, but despite his best efforts, that terrible sadness remained in her eyes.

"Frank taught me how to play, but he only knew three chords." Michael demonstrated quickly and smiled. "Musical genius doesn't exactly run in the family."

"Sing like Jiminy Cricket, Daddy!" Ben shouted.

"Yeah," Marie said, shifting so she could look up to Jessy. "Daddy sings the wish song real pretty."

"Well, I wouldn't say that—" Michael lowered his head in playful 'aw-shucks' shyness. He looked up to Jessy and winked, then began strumming the guitar again, the random notes suddenly familiar. It was the same song he had hummed for her on that first night together, when her fever had risen so frighteningly high and he'd soothed her fears.

It was the song Jessy had always associated with one of her best memories of being a little girl—the first time she had gone to the movies with her parents. She had been fascinated by the story of the little wooden boy who became real, and the Jiminy Cricket song, "When You Wish Upon A Star," had been her favorite song in the world.

Michael began to sing softly, his voice a pleasant tenor, sweetly hopeful and plaintive all at once as he sang of dreams coming true. He kept his gaze on Jessy, singing only to her.

And suddenly it was almost too much to bear. With Ben and Marie cuddled against her so close, she felt warm and safe, even loved. They were falling asleep against her, their heads nestled into her shoulders, lulled by the softness of Michael's voice as he sang. She stroked their silky hair, closing her eyes for a moment as she felt the steady rise and fall of their breathing, as their warmth seeped into her and made her realize what she had been missing for so long.

She'd realized a long time ago that she would more than likely never have children, even though she had longed for someone to love and protect ever since she was a young girl. As the years passed and she grew to understand reality and her place in the world, she understood that the likelihood of her ever becoming a mother grew slimmer with each passing year. She wanted the entire package— loving husband included—and could not settle for anything less.

But now, with Ben and Marie and Libby, she felt as if fate had decided to play a cruel joke on her. The kids trusted her, loved her with that open, boundless love that only children could give. Being here, with Michael and his family, was everything she had ever wanted—but it was only an illusion. Despite her feelings for the children, even her feelings for Michael, she knew that she was only filling in for Ann. This was Ann's family, not hers.

Michael's song faded into silence. For a moment, Jessy kept her eyes closed, listening to the howl of the wind just outside the window, the soft tapping of snow against the glass. She had never felt so warm, so safe, in her life. She realized at that moment that she had to try to remember every last little detail, right down to the scent of baby shampoo in Marie and Ben's hair. She knew that this sense of security, of absolute rightness with the world, would probably never come to her again, except in memories. They would be all that remained.

"They're asleep," Michael said softly.

Jessy opened her eyes, blinking back her tears as she tried a half-smile. "So are my arms."

Michael said nothing as he put down the guitar and gently picked Ben up, tucking him carefully into his own bed. He pulled the bright dinosaur sheets and blanket up to the boy's chin, pausing a moment to lightly touch Ben's cheek and kiss his forehead.

Something inside Jessy twisted. She hadn't known she could hurt any more than she'd already hurt.

Michael came back to Marie's bed and lifted her from Jessy's arm. Jessy stood and pulled down the covers as he eased Marie back against the pillows. Jessy helped him tuck her in and Michael looked up to her with a smile.

"Thanks," he whispered. "Two's better than one when it comes to this."

Jessy managed a half-hearted smile as Michael leaned over and kissed Marie's brow. Marie stirred, eyes fluttering as her gaze found Jessy.

"Jessy—" she murmured sleepily.

Jessy knelt beside the bed, smiling as she brushed a few curls from Marie's eyes. "Right here, sweetie."

"Do you want to know what I want for Christmas?"

Jessy glanced to Michael, then back to Marie again. "I'd like to know, honey. What do you want for Christmas?"

Marie slowly smiled, eyes already closing again as she struggled to stay awake. "I want you to stay forever and ever and be our other mommy."

Jessy felt as if a sledgehammer had slammed into her stomach. She recovered swiftly, smiling again as she kissed Marie's cheek.

"Well, sweetie—" she began, voice shaky.

"Why don't you ask Santa Claus about it in your letter," Michael said quietly, flashing a quick smile to Jessy as he leaned in to give Marie another kiss. "Now go to sleep, jellybean."

"G'night, Daddy," Marie whispered, turning onto her side as she gave into sleep again. "'Night, Jessy."

Jessy smiled sadly and touched Marie's cheek, brushing the hair away from her eyes. Then she slowly rose, keeping her gaze averted from Michael's. She took a deep breath, then managed to look at him again.

And before he could speak, she turned away, hurrying out of the room without looking back.

Chapter Thirteen

MICHAEL TOOK THE STAIRS two at a time as he raced after Jessy. Lyssa was curled up on the couch in the living room, her nose buried in a romance novel.

Michael turned, ready to search the kitchen, when Lyssa spoke.

"If you're looking for Jessy," she said mildly, not raising her gaze from her book, "she grabbed her coat and went outside."

"She what?" Michael was already opening the coat closet and dragging out a heavy parka. "It's freezing out there. Why didn't you stop her?"

Lyssa shrugged and finally looked up, hooking a finger into her novel to save her place. "I figured you had something to work out with her." She arched an eyebrow. "Or something to tell her."

"Like what?" Michael grunted as he tugged on a pair of scuffed cowboy boots.

"I think you know *what.*" Lyssa opened her novel again and settled into it. "Big smart guy like you should've figured that out ages ago."

With a faint shake of his head Michael shrugged into a denim jacket, scowling as he hurried to the door. At least Jessy couldn't have gotten very far, although the thought of her wandering around lost in the night gave him a sick feeling deep in his gut. He stepped onto the front porch and a gust of icy wind sucked his breath away as he struggled to pull his gloves on over his already aching hands. Scanning the front yard, he saw nothing but moonlight sparkling on the unmarred crust of snow. No footprints.

Then he heard it. A slow, creaking sound. Faint but steady.

Frowning, Michael followed the sound, turning the corner of the wraparound porch to find Jessy sitting in the bench swing, bathed in the glow of the multi-colored Christmas lights lining the porch railings. She huddled in her heavy coat, almost disappearing within its folds, her face and head covered by a blue crocheted scarf.

For a moment she looked like a lost child, alone and terribly lonely.

Michael slowly walked towards her, his hands shoved into his pockets, his chin dipped low into his coat collar. Silvery snow dusted the porch, swirling in random breezes.

"Mind some company?" he asked, sitting beside her on the swing and hissing involuntarily at the feel of icy wood. Jessy glanced over to him, and even in the dim light of the Christmas bulbs he could see that her cheeks and eyes were wet. "You okay?"

"Peachy," she muttered, lowering her head again.

"Want to talk about it?"

Jessy said nothing for a moment as she swung her gaze back to him. Finally she looked away, staring out at the flat expanse of snow that surrounded the house.

"That was a rotten thing for you to do," she said softly.

"I know."

"You know this is what I have to do."

"No, you don't."

"Yes, I do." Jessy finally looked at him again, struggling to control the strange swell of anger and fear and grief that threatened to overwhelm her. "Ann—"

"Is just something we're going to have to deal with," Michael said quietly. "You can't hide behind that excuse anymore."

Jessy said nothing for a moment, sighing instead. She sniffed, clearing the tears from her throat, and looked down at her gloved hands, clasped tightly in her lap.

"Okay," she said finally, looking up to him once again. "You're right. No more excuses."

Michael took her hand, lacing her fingers with his. "What are you afraid of, Jessy?"

She gazed at him for a moment, and even in the shadowy moonlight Michael could see the raw pain in her eyes. But when she spoke her voice was surprisingly calm, with only the faintest hint of tears.

"I'm afraid—" She hesitated for a moment, shaking her head. "I don't know how to explain it to myself, much less to you."

Michael said nothing, waiting for her to continue. For just a moment Jessy almost wished that they were arguing again. At least when they fought she could wrap herself in self-righteous anger and distance herself from him. Now, talking like this, she felt uncomfortably vulnerable. She knew she would tell Michael the truth about her feelings, felt the urge to say it rising within her like a bubble. Ever since that first night together in the motel, she had known it would come to this. Now all she had to do was find the courage to say it—and the strength to accept whatever the repercussions might be.

"I'm afraid—of losing you," she finally said, voice so soft it was almost carried away by the wind. "All of you."

"Go on," Michael whispered.

Jessy took a deep breath and sighed. "When my family died—I lost everything in the world that I loved. I never wanted to go through that kind of pain again, ever. So I kept to myself, and I kept telling myself that it was okay to be alone, that I was doing myself a favor because if I didn't let anyone get too close, then I wouldn't have to deal with losing anyone again."

Michael gave her hand a gentle squeeze. "But now?"

Jessy smiled sadly, shaking her head. "Now everything's changed. I—" she hesitated a moment, swallowing back tears. "I can't go back to being alone anymore."

Jessy's voice faded away as she gazed at him a moment longer, as if trying to will him into understanding. Then, unexpectedly, she rose and walked away from him, hurrying down the snowy steps. Michael quickly followed, catching up with her easily as she trudged through the snow.

"Michael, I need to think—" Jessy didn't look over to him, keeping her eyes focused directly ahead of her.

"And I'm supposed to let you wander around the farm by yourself?"

Jessy stopped so abruptly that Michael didn't realize it until he was several steps ahead of her.

"I can't do this, Michael. I *can't.*" Jessy's voice was as soft as the whisper of the falling snow. "I want to stay. I really do. But—"

"But you can't," Michael said softly, walking back to her. "*Why,* Jess? Just tell me why."

"I don't know—" The hopeless frustration in her voice, the utter bewilderment, broke Michael's heart all over again. She raised her gaze to him again, her eyes wet with tears. "I wish I did—but I don't. I just know that I can't stay here."

Michael moved to wrap his arms around her, meaning to offer comfort, but Jessy pulled away from him.

"No," she whispered. "Please—don't make this any harder than it has to be. Would you please take me to town now?"

"You're actually going?"

Jessy glanced up, barely meeting his eyes. "I need to go now. While I still can."

And with that, she walked away.

TEN MINUTES later, Jessy was in the Bronco. Seatbelt fastened. Eyes staring straight ahead. Totally silent.

Michael purposely kept his thoughts to himself, giving both of them time to settle their emotions down to a dull roar. He'd never felt so helpless and frustrated and angry in his entire life—not even during the divorce from Ann. This—this was beyond all his experience with women. He knew Jessy wanted to stay with him and his family. He knew she had feelings for him, just as he had feelings for her. If she'd just give it a chance—

But then again, why should she? What had he done to prove how he felt to her? He'd kissed her, yes, but he hadn't found the courage to tell her that he was falling in love with her. He hadn't found the nerve to tell her that he wanted, more than anything in the world, for her to stay with him and his family forever. Somehow, for some reason, he'd expected her to just *know*, to be able to read his thoughts through his actions and know that he cared deeply for her. It had never occurred to him that Jessy's upbringing had been worlds away from his, that she had not had the privilege of being raised in a family that had the luxury of taking each other's love for granted.

Jessy needed to be told beyond a shadow of a doubt that she was loved. He understood that now.

He also understood that her concern about Ann taking the kids was simply a way of hiding her own fears of allowing herself the vulnerability of getting too close to him and his family. For Jessy, life would be easier if she didn't get involved. To her, love equaled pain—so to avoid the agony of grief again, she would just be numb. And instead of living, she would merely exist.

As he drove, Michael chanced a quick glance at Jessy. She sat ramrod straight, her beautiful chestnut hair loose and spilling over her shoulders in soft waves. She sensed his gaze and grimly smiled.

"I warned you about me," she said quietly, a faint note of sour humor in her tone. It was enough to give Michael a glimmer of hope.

"Yes, you did," Michael said. "But I'm not one to listen to warnings."

Jessy almost smiled at that, looking straight ahead instead of at Michael. "I don't know what else to say to you, Michael."

"I don't either," he said, swinging his own gaze back to the road. "That's why I want you to listen to me now and hear what I have to say."

The unusual forcefulness of his words caught Jessy off-guard. She frowned faintly, but said nothing. For once, she didn't attempt to argue.

Michael pulled the Bronco onto the shoulder of the road and cut the engine. An uneasy silence settled between them as the engine ticked and snow softly tapped against the windows.

"I know why you're afraid," he said, voice as soft as a caress. "I understand."

Michael undid his seatbelt and half-turned in his seat, facing Jessy. It had been so long since he'd talked about this, years since he'd even allowed himself to dwell on it—but Jessy needed to hear it. And maybe he needed to share it.

"When Libby and Marie and Ben were born," he said quietly, "I didn't think it was possible to love anyone as much as I loved them. From the moment they were born, I knew that I was taking a risk by loving them so much. Every time they bumped their head or caught a cold, it reminded me just how easily I could lose them."

Jessy remained silent, gazing steadily at Michael. He looked away, eyes shining with sudden tears. He gritted his teeth for a moment, steadied himself to continue.

"We almost lost Libby," he finally said. "She was just a few months old, just a little thing. One second she was smiling at me in her crib and the next—" His voice caught and he swallowed hard. Jessy reached out to smooth down his hair, a simple gesture that suddenly meant the world.

"What happened?" she asked softly.

"Convulsions," Michael said simply, meeting Jessy's gaze again. "Her temperature spiked to a hundred and one by the time we got her to the hospital. Ann and I spent the night in the ER while they packed Libby in ice and reduced her fever. Every time I saw a doctor walk by, I was afraid he was going to tell me that my little girl had died."

Jessy reached out, covering his hand with hers. He smiled slightly, grateful for her touch.

"It wasn't until we lost my dad that I understood how the world worked," Michael said, his voice not much more than a whisper. "There's a price we have to pay, a trade-off. If we're going to be happy or love somebody or be loved—we have to be willing to accept the fact that one day it's going to end."

Jessy nodded slowly. "But when it ends—it hurts so much—"

"It should," Michael said, a faint smile slanting over his lips. "That pain is what reminds us of how much we loved. Yes, it hurts to let go and face the end of that love—but I don't believe that it ever really ends. It just changes."

Jessy thought of her parents, gone for so many years, yet still so alive in her heart and memories. Michael was right; she still loved her parents as much as she ever had, if not more. And she knew—felt in her heart—that wherever they were, they still loved her.

"You have to take that chance, Jessy." Michael touched her cheek, cupping it gently in his palm. "I know you've had a lot of pain in your life—but you're entitled to some happiness, too. If you don't allow yourself that, then—then all the pain was for nothing."

Jessy studied him for a few moments, feeling something deep inside her linking to him. He was speaking the truth, a truth she had tried to convince herself of time and time again. "You think so, huh?" she asked with a faint, lopsided smile.

"I know so." Michael felt an almost sickening lurch of fear in his belly as he realized that now was the time to tell her how he felt. There would be no better chance, no more perfect opportunity. "Jessy—"

His voice trailed away and she waited for him to continue, gazing at him with guileless, wide eyes. Her breath had caught, as if she somehow sensed what he was about to say.

But the words wouldn't come.

"Don't run away from us," he said instead, his slight smile fading even more. "The kids don't want you to go. Stay until Christmas at least—please. Then you can do whatever you want. Just—think about it."

Michael heard the pleading tone in his own voice and forced himself to stop before he could embarrass them both. For all his talk of taking risks, he couldn't bring himself to take that chance yet—just in case she didn't feel the same.

Jessy said nothing, keeping her eyes averted as she finally, slowly, nodded her head. Michael had the very bad feeling that somehow, without meaning to, he had hurt her even more by not being completely honest. He had let the moment pass, and now it was too late to fix it.

"Jessy," he said softly, taking her hand before she could move away from him. "I told you I'd give you all the time you need—all the time we need—and I meant it. I promise you."

She nodded, struggling for control of her emotions, but said nothing.

"So what do we do now?" Michael asked, voice barely more than a whisper. "Do I drive you into town, or do I take you home?"

Jessy closed her eyes for a moment, a tear trickling silently down her cheek. Her silence seemed to last an eternity to Michael. She could say anything right now. With her decision, she could either destroy the fragile thing they had created, or she could make everything right again.

"Take me home," she finally whispered. "Just—take me home."

Resisting the urge to laugh, to take her into his arms and shout his relief to the world, Michael simply nodded.

"Yeah," he said softly. "Let's go home."

Chapter Fourteen

MICHAEL HELD TO his promise. The rest of the week passed in a pleasant whirl of Christmas shopping and school pageants and cookie decorating, and Michael never again mentioned their argument or the reasons behind it. If anything, he was more wonderful than ever, as friendly and caring and generous as always. He kept his thoughts and feelings to himself, and if Jessy glanced up and caught him studying her, he merely looked away without a comment. Every night, after the kids were put to bed, they sat up and watched television for a while—usually while Lyssa dozed in her easychair—and then went their separate ways to bed. Michael never tried to kiss her or touch her or do anything that might scare her away.

And after a week of it, Jessy was just about to lose her mind.

It drove her crazy to be close to him, to catch a whiff of his soap or feel the faintest accidental brush of his hand against hers. The memory of that last kiss they'd shared in the garage haunted her. Every time she saw him smile, every time she heard his voice, she was jolted with total recall of how it had felt to kiss him, how sweet his lips had tasted, how gentle his hands had been—

Crazy. She was going crazy. He'd said he'd give her time, so he'd given her time. Plenty of time. More time than she'd needed to realize that she wanted to be with Michael, that it was too late for her to be afraid of getting too close to him. Now she wanted him to kiss her again. She wanted him to make advances and do all the things that she'd always dreamed a man might do—

But he was still giving her time.

Be careful what you ask for, she thought as she shook the thoughts out of her mind and turned her attention to the sizzling griddle on the stove. With the tip of her tongue poking from the corner of her mouth and her forehead wrinkled in exaggerated concentration, Jessy carefully poured pancake batter onto the griddle. Her audience, Ben and Marie, sat high on the stools at the breakfast nook, giggling at her silliness. Libby, nose buried in a glossy teen magazine, was oblivious.

"Make me a cat pancake!" Ben said, grinning broadly.

Jessy wrinkled up her nose in a playful grimace. "A cat pancake? Eww—yuck! I'll make blueberry or banana, but cat-flavored—?"

Ben's chuckle made Jessy's heart feel lighter, banishing the more frustrating thoughts of Michael to the back of her mind. Even though she had the feeling that something was building between them—something big and scary and completely unfamiliar to her—she welcomed the distraction of the kids.

"How about snowmen pancakes?" Maria asked, leaning on her elbows and half-lying over the counter. "Gramma makes them all the time."

Jessy glanced over to Lyssa, who sat at the breakfast nook with the morning paper spread out over the table. Lyssa looked over the rim of her bifocals and smiled. "I'm a culinary genius. What can I say?"

Jessy laughed and quickly glanced around the kitchen, smile widening when she saw the basket filled with old-fashioned metal cookie cutters in the shapes of Christmas trees, Santas, reindeers, and sleighs. Perfect.

"I don't know if I can do snowmen," she said to Ben and Marie, "but how about some Christmas pancakes instead?"

As Ben and Marie watched, fascinated, Jessy placed the cookie cutters onto the griddle and filled them with batter. She made Santas with blueberry eyes and Christmas trees decorated with strawberry slices and bits of banana. She was just about to pour batter into the reindeer cookie cutter to make a strawberry-nosed Rudolph when Michael burst through the back door, a huge grin on his face as he quickly stomped snow from his boots and shook it from his hair.

"Mom, could you give Doc Neilson a call?" he said, yanking off his gloves. "We're about to add to the family."

Lyssa's glasses slid off the end of her nose. "Lolita's in labor?"

"As we speak." Michael grinned over to Jessy, reading her puzzled expression instantly. "Lolita's one of the cows. She's about to drop a calf and I'm afraid it might be breech."

Lyssa quickly made the phone call as Michael joined Jessy at the stove, sampling a Santa pancake. "This is actually good," he said through a mouthful.

"You sound surprised." Jessy said and smiled. "I happen to be an excellent cook. You don't get to be my size without—" She caught the sudden disapproval in Michael's eyes and let the rest of the sentence trail away. "Sorry—habit."

"It's a bad habit."

"I know, I know—" Jessy batted her eyes as she cocked her head and smiled up at him. "Forgive me?"

"Well—" Michael slowly smiled. "I'll have to think about it."

Their smiles locked and held for a long, sweet moment. For just an instant, a heartbeat, it felt as if anything could be possible between them.

"Are you feeling better about—things?" Michael asked softly, standing so close to Jessy that she had to almost crane her head to look into his eyes. With Lyssa on the phone, Libby preoccupied with her magazine, and the twins playing with their food, it was almost as if they had the world to themselves. At least, it felt close enough for Jessy.

"Yes," she said, taking a deep breath and inhaling deeply all of Michael's good smells—soap, fresh hay, skin. He hadn't yet shaved that morning, so a stubbly growth of beard darkened his cheeks and chin and throat. He hadn't bothered to brush his hair either and it stood at all angles, styled by the wind and snow. He looked as if he had just rolled out of bed after a particularly strenuous night—and Jessy had to rein her thoughts in before they could go any further. "Much better."

Michael slowly smiled down at her, as if he could read her thoughts. "So I've given you enough time and space and all that other jazz? You've thought about everything?"

"Mucho thought," Jessy said, her own smile growing. He shifted a little closer to her, still smiling in a way that made her heart trip-hammer.

"So what have you decided?" he murmured, brushing a stray hair from Jessy's temple, his fingertips lingering along the line of her cheek. One look into his eyes told her that he knew exactly what kind of reaction that gesture would cause. And he wasn't far wrong. All of a sudden she forgot how to speak English.

"I'm—I mean—I guess I'm—"

"Doctor's on his way," Lyssa announced, turning around just as Michael was moving in closer. "Oh—don't let me interrupt."

Michael grinned and tipped a quick wink to Jessy, then turned to Lyssa. And just like that, the spell was broken and Jessy regained the use of her brain. She sagged a little against the counter, pleasantly overwhelmed by whatever had just happened.

"Guess I'd better go deliver me a calf," Michael said, tugging on his gloves again. "Libs? Would my future veterinarian like to come watch?"

Libby looked up from her magazine. "Is it all gross and yucky?"

"You'd better believe it."

Libby suddenly smiled. "Cool."

"Can we go?" Marie asked, tugging at Michael's coat. "Please, Daddy?"

"Not this time, sweetie." Michael knelt in front of Ben and Marie, anticipating their pouts as he smiled. "I know Lolita's your favorite, but she needs to be by herself for a while so she can have her baby and be safe."

"Can we visit her after she has the baby?" Ben asked.

"Of course. I think she'd be disappointed if you didn't." Michael kissed their cheeks and gave them each a quick tickle. "But right now, I want you two to eat your breakfast so we can go Christmas shopping this afternoon. Right?"

"Right!" they chorused, smiling as they climbed back up on the barstools. Michael straightened and turned back to Jessy. For a moment they gazed at each other, connected in that moment of cozy domesticity.

And right then, she couldn't resist a moment longer.

"Hurry back," she finally said, stretching up on tiptoe to quickly kiss Michael's cheek. He blinked in surprise, then frowned faintly to egg on Ben and Marie's giggles.

"You call that a goodbye kiss?" he muttered, smiling faintly as he snagged his arm around Jessy's waist and pulled her flush against his side, gazing melodramatically into her eyes for a moment. Jessy, caught completely off-guard, laughed.

"Michael—"

Before she could say another word, Michael dipped her deeply, as if they were doing a tango in an old movie, and slowly, thoroughly kissed her. Jessy forgot she was supposed to be self-conscious of her weight, feeling as if her entire body had dissolved into a boneless rag, supported entirely in Michael's strong arms, aware of absolutely nothing but the feel of his lips on hers. Everything else in the world melted away.

When it ended, Jessy breathlessly gazed up at him. Michael just smiled.

"Now *that's* a kiss," he said, winking as he helped her stand again. Jessy had to lean against the countertop to keep her trembling knees from giving out on her.

"Wow," she whispered.

Michael laughed and kissed her again, the scratch of his stubble tickling her nose. "I'll be back in a bit. Keep some pancakes warm for me, please."

Jessy managed a weak nod. "Sure—"

With another wink, Michael left the house, followed by Libby. Jessy watched him go and then sank onto a stool, dazed and flushed and tingling from the lips down. Ben and Marie peeked at her through their hands, giggling. Lyssa just grinned as she poured a cup of coffee for Jessy and handed it to her.

"And that's what he does in front of family," Lyssa said and *tsked* playfully. "Remind me to have you two chaperoned at all times."

Jessy laughed. With the thoughts running through her mind just then, a chaperone might not be such a bad idea after all.

"DADDY! It's Santa Claus!" Ben gave Michael's hand a mighty tug as he pointed towards the street corner, where a Salvation Army Santa stood ringing a handbell.

Marie, holding Jessy's hand, frowned faintly. "How can Santa be here and at the North Pole at the same time?"

As they walked along the town square, Michael glanced over to Jessy and smiled, his eyebrows raising as if to say *How am I gonna get out of this one?*

"Well—" Michael cleared his throat and shrugged uncomfortably as he looked down and met Marie's questioning gaze. "Santa is, uh, a busy guy—"

"But how can he be here and be at the mall and be at the North Pole making toys all at the same time?" Marie asked.

"Maybe he's been clowned," Ben said softly, voice dropping with awe.

"Cloned," Michael corrected, smiling. "And no, there's only one Santa."

Marie wasn't satisfied. "Then how—"

"Elves," Jessy said quickly, giving Marie's hand a light squeeze. "Santa has a secret group of specially trained elves who go out and make all his public appearances for him."

"Really?" Both Ben and Marie frowned.

"Jessy's right," Michael said, nodding. "Like I said, Santa's a busy guy. He can't go gallivanting all over the world to ring bells or sit in toy stores, so he has his elves go for him."

"Oh." Marie suddenly smiled as everything clicked. "Okay."

Michael and Jessy looked at each other over the children's heads and shared a relieved smile. He mouthed a silent "thank you" and Jessy grinned, shrugging. She had enjoyed every last second of their trip into the town of Scottsview—which was, to be honest, like taking a trip into a Norman Rockwell painting. Every storefront was decorated beautifully for Christmas and Hanukkah, with wreaths hanging from each street lamp and multi-colored lights criss-crossing the streets. For the first time in far too many years, Jessy actually felt excited about Christmas.

"Oooh—" Libby, walking ahead of them, had stopped in front of a jewelry store window. "Look, Dad."

The window was decorated as a living room, complete with Christmas tree and fireplace and a life-size Santa caught in the act of leaving gifts. The tree was decorated with exquisitely crafted blown-glass ornaments, topped by a beautiful flame-haired angel. Libby's eye had been caught by the diamond necklace dangling from Santa's hand, but the ornaments had drawn Jessy's attention. Michael noticed her sudden fascination and smiled.

"It's called a Bride's Tree," he said, slipping an arm around Jessy's shoulders. "There's an old German tradition that says that a couple's first Christmas tree should have these twelve ornaments to bring happiness and good luck to the marriage."

Jessy glanced over to Michael, feeling suddenly self-conscious. "They're beautiful," she said softly.

"Each ornament symbolizes something special," Michael continued, his fingertips lazily grazing the nape of Jessy's neck. "If I remember correctly, the bird stands for joy, the rabbit for hope, the rose for affection, the flower basket for good wishes, the heart for true love—"

Michael's voice trailed away as he turned his attention to Jessy again, hesitating for a moment as he saw the wistful longing in her eyes. His sudden silence caught her off-guard. She looked away from the Bride's Tree and saw that Michael was openly gazing at her.

"What's wrong?" she asked, lips curving in a faintly sardonic smile.

"Not a thing," he said quietly, leaning forward to press a soft kiss against her forehead, taking her into his arms. "I have to stop by the toy store and do the Santa thing. Would you mind keeping an eye on the kids for me? I'll make it worth your while—"

Jessy smiled up at him, feeling suddenly weightless as she

laughed. "Oh, I believe I could be coerced into that."

With a devilish grin, Michael cocked an eyebrow and leaned in close, the warmth of their breath mingling in a way that was almost more intimate than a kiss. "I'll save the coercion for later, then."

Jessy felt her smile curling in a way that felt totally alien, yet wonderfully seductive. "Mr. Forrester," she said softly. "The children are watching."

"So they are," he said and brushed his lips over hers, lingering sweetly for just a moment before pulling away. Jessy smiled again as they separated. "I'll meet you guys for lunch in an hour."

"Deal."

He quickly kissed her again and then—with a wink and a grin to Libby, Marie, and Ben—headed down the snowy street. Jessy watched him go, then smiled and turned back to the kids.

"So—how about we go talk to Santa?" Jessy asked.

"You mean Santa's elf," Marie corrected.

"Right. Santa's elf."

With Libby leading the way and trying not to look like she was actually with them, Ben and Marie impatiently tugged Jessy into the department store. A blast of over-heated air struck them, but the kids were too excited to notice. They had caught sight of Santa as he sat majestically on a throne of candy canes and artificial snow. All else had ceased to matter.

Jessy, meanwhile, had caught sight of the line that stretched through three aisles. Stifling a groan, she led the kids to the end of the line and settled in for the wait.

"Do I have to stay here?" Libby asked, sighing melodramatically.

"Don't tell me you don't want to tell Santa what you want for Christmas," Jessy teased, managing to coax a reluctant smile from Libby.

"Can I go talk to my friends? They're right over there—"

Jessy followed Libby's pointing hand and saw two young girls standing at a cosmetics counter. They waved when they finally noticed Libby and gestured for her to join them.

"Libby, honey—I don't know. Your dad wanted me to keep an

eye on you guys—"

"I'll just be over there. I promise I won't go anywhere else." Libby tried the big puppy-eyes look that worked so well on her father. "Please, Jessy? You can see me from the line—"

Jessy hesitated a moment, then relented with a nod. "Okay—but promise you'll stay right there."

Libby's smile brightened. "I promise. Thanks, Jessy!"

Jessy kept an eye on Libby as she hurried over to her friends, so anxious to experiment with the trial perfume and makeup at the counter. She remembered all too clearly how it felt at that age—too old to do kid stuff like sit on Santa's lap, but too young to flirt with boys and wear makeup.

They shuffled forward in the line and Jessy was pleasantly surprised by how well-behaved Ben and Marie were—especially in comparison to some of the other children in line, who were so hopped up on sugar and excitement that they practically climbed the walls. Ben and Marie passed the time by playing rock-paper-scissors against Jessy's legs, and Jessy took the opportunity to do a little people watching, allowing her imagination to fill in the blanks. She hadn't realized how much she missed singing Christmas carols or buying gifts—and more than that; she hadn't realized how much she had missed the feeling of family, of tradition. Michael had given all that and more to her. His gift was the gift of his family.

She realized that she had lost sight of Libby and scanned the crowd. There were her friends—but where was Libby?

Jessy's heart jumped into her throat as she stood on tiptoes and craned her neck to look over the crowd. The store suddenly seemed jam-packed, full of unsmiling strangers. What was she thinking to let her go off by herself? She should have known this might happen.

"Oh—I might have known."

Ann's voice, brimming with disdain, seemed somehow louder than the roar of the crowd, as unwelcome as a ice cube down the spine. Jessy turned to see Ann leading Libby through the crowd, protectively keeping one hand on the girl's shoulder while holding her hand. Libby looked utterly mortified.

"Mom—I told you, I was talking to my friends. I'm not lost."

Ann ignored her. She kept her glare focused exclusively on Jessy. "What are you doing with my children?"

"Mom!" Marie reached up for a hug—which Ann also ignored, too distracted in her self-righteous fury. Jessy caught the flash of hurt in Marie's eyes and knelt down beside her.

"It's your turn, Marie. Why don't you and Ben go together. Then we'll meet your dad for pizza."

Marie glanced up to her mother quickly, then and walked hand in hand with Ben to sit on Santa's lap. Once she was away, Jessy smiled at Libby.

"Would you mind keeping an eye on them while I talk to your mom?"

"Whatever." Libby wrenched herself away from Ann and stomped over to stand near Santa's throne, well out of earshot. Just to make sure, Jessy walked away from the front of the line, Ann furiously following.

"I cannot believe this!" Ann didn't bother to modulate her volume and several shoppers turned to look. Jessy tried to pretend they didn't exist, keeping her attention focused on Ann. "What are you doing with my children?"

"We're shopping. They wanted to see Santa." Jessy struggled to maintain a semblance of patience in her voice. "Libby was with her friends—"

"You have no right to do this!"

Puzzled, Jessy shook her head slightly. "No right to do *what?*"

"To take my place. You're not their mother. I am."

"Then why don't you act like it once in a while, instead of just when it suits you." Jessy's temper flared, but she didn't bother to try to control it. "And I'm *not* taking your place. Your kids love you. You don't deserve it, but they do."

Before Jessy knew what was coming, Ann slapped her.

Tears shone in Ann's eyes and she literally trembled with rage. Jessy was struck dumb with shock. The only thing that stopped her from returning the blow was knowing that the kids would see. She could hear the murmurs of shoppers all around them, feel their stares. Ann seemed completely oblivious to it all.

"Michael doesn't love you," Ann finally managed to say. "If you think that he does, then you're as stupid as you look."

Jessy opened her mouth to speak, but Ann interrupted her.

"Do you know why he's with you now? Because he felt sorry for you. Not because he wants a relationship with you." Ann's eyes glittered as a smile twitched at her lips. "I bet he didn't tell you that we're still sleeping together, did he? I'll bet he didn't mention that whenever I come to town to see the kids, I stay at the house. In his bed."

Jessy felt as if she'd been slapped again. But this stung more.

"You are not taking my place in the family. Michael will never love you as much as he loves me. My children will never love you as much as they love me." Ann's eyes blazed. "I'm not giving him up."

"You walked out on him and the kids," Jessy said quietly. *"You* are the one who decided it was over. You broke their hearts."

Ann said nothing for a moment, seething. When she finally spoke, the calmness in her tone seemed unnatural.

"Walk away from them now."

Jessy matched her glare, unblinking. "No."

"No?" Ann slowly, unpleasantly, smiled. "Fine. Then you can be the one Michael blames when I take his children away from him. You can be the one he hates when he never sees the kids again. Because I'll do it. If you stay with him, if you think you have some kind of fairy tale future together, then I will sue him for custody of the kids and he will have to beg me to spend time with them. Is that what you want?"

Jessy couldn't speak. Ann's eyes were coldly calm. She would do it. She would take Michael's kids away from him just for spite. Despite all her claims to still love him, she would easily be able to hurt him like that.

Ann's smile crooked slightly as Marie and Ben returned, followed by Libby. "Have a merry Christmas, Jessy. Remember what I said."

And without a word to her children, Ann walked away.

Feeling shellshocked, Jessy took Marie and Ben's hands and led the kids out of the department store. They sensed something was wrong and filled the silence with chatter about Santa and the elves. Even Libby.

They didn't mention their mother.

It wasn't until they'd finally stepped out of the close confines of the store that Jessy felt a little better, a little less claustrophobic. But even as she herded the kids across the street to the pizza parlor they had chosen for lunch, she looked over her shoulder, unable to shake the feeling that Ann was still watching her.

Would she try to take the kids? Could Ann actually do something so awful to Michael?

Jessy remembered the pain and anger in Ann's eyes and knew that she was perfectly capable of hurting him so badly. If it got her what she wanted, she would do it in a heartbeat.

Once inside the pizza place, she struggled to relax a bit but failed miserably. The restaurant was bright and loud and filled with people laughing and talking and having a wonderful time, and Jessy felt as if she were an alien from another world, surrounded by a culture she could not understand. Laughing was not something she'd be doing again anytime soon.

She couldn't get the image of Michael and Ann out of her head. Surely it couldn't be true—Michael didn't seem like the kind of guy who would continue to sleep with his ex-wife just for convenience's sake. He'd sleep with her because he still loved her.

That realization didn't help matters.

Ben and Marie bounced excitedly, singing along to "Jingle Bell Rock" as it blared over the speaker system. Jessy helped them out of their coats and mittens and gave them a handful of quarters to spend on the video games on the other side of the room. What would they think about their mom and dad getting back together? Wasn't that the hope of every kid whose parents divorced? That one day they'd be a family again?

Was she getting in the way of that?

When Michael entered, she felt like running away. This was getting too complicated. She couldn't be the reason Michael lost his kids. She had no doubt Ann would do whatever she had to do to make Michael pay for the mistakes she had made.

Jessy felt her stomach churn and thought she might throw up.

"Hey," he said, smiling as he slid into the booth beside Libby. "You guys have fun?"

Ben and Marie immediately launched into a retelling of their encounter with the Santa imposter. Michael listened intently, nodding and making the appropriate sounds, but Jessy couldn't keep her attention focused on the kids. She kept glancing at the door, feeling as tensely wound as a clock spring.

She didn't hear Michael when he asked her a question. Or when he repeated the question. It wasn't until he whistled and waved his hand in front of her eyes that the spell was broken and she finally looked away from the door.

"What? I'm sorry—what did you say?" She tried to smile but couldn't hide the strained tone of her voice.

Michael studied her a moment longer, then looked to Libby. "How about taking Ben and Marie over to the jukebox?" he asked, fishing in his jeans pocket for a handful of quarters.

Libby grumbled as she slid out of the booth, taking Ben and Marie by the hands. "If you want us to leave, you can just say so."

"You're a funny kid, Libs." Michael grinned and handed her the quarters. "Go easy on the boy bands, please."

As the kids left the table, Michael turned his full attention back to Jessy. "Okay. Spill it. What's going on?"

"Nothing," she said softly, unable to meet his eyes.

"Uh-huh. Right." Michael reached over and covered her hands with his, startling her.

Jessy gazed at Michael for a few moments, stalling for time as she took a deep breath and slowly released it.

"While we were in line for Santa," she said calmly, trying her best to sound casual and nonchalant, "I ran into Ann. We had a few—words."

Michael's smile faded. "What did she say?"

"She was angry because I was with the kids—"

Michael took Jessy's hands, holding them lightly. Jessy focused her attention on the warmth of his palms, the soft roughness of his skin. How could something as simple as holding his hand make her feel so much safer?

"And she told me to walk away now." Jessy chanced a quick glance up to Michael's eyes. "Or else she'd take your kids away."

Without saying a word, Michael scooted around the circular booth, draping an arm around Jessy's shoulder, holding her close. She could feel his tenseness, the tightness of his muscles as he fought to control his anger.

"She's not going to do that," he finally said. "She can't."

"I don't want to be the reason you lose your family." Jessy looked up at him. "She wants to come back, Michael."

Michael gazed into her eyes for a few moments. "Everything will be okay, Jess. I promise."

"You can't just dismiss it that easily. She's mad, Michael, and she's going to take it out on you and the kids. She wants her way."

"And you think we should just give in to her? You think the best solution to this is you leaving us and Ann coming back for a few weeks—or until she gets bored of us again?"

Jessy looked away from him, unable to meet his eyes. "I think I should go—"

"For God's sake, Jess—haven't we been through this song and dance before?"

"I don't belong here—"

"That's not true and you know it."

Jessy said nothing for a moment. She slid her hand out of Michael's and covered her face. She wanted to hide from everything.

"I think the reason you want to go is because you're still afraid." Michael's tone softened and he reached for Jessy's hands, lowering them so he could look into her eyes. "It has nothing to do with Ann."

Jessy couldn't deny the truth of that. She was scared to death of the new life that was slowly revealing itself to her. What if she and Michael got serious? Was she ready to be a mother to a ready-made family? Was she ready to share her life with someone? After so many years of being alone, the thought of being with someone twenty-four hours a day terrified her. What if they got sick of each other? What if they started noticing each other's not-so-pleasant qualities?

In her mind, she had already imagined the breakup with Michael. She just couldn't imagine the in-between parts.

"Jess—I need you to stay. I want you to stay."

The words, so softly spoken, seemed to resonate throughout Jessy's entire body, more powerful than she could have ever expected. Her fears eased slightly, giving way to a whisper of hope. All her life, she had dreamed of having someone to love, someone to take care of, someone to trust. It had never occurred to her that it could actually happen.

"Okay," she whispered, sinking back into the circle of his arms again, allowing herself to believe him.

Chapter Fifteen

SOMETHING SNEAKY'S going on here, Michael thought, folding his arms over his chest as he watched his mother herd the kids into the kitchen, where the smells of gingerbread and fudge already filled the air. Cookie decorating was next on the agenda, with each of them getting their own bowl of frosting to lick. The kids—Libby included—were delighted. If Michael hadn't known any better, he'd suspect that she was attempting to give him and Jessy a chance to be alone. After last week's experience with Ann in town, he was grateful.

"Here you go," Lyssa said as she handed Michael a well-stocked picnic basket. "I thought you and Jessy might like to have your dinner while you show her the farm."

Michael smiled. "While I show her the farm?"

"Of course." Lyssa looked at him as though he was a child. "Don't tell me you haven't thought about taking her out to see the barns—"

"The barns?" Michael frowned, not quite following his mother's reasoning. He glanced over to Jessy and she shrugged helplessly, the faintest tinge of a blush in her cheeks.

"I thought you might want to take Jessy along as you do your chores," Lyssa said and smiled.

"But I've done most of the chores—"

"Don't you have *something* to do out there?" Lyssa raised an eyebrow as her smile twisted slightly, doing her darnedest to be subtle and failing miserably. Michael finally realized what she was trying to do and grinned.

"Oh, right—I guess I do have to take care of some—things." He laughed at himself and kissed Lyssa's cheek. "Good idea, Mom."

Lyssa, smiling, swatted Michael's backside. "Then get going, Mister."

"Yes, ma'am." Grinning broadly, Michael glanced to Jessy and raised his eyebrows. "So—would you like to have the grand tour of Forrester Acres?"

"Why, what a good idea," Jessy said, playing along. "And so spontaneous, too."

"Great," Lyssa muttered, good-naturedly grumpy. "Now there's *two* of 'em."

Michael kissed Lyssa's cheek once more, and then he and Jessy were off on the tour. The sun had begun to set already, the afternoon darkened by low-hanging snow clouds, but Jessy didn't feel the cold. As they walked, hand in hand, Jessy didn't care if it snowed, rained or typhooned.

The farm looked as though it could have been a model for Currier and Ives, all rolling hills and snowy valleys and split-rail fences. In the backyard, a barren willow tree stood out in stark contrast to the snow; an old tractor tire slowly swung from one of its skeletal branches, waiting for summer. Michael told her stories about his childhood, the summer days spent fishing for trout and swimming in the pond, the summer nights camping in the treehouse hidden amid the thicket of trees surrounding the pond. It had been a child's paradise, and as Michael shared his memories with Jessy, he realized that in many ways, it still was.

Every time Jessy's eyes widened in delight, every time she laughed with him at one of his memories or gazed silently at the rolling hills and valleys, Michael wondered if she could be happy with him, with life on a farm. Ann had tried to be satisfied, but the quiet life had eventually stifled her. Would Jessy be the same?

Somehow, in his heart, Michael knew that she would not be like Ann. If Jessy shared his feelings, she would love him and his family no matter where they lived or what they did—and he knew now that he wanted her to be a part of his life, of his children's lives.

As the last of the sunlight faded, Michael and Jessy finally reached his favorite place, the old barn he and the kids had rebuilt and used as a getaway. The two-story barn had been abandoned when business expanded and they needed a more modern shed for the cows, so Michael had repaired the barn as a place to escape when the pressures of running the farm got the best of him. He was planning on moving his art supplies to the upper loft in the spring, once the snow thawed and the scenery grew more scenic again.

He pulled the barn door open just enough for them to slip through and followed Jessy inside. She stood in the middle of the straw-strewn floor, eyes closed as she took a deep breath of the sweet, hay-scented air, a smile of pure contentment on her lips. A half-repaired truck sat in the back of the barn, close to a pyramid of hay bales that led up to the loft. A wooden swing hung from the rafters, the wide plank swaying gently in the gust of cold air, beckoning irresistibly.

Jessy shrugged out of her coat and gingerly climbed onto the swing, holding tight to the ropes as she pushed off and began to swing. Michael smiled as he set the picnic basket down and took off his own jacket, lighting a lantern before taking a seat on a bale of hay. He loved watching her as she swung, laughing as she spun and twisted on the swing. For a moment, Michael was captivated by the sight of her, wondering how many times in her life she had ever been so carefree, so happy.

"I used to have one of these when I was a kid," Jessy said, laughing as the rope uncoiled and sent her spinning in the opposite direction.

Michael stood and caught the swing, slowly pulling Jessy closer to him. The smile remained on her lips, but something changed in her eyes. Finally he was beginning to know the signs, the secret signals that she didn't even know she was giving him. Right now, she wanted him to kiss her. He could read it in the widening of her eyes, the parting of her lips, the quickening of her breath.

"Stand up for a second." Michael grabbed the rope to steady the swing and straddled the plank as Jessy stood. Without a word he turned her to face him, then settled down on the seat and gestured for Jessy to do the same. She awkwardly sat astraddle the plank, cheeks pinkening as she realized how close they were, then darkening as Michael gently lifted each of her legs, repositioning them over his thighs. Jessy never looked away from him, the mixture of innocence and uncertain desire in her eyes affecting him instantly.

"This is cozy," she said softly, a faint smile curling the corner of her lips. Only a few inches separated them as they gazed at each other, the swing slowly twisting and turning, swaying back and forth as Michael gently propelled them. He slipped his arms around Jessy's waist, pulling her even closer. Her eyes widened slightly, but she settled against him, waiting for his next move.

Michael was momentarily at a loss, stunned by her trust, by her breathless expectation. His desire to touch her, to make love to her, had grown almost exponentially over the past few days, building to such a fever pitch that just the sight of her was enough to create a flurry of distracting fantasies. He hadn't realized how much he could want a woman until now.

And now he wanted Jessy. In his heart, in his gut, he knew he wasn't rushing things, that there was no timetable, but until this moment he hadn't been able to gauge Jessy's feelings. Now, if he was truly seeing what he thought he was seeing in her eyes, she wanted him as much as he wanted her. And maybe she even loved him as much as he loved her.

The realization was as frightening and exciting as it was sobering.

"What's wrong?" she asked softly, touching his creased forehead, smoothing her fingertips over his skin. At her touch, he felt his body respond, every muscle tensing, every nerve flaring into life. He gazed at her for a few moments before speaking, greedily drinking in her soft smile, her warm eyes. He dimly remembered the horrible things Ann had said about Jessy and wondered how anyone could look at her and not see how beautiful she was.

"Remember when you told me that you weren't used to this sort of thing?" Michael smiled faintly as he spoke, even though he felt as if his stomach had twisted into a knot. He was more than nervous. He was terrified.

"I remember it well," she said, her full lips curving in a way that sent darting pangs of desire through his body. "Why?"

Michael said nothing for a moment as Jessy rested her hands on his hips. His breath caught. He'd forgotten what it was like to feel such overwhelming need for a woman; in the years since his divorce he'd lived the life of a monk, not even bothering to consider anything as unnecessary and frivolous as sex. He'd concentrated on his children and his work and nothing more.

Now he felt those two years of celibacy catching up with him all at once. With a vengeance.

Without thinking twice Michael leaned closer to Jessy and kissed her, the movement sending the swing swaying anew. Their lips brushed softly against each other, breaths mingling, shifting with the movement of the swing. Michael deepened the kiss, tasting Jessy's mouth with slow, measured strokes of his tongue, feeling her timid but aroused response. Wrapping his arms around her, Michael urged Jessy closer, until she was nearly sitting on his lap. The feel of her moving against him was almost too much to bear. Involuntarily, he shifted, straining to be even closer—

And Jessy abruptly broke away from the kiss, eyes huge as realization of what they were doing, what *she* was doing, hit her. She looked at him with an odd mixture of fear and desire, silently questioning. Michael didn't move, couldn't move. All he could do was stare back at her and feel more and more like a creep with every passing moment. She wasn't ready for this. He'd known she wasn't ready, he'd promised not to rush her into anything, to take it slow—and now this. No wonder she was looking at him like that.

"Jessy—" He couldn't seem to raise his voice above a murmur, his lips and tongue thick, numb. "I don't know—I mean—"

Jessy shook her head slightly, cutting off his fumbling apology, and carefully stood, her cheeks crimson as she slipped away from him. She kept her head down, her eyes averted, trembling as she rubbed at her mouth and took slow, deliberate breaths. Shakily, she took a few steps away from the swing, keeping her back to him.

Michael climbed off the swing, feeling more miserable with each passing moment. Damn it, why did he have to act like a teenager in heat? Why did he have to take so much for granted?

"Jessy," he said again, his voice a little stronger.

She didn't look at him. The sheer awkwardness of the moment was unbearable. Michael wished he could rewind the last ten minutes and start all over again. At the very least, he wished he could give himself a good swift kick in the butt.

Especially when she finally faced him again. He had never seen her look so alone—or so lonely.

"Don't apologize," she said quietly, a faint but grim smile curling the corner of her lips. "It's me—I'm not—"

"No, Jess—"

Jessy picked up her jacket and started walking towards the door. "I don't think I can do this," she whispered, almost to herself.

Michael caught her arm gently and she stopped without turning to face him. What had she gone through? What had Wilks done to her?

"I need to talk to you about this," he said softly. "Please, Jessy—give me that much."

Jessy finally raised her gaze to his, holding it for a long time, and Michael could see every flicker of indecision and fear. His heartbeat felt sluggish and sick as he waited for her to respond. He didn't want to lose her now that they were so close to finally building something together, but he had the very bad feeling that with one wrong word, one wrong touch, he could lose her forever.

"Okay," she finally whispered. She averted her eyes from his gaze, but Michael caught the flare of hope she was trying to hide. "Let's talk."

Michael reached out and took her hand. She squeezed it tightly, as if she were afraid to let it go.

"I know a place," he said and smiled.

CLIMBING A MOUNTAIN of hay was not one of Jessy's finer moments, but she managed to haul herself over the bales with a minimum of clumsiness. A horrible anticipation had settled over her, impatient to hear whatever it was Michael was planning to say to her. She knew what she *hoped* he might say—but she also knew better than to expect too much.

In all honesty, she was stunned by her reaction to the kiss on the swing and the abrupt turmoil it had triggered. That one kiss had left her feeling weak and frightened and hungry for more. She knew that Michael had misread her actions, probably believing that she had pulled away because she had been scared of his obvious arousal, but that was far from the truth. The rush of desire she had felt for him had left her feeling pole-axed, as if someone had taken control of her mind and body and thrown all her caution and timidity out the window. She'd only pulled away because she had been astonished by her own arousal, not Michael's—although that had been a revelation in and of itself. She had never dreamed that a man could want her, had never imagined that anything she could do would make a man desire her so much.

But it was happening. And she had to deal with it.

"Here we are," Michael said as he helped Jessy up to the final bale. There were bits of hay in his tousled hair, sticking to his sweaty brow; Jessy had the sudden thought that he looked like every farmer's daughter's dream date. "My oasis."

On the top of the piled hay, high above the barn floor, Michael had created a refuge of sorts, a hollowed out nest lined with thick blankets and pillows of all shapes and sizes. Paperback novels were scattered around the nest's rim, along with a battery-powered lamp and a stack of newspapers and magazines.

Jessy smiled despite herself as she looked at Michael, who had switched on a small battery-powered lamp. She could imagine Michael sprawled among the pillows, reading as the kids played on the swing below, napping on those rare afternoons when there was nothing more pressing to do.

"I fixed this up during the divorce," Michael said, stepping into the nest. He held his hand to Jessy, helping her down. The whole thing felt surprisingly steady and solid beneath her feet. "I spent a lot of time up here, just thinking about everything."

It felt like he was stalling, so Jessy remained silent, watching as

Michael settled down against the pillows and opened the picnic basket. He looked up to her, expectant, and Jessy realized that he wanted her to sit with him. She awkwardly lowered herself to the blankets, surprised by how comfortably the nest was padded. It almost felt like a feather bed.

They remained unnaturally silent as Michael rooted through the picnic basket, taking out the sandwiches and coffee thermos that Lyssa had packed for them. The sudden change of mood—from pulsing desire to aimless chit-chat—bewildered Jessy. How could two people go from such rampant lust to casual conversation without making mention of such a drastic mood swing? The urge to say something, to question Michael, was enough to make her squirm.

"So," Michael said as he poured Jessy a mug of coffee and handed it to her. "Here we are."

"Yep." She sipped at the coffee, keeping her eyes riveted on Michael. "Here we are."

The silence that descended upon them was nearly stifling. Jessy drank her coffee slowly, her stomach churning, watching as Michael plucked an orange out of the basket and began to idly peel it. A thousand scenarios unspooled in her mind, a thousand possible ways for Michael to change her life forever. Whatever he was going to say, good or bad, it would be momentous. At least, that's how it felt. The waiting, the anticipation, ratcheted up her dread by the millisecond.

"I wish I'd known you when I was a kid," Michael said suddenly, popping a section of orange into his mouth.

Jessy smiled slightly, more confused than ever, and slowly shook her head. "No, you don't," she said, looking away from Michael.

"Why not?" Michael leaned against the side of the nest, stuffing a pillow beneath his arm as he propped his temple against his hand. "Would you have gone to the prom with me?"

Jessy's gaze shot to his again, the faint smile on her lips fading. "You wouldn't have asked me."

Michael frowned, scooting the basket out of the way as he moved closer to Jessy. "Why's that?"

"Well—" Jessy cleared her throat, taking a steadying breath before she looked squarely at Michael again. "Let's just say that not too many sixteen-year-old boys want to be seen with a girl who has the figure of a sumo wrestler."

"You sound pretty sure about that," Michael said after a moment. The flatness of his tone startled Jessy into looking at him again. He watched her intently, his gaze challenging her.

"Don't tell me you haven't noticed my weight," she said quietly. There it was, finally spoken aloud.

Michael kept his gaze steady on hers. "All right—I won't."

His answer rattled Jessy, but she refused to let it show. She'd had a lifetime of practice keeping her true emotions hidden. But since Michael seemed to be in the mood for speaking frankly—

"You know, that's what really surprises me about you," she said, forcing a casualness into her voice that she did not feel. She felt as if she were picking her way through a minefield. "You act like my weight doesn't matter—"

"It *doesn't* matter." Michael took her hand in his, squeezing it gently. Jessy kept herself very still, unable to respond to his touch. This was the conversation she had dreaded from the beginning. "Honey, it really doesn't matter to me."

"Are you sure?" Jessy's gaze was direct, unflinching. She had the unsettling sense that this was the point of no return, that whatever was said beyond this moment would affect their relationship drastically. For an instant, she wanted to turn back, to stop right now—but she knew in her heart that she couldn't. This was an issue that she needed to resolve right here, right now, if she wanted to have any kind of peace of mind.

"It does matter," she said, voice soft. She threaded her fingers through his, bracketing his hand with hers. "Michael—I weigh two hundred and twenty pounds, and that has mattered to every person, every man, who has ever looked at me. There has never been a day that it hasn't."

Michael said nothing, simply watching her, and she felt excruciatingly vulnerable. But she couldn't stop now.

"When you're this fat," she said quietly, unable to hide the pain, the bitterness in her voice, "people don't look at you. They look over you. Men seem to be afraid that if they make eye contact, I'll suddenly develop a fixation on them or embarrass them in front of their friends. They don't want to be seen with any woman who might be less than perfect, who's not beautiful and slim and—"

"You're being unfair." Anger hummed beneath the soft tone of Michael's voice. "Don't make assumptions about me, Jessy, because you're wrong. Maybe you've known some narrow-minded jerks, but I'm not like that."

"How many fat girls have you dated in your life, Michael?"

Michael's anger deflated almost instantly. He didn't answer, sliding his gaze away from hers for a moment.

"That's what I thought," Jessy said grimly.

"You're not being fair."

"So I'm wrong?"

Michael looked back to her again. "No," he said softly. "You're not wrong."

"I didn't think so." Jessy didn't like the coldness of her tone, but couldn't help it. She knew that Michael didn't deserve this kind of attack, but couldn't stop herself. This was something she'd had to live with her entire life. A few kind words from Michael, no matter how much she cared for him, couldn't reverse so many years of pain.

"Charlie Wilks was obviously a saint among men, then," Michael finally said after a few moments of silence.

"What are you talking about?"

"I'm talking about good old lover-boy Charlie." Michael's voice remained flat, expressionless, impossible for Jessy to read. "He must have been some swell guy to have put up with you all that time you dated. I just wonder how he could stand being with you."

Pain flashed in Jessy's eyes, but she said nothing. Michael wouldn't let her look away from him, his gaze penetrating, angrier than she'd ever seen.

"I mean, never mind the fact that you have the most beautiful smile I've ever seen," Michael continued. "Or the fact that you have a wonderful sense of humor. And never mind the fact that any half-way intelligent man should get down on his knees and thank God if you decided to fall in love with him. Never mind any of that. Apparently Charlie, despite being a total idiot, could see beyond your weight to all those other things, so I guess that makes him pretty much a prince among the rest of us jerks, right?"

Jessy stared at him for a few long moments, afraid to speak, afraid to say the wrong thing, afraid to believe what he said could be true.

"If we hadn't met on the bus," she finally said, slipping her hands away from his, "if you had just seen me on the street, you wouldn't have given me a second look."

"You don't know that."

"Yes, I do." Jessy smiled sadly. "I do."

Michael fell silent for a few moments, studying the half-eaten orange in his hand. "When I was a kid in high school," he said softly, "I weighed about ninety pounds, and twenty pounds of that was pimples. I wanted to play football more than anything, but the coach wouldn't even let me on the field. Girls ignored me because I was too skinny, too weird. I wore head-gear braces until the day of graduation, and I didn't have my first real date with a girl until my second year of college—Ann."

He looked up to Jessy again, arching an eyebrow. "So you tell me. Would you have dated *me* in high school?"

Jessy didn't answer. His point had been made.

Michael gazed at her for a few moments, his eyes remaining solemn. "The woman that you are now," he said softly, "is the woman that I'm in love with. That's all that matters."

The enormity of his words stunned her into silence. She could not speak, could not react, could not even breathe.

Michael reached out to touch her cheek, skimming the line of her cheekbone with his thumb, cradling her face in his hand. The gentleness of his touch, his gaze, was suddenly too much for her to bear. All her life, she had hoped, dreamed, that one day someone would say something like that to her. How many years had she wished that someone would love her for who she was and not how she looked?

It all seemed unreal. For a moment, she actually thought she was asleep and dreaming.

"I love you, Jessy," Michael whispered, leaning his forehead against hers for a moment as he slowly smiled. "I love you for all kinds of reasons, and I'd be lying if I said that the way you look isn't one of them. But it's not the *only* one—and I couldn't even begin to tell you all of the others."

Jessy could not speak, could not find the words that would tell Michael how much his acceptance meant to her. She couldn't explain to him how she felt finally free, finally whole. She had always been so afraid that she might never be allowed to love anyone the way that she wanted, that she would grow old and bitter and lonely and alone. Until she met Michael, she had been well on her way to that future.

But not anymore. Miraculously enough—not anymore.

"I love you," she managed to whisper, tears burning her eyes, blurring her vision. "I love you so much—"

Smiling faintly, Michael kissed away her tears, brushing his lips against hers, trailing a line of soft kisses over the curve of her cheekbone as he gathered her close in his arms. Jessy's eyes closed as he held her tightly, her tenuous control slipping away as she felt that unfamiliar desire growing within her once again. But now it was different. Now she knew that he wanted her for *her*, for her heart and soul.

And knowing that made all the difference.

Chapter Sixteen

PULLING AWAY from his embrace, she touched his cheek in wonder, flattening her palm against the faint scratchiness of his stubbled skin. She saw her own desire mirrored in his expression and urged his mouth back to hers once more, kissing slowly, almost lazily. She felt his fingertips against her throat, lightly stroking the throb of her pulse before his hand shaped itself to the curve of her neck. He made a soft sound of need, a low growl that Jessy felt against her lips like a sigh, his breath hot and sweet and tasting faintly of oranges.

His mouth continued its slow, deliberate teasing. Knowing that he was aware of her pleasure, that he kept watching her as she kissed him, made her impatient for more. His hand slid up the curve of her throat, his touch so gentle, so careful, that she felt as though she were some fragile treasure in his hands. She could not look away from his eyes, could not look away from the desire she saw in his gaze. The intensity of her own desire frightened her. As his mouth and eyes teased her, she felt the desire, the pure animal need, overwhelming her.

Growing bolder with each stroke of his lips over hers, Jessy touched the buttons of his chambray shirt, her fingers trembling, and saw the instant change in his eyes. She realized at that moment that she had given him silent permission to go on, to end the teasing. Michael lifted his head, watching her for a few long moments, his hand cradling her cheek as his fingers tangled in her hair. The naked longing in his eyes made Jessy's heart beat harder, made every inch of her body burn with the need to touch him. The knowledge that she *could* touch him, that she could give him as much pleasure as he was giving her, was a heady drug.

She sighed, breath catching, as she trailed her fingertips over his chest. She could feel the heat of his skin through the fabric, feel the hardness of muscle beneath the taut material, the strong pounding of his heart. Michael half-lay beside her, propped up by a mound of pillows, watching her with hooded eyes as she touched him. Jessy hesitated only a moment before unbuttoning the first button of his shirt—then the second—and the third. She slipped her hand inside the wide V, tentatively touching the soft mat of springy dark hair on his chest. His breath caught for a moment, then came faster by degrees, chest rising and falling beneath her questing hand as he fought for control.

For a moment Jessy wasn't sure what she should do next. Michael's reaction had startled her, and as her gaze swept over his body, she saw clearly the proof of his arousal, proof that she had felt so intimately earlier on the swing. She dragged her gaze up to his eyes again. The heat of his stare was almost frightening, almost overwhelming, and with any other man but Michael, she would have been terrified.

But she knew that this moment, if nothing else in her life, was right. This moment. This experience. This man.

Michael swiftly rose up on his knees beside Jessy before she could react. His movements jerky with impatience, he tugged his shirt from his jeans, unbuttoning the remaining buttons with a swipe of his hand. For a moment, Jessy could only stare up at him, transfixed by the hard, sculpted muscle of his chest, by the lightly furred flatness of his stomach. He was so perfect in her eyes, so beautiful, that for a heartbeat she felt almost too self-conscious to touch him.

Then he extended his hand to her, urging her to her knees to join him. His chest rose and fell with deep, controlled breaths. His eyes held steady on hers, dark and filled with hunger.

Jessy slowly rose to her knees, so close to him that their thighs touched, their bellies brushed. So close to him that she could feel the pounding of his heartbeat against her breasts. She felt as though she had been drugged, every movement languorous, every touch a slow torture of pleasure. Michael's arms surrounded her, pulling her closer, flattening her body against his as his head dipped down to her throat. Jessy gasped aloud at the feel of his mouth and tongue working wetly over her skin, her eyes opening wider as she pressed her palms against the heat of his chest, fingers digging into the firm muscle of his shoulders. She bracketed his face with her hands and silently urged his mouth back to hers once more.

The kiss was slow, deep, and as Michael's lips slanted over hers, Jessy's hands trailed over the hard curve of his shoulders to his chest, palms lightly brushing over the soft mat of hair, over the sides of his stomach to his back. His skin was the softest she had ever felt, like warm silk. Michael's hands had drifted over her hips, sliding up beneath her breasts, cupping them gently through her blouse. The feel of his hands touching her so intimately, the knowledge that she was free to touch him as she liked, was a revelation.

"Jessy—" Michael's voice was a hoarse growl against her lips. He pulled his head away only slightly, as if he couldn't bear to break the contact between them, kissing her with each word as he whispered, "I want you—"

Jessy managed a weak nod, breaths coming in quick gasps. She gazed at him, seeing the love, the tenderness in his expression. She wasn't sure what she was expected to do now, wasn't sure what he wanted her to do, but she knew that there was nothing to be afraid of with Michael. She knew that with a certainty that she felt to her very core.

"Jessy—" He trailed his open mouth along the line of her jaw, nuzzling just beneath her ear for a moment. "I want to make love to you."

His hands kneaded her breasts as he spoke, his words and touch sending shivers of pleasure through her body. His hips moved against hers, a faint rocking back and forth, hard against soft, that communicated his desire far more eloquently than mere words. She felt his tongue flick over her throat and knew that she would follow him anywhere, that she would do anything for him.

She felt his hands slipping up to the top button of her blouse, felt his fingers swiftly separating the material, grazing over her skin. He lifted his mouth to hers once again, kissing her so gently that she only barely felt his lips brushing hers. Sensation overwhelmed her, taking her breath away. She was only dimly aware of her blouse opening completely, of the rush of cool air against her exposed stomach and chest. Michael's hands skimmed over her shoulders and down her arms, sweeping the blouse away. He trailed open-mouthed kisses over her chin, down her throat, his lips moving over the line of her collarbone and onto the upper swell of her breasts.

And that's when the barn door slammed shut and Libby's shout shattered the moment. "Dad! Mom's here! She says she needs to talk to you about something!"

Michael and Jessy jerked away from each other as if scalded, suddenly awkward. Jessy pulled together her blouse, pressing a hand against her over-heated cheeks, as Michael grabbed his shirt and leaned out of the nest.

"Go on back to the house, darlin'. Tell your mom I'll be right there."

Libby peered up at him. "What are you doing up there?"

"Now's not the time for twenty questions, babe. Go on back."

Shrugging, Libby gave the swing an idle push and scuffed her way out of the barn. Michael watched her go, waiting for the door to close before looking to Jessy again. She kept her gaze averted from his.

"What's wrong?" he asked softly.

Jessy shook her head, her hands trembling as she buttoned her blouse. "Nothing."

"Mmm-hmm. C'mere." Michael crawled over to Jessy and gently lowered her hands from her buttons, undoing them again as Jessy gaped at him. "You're buttoning them up all crooked," he said as he began redoing them.

"What are we doing?" Jessy said quietly.

"Well, until my daughter's impeccable timing kicked in, we

were about to make love." Michael glanced up at her and smiled. "At least, it seemed that way to me."

"No—I mean—what is this. With us." Jessy closed her hands over his, stilling them at her breasts. "Did you mean what you said?"

Michael's smile faltered slightly. "I'm not following—"

"When you said that you loved me—did you mean it, or were you just saying it to—"

"To what?" Michael's expression hardened as he slid his hands away from hers. "To get you to go to bed with me? Do you think I make a habit of bringing women up here?"

Jessy's cheeks blazed. She hadn't expected him to react with such defensiveness. "I don't know what to think."

Michael leaned back slightly, the anger fading from his expression as quickly as it had appeared. He reached out to Jessy, cradling her cheek in one big, warm hand. For a few moments, he didn't speak, didn't look away from her eyes.

"I don't say anything unless I mean it," he finally said, his voice almost a whisper. He met Jessy's gaze again. "I love you, Jessy. Question it all you want. Obsess over the intonation and the context and the phrasing all you want. But in the end, it's just that simple. I love you."

Before Jessy could speak, before the tears welling in her eyes had a chance to fall, Michael leaned forward and kissed her again. And with that one, gentle kiss, Jessy finally believed him.

THEY WALKED back to the house in a pleasant silence, holding hands, nuzzling close. Everything had changed. *Everything*. Jessy half-suspected that if she looked in a mirror, she wouldn't even recognize herself. She definitely didn't feel like herself anymore. Where she had once felt empty, almost incomplete, she now felt a serene sense of calm. All she had to do was look at Michael, see the love in his eyes, and suddenly she was invincible. Bulletproof. Able to leap over tall buildings and perform minor miracles.

Jessy smiled at herself and glanced over to Michael. Without saying a word, he seemed to understand. He grinned, pulling her closer, and she tucked her head against his shoulder as he wrapped his arm around her. She could barely remember the time when she thought Michael and Ann had fit so perfectly together; now it seemed like he had been made for her and her alone.

She held his palm to her lips and pressed a quick kiss against it, her breath warm against his cold skin.

"What's that for?" Michael asked, smiling.

Jessy grinned and gazed up at him. "I need a reason?"

They rounded the corner of the house and saw Ann's car, parked haphazardly behind Michael's Bronco. Jessy felt her good spirits fading.

"Are you okay?" Michael asked, noticing her sudden somberness.

Jessy nodded, forcing the smile back to her lips. "Just gearing up for round two."

"Well, whatever happens—" Michael bracketed Jessy's face in his hands and rested his forehead against hers, gazing steadily into her eyes. "It's me and you. You and me. Don't let her get to you. Don't let her make you doubt anything. I love you, you love me—and I sound like Barney the dinosaur so I'm going to shut up now."

Jessy laughed and wrapped her arms around him, holding him tightly as he stroked her hair and kissed her temple. "It'll be okay, honey. I promise."

"I know," Jessy whispered, voice muffled against his throat. As long as he held her that way, she knew everything really would be okay.

"Sooner we go in, the sooner it's done," Michael said, forcing lightness into his voice as Jessy looked up at him again. "After all— I think we have some unfinished business to attend to later, don't you?"

The memory of what they'd shared in the barn sent a thrill through Jessy's body. And just imagining what else they could do—

"Yes, I do," she said and smiled. "Let's get this over with."

IF LYSSA'S SMILE had been any more brittle, her face would have shattered. She met Jessy and Michael at the front door, composed and gracious, but with a look in her eyes that betrayed her true feelings.

Jessy's first thought was that Ann had come for the children. She had made good on her threat and had come to take the kids away.

"Lyssa?" Jessy reached out to her, taking her hand. "What's going on? Are you okay?"

"Oh, I'm fine, sweetie. Just fine." Lyssa's pleasant tone had an undertone of rage that chilled Jessy to the bone. Lyssa looked at Michael, the smile finally fading. "Ann's here."

"What does she want?"

"She wouldn't tell me. But she brought a lawyer."

A sudden, sickening sense of foreboding slammed into Jessy. Helpless to control her fear, she followed Lyssa and Michael into the living room. Ann sat perfectly composed on the couch, sipping at a mug of coffee, smiling tightly when Michael entered the room.

"What is this, Ann?" Michael glanced at the man sitting beside her and grimaced. He wore an expensive suit that cost more than the farm's tractor and looked utterly emotionless. "You brought a lawyer into it?"

"*This* is Edward Jameson." She smiled brilliantly as she touched Jameson's shoulder. "When I told him about your new girlfriend living here, he was very interested in taking my case."

"What have you done?" Jessy whispered.

"This is ridiculous, Ann." Michael's voice was tight with barely restrained anger.

"Is it? You've brought a stranger into the house with my children. I don't want them exposed to your sexual relationship—"

"She's sleeping in the guest bedroom!"

"And I guess that's exactly what you want everyone to think." She looked him up and down, smirking. "Care to explain why you've both got straw in your hair and your shirt's buttoned wrong?"

Jessy felt her face go crimson. "Nothing happened, Ann."

"Right." She turned to Jameson, suddenly pained. "She was with my children last week, shopping, and she told them to call her 'Mommy.' She told them that their real mommy didn't love them anymore and that I hated them!"

Jessy gasped. "That's a lie."

"Michael, did she tell you about her aunt?"

"What are you talking about?"

"She used to hurt her aunt," Ann said, ignoring Jessy as she spoke directly to Michael. "I did some digging into her background. Her aunt was taken from her and put into a nursing home, where she died."

"What?" Jessy suddenly felt as if she couldn't breathe. She saw nothing in Ann's expression but pure malice. "No! My aunt had pancreatic cancer. She was in too much pain to stay at home. I had to put her in a nursing home so they could manage her medicine—"

"Thank God I checked her background," Ann said, casually crossing her legs and sprawling back on the couch. "To think that you've allowed this woman so much access to our children—"

"That's enough, Ann." A muscle jumped in Michael's jaw as he looked at his ex-wife. "I want you out of my house. Now."

Ann shrugged. "Whatever, Michael—dig your own grave."

"What does that mean?"

Ann's smug smile widened. "Look at the situation, babe. The farm's losing money. You're living with a bimbo who probably killed her own aunt. My children are being exposed to all manner of depravity and sin." She laughed quietly. "Tell me what judge wouldn't award full custody to me."

"You wouldn't do that to me."

"You've done it to yourself," Ann said coldly.

"But we're not doing anything wrong." Jessy looked to the lawyer, hoping to see some kind of empathy there. He stared impassively back at her. "Ann, there's got to be some other way to handle this."

"No, there isn't." Ann kept her eyes on Michael. "I'll take the kids and you know it. I'll move them to Chicago and you'll never see them. Unless—"

"Unless what?"

Ann slowly smiled, but her eyes were cold. "You know what you need to do, Michael. You know my terms."

"I think it's time for you to leave," Michael said quietly. "You're not welcome here. Either of you."

Ann grabbed her purse and stood, focusing her anger not at Michael, but squarely on Jessy. She took her time as she walked across the room, never looking away from Jessy's eyes. Jessy thought she had never seen such anger, such frustration.

"You don't belong here," Ann said finally, her voice low and seething with rage. "I don't know how you've managed to delude yourself that Michael has any feelings for you, but I can assure you that he doesn't. A man will say just about anything when he's desperate to get laid."

"That's not the way it is," Jessy said quietly.

"Sure, it isn't," Ann smirked, looking Jessy up and down. "So tell me, Jessy—have you slept with him yet? Frankly, I'd be surprised if Michael was able to get it up for a fat cow like you, but hey—when you're desperate, just about anything will do, won't it? He's settling for you, honey. And you're taking advantage of it."

Jessy shook her head slightly, the faintest trace of a sad smile on her lips. For the first time in her life, words did not hurt her. And for the first time, she knew exactly what to say.

"Ann," Jessy said softly, with no trace of anger, no hint of rage. "You're pathetic."

Ann's mouth closed with a snap. Glancing quickly to Michael and seeing no support there, she stormed past them. She stopped at the door and turned to face them again. Nothing was said, but Jessy could read the look in her eyes. It wasn't over. It wasn't over because Ann hadn't decided that it was over.

Ann turned to Michael, her blue eyes ice cold. "And I *will* still be here tonight to take the kids to the recital. I still have the right to do *that*, at least."

Then she was gone. And for the first time since stepping into the house and seeing Ann's sneering face, Jessy could breathe again.

HOURS LATER, the shock of Ann's ultimatum had still not worn off.

Lyssa had kept the kids upstairs, busying them by helping them wrap Christmas presents, while Michael had tiptoed carefully around Jessy, so solicitous and concerned that she finally had to ask him to leave her be for a while. She didn't want his pity. She didn't want his questions. She just wanted to be alone, to be allowed to sort everything out in her mind. It was bad enough that Ann could even imply that she'd ever try to hurt Aunt Amelia—she couldn't bear the thought that anyone could actually think she was capable of doing such a thing.

Yet Ann had easily, almost eagerly, lied about it.

What if Michael chose to believe her?

And what if the rest of Ann's words were true? What if Michael *was* settling for her? Now that he'd told her he loved her, the entire relationship had changed. Now that they'd crossed that boundary the stakes had been raised to impossible heights. Now there was no distancing herself. Now she could be hurt more than she'd ever imagined possible.

Ann had picked up the kids for the school recital at six o'clock, saying absolutely nothing to either Michael or Jessy. The kids had noticed the tension, of course, and remained quiet and timid. Jessy had tried to be cheerful, telling Libby how pretty she looked in her dress and how she'd knock 'em dead with her singing, but Libby had only responded with the faintest of smiles, as if she were afraid to anger her mother if she were friendly with Jessy.

It had been awkward and painful and horrible, and it was a preview of the rest of their lives, if Ann had her way.

Michael stepped into the living room, as if her thoughts had somehow summoned him. The grandfather clock in the foyer chimed, muffled tones ringing out the quarter-hour. Fifteen after ten. Everyone else in the house had long since gone to bed. Ann, once again, was late bringing the kids home.

"Why did she do it?" Jessy whispered, staring into the flickering flames of the fireplace. The dance of light had comforted her, alone in the amber-tinted darkness.

"Fear. Jealousy." Michael kept his voice low, soothing, as he sat beside her on the couch. Jessy remained cocooned in the couch corner, a pillow under her head, her eyes fixed on the fire. "You threatened her, so she did what she thought she had to do."

Jessy slowly sat up, turning to face Michael fully. "Are you defending her?"

"No," Michael said quietly. "What she did—what she's done—is inexcusable. But it is understandable. She never knew what she had with me and the kids until she saw you taking her place."

"I'm not taking Ann's place. I could never—"

"I don't mean it that way. No one thinks you're trying to do that." Michael took Jessy's hand, holding it loosely in his. "She saw that I could be happy with someone that wasn't her. She saw that the kids could be happy. And it hurt her."

Jessy turned her attention back to the fire. "I heard what she said to you last night," she said softly. She didn't dare look at him, didn't dare try to gauge his reaction. "I saw you kissing her."

Michael said nothing for a moment. Jessy slipped her hand out of his. Suddenly she felt very cold, very alone.

"I know you loved her," she continued, voice little more than a whisper. "I know you probably still do—a little. Even after all this."

"Jessy, why does it always have to come back to that?"

"Because I don't think I can do this, Michael." Jessy finally turned her gaze back to his again. "I can't compete with her, even if it's all in my mind. I look at you now and all I can see is the way you looked when you kissed her."

"And how was that?"

"Like you belonged together," Jessy said simply. "You both looked like you belonged with each other."

Michael silently studied her, his gaze lingering on her face so long that she began to feel intensely self-conscious. She knew better than to think she could explain her feelings to him. She didn't know if she *could* explain them.

"And what about us?" Michael finally asked. "Don't you think *we* belong together?"

Jessy looked back to the fire. "I don't know."

"What do you want to happen here, Jess?" Michael smiled humorlessly, shaking his head. "I don't know what else to do."

"Neither do I."

They sat in silence, gazing at the crackling fire, listening to the sound of the wind whistling through the eaves, the soft tap of snow against the windows. The grandfather clock chimed midnight.

"It's Christmas Eve," Michael said quietly. "Are you still going to leave after Christmas?"

Jessy didn't answer. Couldn't answer.

"You know you don't have to go."

She managed a slow nod.

"You know I want you to stay."

"Yes," she managed to whisper.

"You know that I love you."

Jessy turned her head slightly, not looking directly at Michael. "I know."

Michael said nothing for a few moments. The quiet that enveloped them felt thick, suffocating. All the things that both of them wanted to say, needed to say—neither of them could find the courage to speak aloud.

"Mind if I stay up with you for a little longer?" Michael asked softly, his voice a rough rasp.

Jessy leaned back on the couch, shaking her head as she cast a quick glance in his direction. "I don't mind," she said quietly.

In silence, they sat on opposite ends of the couch, watching the fire pop and spark. When the phone rang, it startled both of them. Michael sighed as he leaned forward to grab the cordless receiver.

"Ann probably wants to keep the kids tonight," he said as he pressed the TALK button. "Hello?"

Jessy couldn't hear the other side of the conversation, but it was clear from Michael's reaction that it was not good news. He lost his color immediately, eyes widening as he sat up straight and gripped the phone tightly.

"Well is she okay?" A long, horrible pause. "What do you mean you don't know? Why aren't you with her?"

Michael rubbed at his eyes, forcing himself to calm down. Jessy gently touched his forearm and he covered her hand with his.

"Okay—where are you? Which hospital?" He listened for a moment. "We'll be there in ten minutes."

He turned off the phone, already on his feet and heading for the door. Jessy was right on his heels.

Chapter Seventeen

JESSY HATED HOSPITALS. She hated the smell of disinfectant. The sound of muted announcements. The painful brightness of the lights. She'd spent so much time in hospitals when her aunt was dying that at one point she felt like she'd never be able to leave, that she'd spend eternity in those brightly lit corridors, tortured by the moans of the dying.

All that came back to her now as she followed Michael into the emergency room. He'd nearly crashed them into a tree on his way there, skidding on the icy roads. He'd driven with his jaw clenched and his hands tight on the wheel. Jessy could only imagine what was going through his mind. As scared as she was for the kids, his fear must have been a million times worse.

They half-ran into the waiting room, where they found Ann sitting with Ben and Marie. All three looked like they'd been put through the wringer, their eyes red and cheeks still wet with tears. When Ann saw Michael, she shot to her feet and threw herself against him.

"Oh, God—Michael!" She began sobbing again, which started Ben and Marie crying once more. Jessy went to them, gathering them both on her lap. She tried not to look at Michael and Ann.

"What happened, Ann?" Michael gently held Ann by the shoulders and pushed her back. "How's Libby?"

"I didn't know she was allergic—"

Jessy's head snapped up. "You let her have shellfish?"

Ann didn't look away from Michael. "We went out to eat after the recital. She ordered some kind of salad—I didn't know!"

"She's been allergic to shellfish since she was three," Michael said, stepping away from Ann. "You should have known that."

Ann was speechless for a moment. "But—I didn't know—"

Michael's eyes were hard as he stared at her. "But you should have."

He turned away from Ann and looked at Jessy. "I'm going to try to find Libby. Would you watch—"

Jessy was nodding and gesturing for him to go before he could finish the sentence. "Go. Go. We're fine."

He hurried away and Ann collapsed in a plastic chair across from Jessy. She kept her head down, one hand rubbing at her brows. She looked utterly miserable. Helpless in the face of Libby's illness. Despite everything, Jessy felt a stab of pity for her.

"I think your mom needs a hug," she whispered to Ben and Marie.

Still sniffling, they slid off Jessy's lap and went to Ann, who began to sob as she gathered them in her arms. Her eyes met Jessy's and, for the first time since she'd met her, Jessy saw no malice or hatred in them.

Just sadness. Deep, overwhelming sadness.

IT WAS well after midnight by the time Libby was released from the ER. She had gone into anaphylactic shock after taking one bite of the seafood salad Ann had allowed her to order. She had her medi-pen with her, but couldn't tell Ann what she needed to do. And Ann hadn't had a clue. If not for the quick reaction of a nurse at a nearby table, Libby might have died.

No one wanted to think about that.

They trailed out of the ER, exhausted but grateful to be leaving. Michael wheeled Libby out to the car as Ann carried Ben and Jessy carried Marie. The kids were asleep. Libby, still pale and weak, could barely keep her eyes open.

Michael hadn't spoken to Ann since arriving at the hospital, and as he loaded the kids into the passenger seats of the truck, he maintained his silence. Jessy could feel anger nearly pulsing off him in waves. Ann must have sensed it too, because she said very little to anyone but the kids. She kept her eyes downcast most of the night, as if ashamed to look at anyone.

Jessy knew that Ann blamed herself. And she sensed that Michael blamed her, as well. It wouldn't do any good to tell either of them that it had just been a very unfortunate accident, and that no one was to blame for anything. Jessy didn't think logic would penetrate Ann's guilt, anyway.

Ann handed Ben to Michael and stepped back as he helped the boy into the truck and fastened his seatbelt.

"Please call me—let me know how Libby's feeling." Ann's voice had an unfamiliar pleading tone.

Michael nodded, still silent as he brushed past Libby and opened the driver's door. Jessy said nothing as she opened the passenger door and climbed into the truck. Ann looked as if she had a million things she wanted to say, but Michael had already dismissed her, slamming the door as he settled in behind the wheel.

They backed out of the parking space, leaving Ann standing alone in the snow and slush. Even in the dimness of the parking lot, Jessy could see the shine of tears on Ann's cheeks.

THEY WORKED in perfect unison as they put the kids to bed—slipping off shoes, tugging on pajamas. Ben and Marie slept through it all, totally exhausted. Jessy kept a close eye on Michael, hoping that his fear would ease up and allow him to at least smile again, but his face remained locked in that grimace, as if he were expecting the worst.

Libby was still awake when they checked in on her. She looked slightly better than earlier, but her eyes were dark-ringed and her cheeks too pale.

"Hey squirt." Michael managed a smile as he sat on the edge of Libby's bed and took her hand. "How are you feeling?"

"Okay, I guess." Libby looked over to Jessy, who hovered in the doorway, unsure if she could enter. "You can come in, too."

Jessy joined them, sitting on the opposite edge of the bed. Michael reached out and smoothed Libby's hair down, gazing at her for a few moments before speaking again. Jessy knew he was remembering the night so many years ago that they'd almost lost her.

"I hear you were great at the recital," he said. His voice sounded gruff, as if he were trying to control his emotions. "Wish I could have been there."

"It was boring, except for my parts." Libby smiled slightly. "I should have known better, huh?"

"About eating seafood? Oh, yeah," Michael chuckled and nodded. "Why'd you order that anyway?"

"I thought maybe I wasn't allergic anymore. A kid at school used to be allergic to peanuts when he was little, and now he can eat them without getting sick. I thought I'd be okay, too."

"Next time you wonder anything like that, let me know first, okay?"

"I'm sorry, Dad."

Michael touseled her hair. "It's okay, Libs."

"Are you mad at me?"

"Never."

Libby hesitated a moment. "What about Mom."

"Your mom—" Michael's voice trailed away. "No, I'm not mad at her, either. I'm just glad you're okay. And that you're home."

"Me, too."

"Okay—I think it's time for you to hit the hay." Michael leaned forward and gave Libby a kiss on the forehead. "Goodnight, troublemaker."

"G'night, Dad."

Jessy rose as Michael stood and followed him to the door.

"Hey, Jessy—?"

As Michael left the room, Jessy turned to face Libby. "Yes, sweetie?"

"I just wanted you to know—I'm okay with you liking my dad."

Jessy smiled. "Thank you, Libby."

"Good night, Jessy." Libby smiled as she turned onto her side, cuddling into her pillow as Jessy turned off the light and closed the door, leaving it slightly ajar. She turned to the hallway and nearly ran into Michael.

"What—"

He was kissing her before she could even think to finish the sentence, and Jessy could feel every bit of fear and anger and tension and stress leaving his body as he pulled her close and wrapped his arms around her. The kiss felt almost desperate, but she returned it with every bit of her soul.

When it was over, he raised his head slightly to look into her eyes and she could see that the old Michael was back. His eyes shone almost mischievously as he gazed at her.

"Thank you," he said after a moment.

"For what? Kissing you?" Jessy grinned. "Not a problem. Trust me."

"No. Thank you for being here tonight."

"Again—not a problem."

He studied her for a moment. "Remember that unfinished business—?" he murmured, leaning forward to kiss her cheek, her throat.

"Mmm-hmm—" Jessy felt absolutely limp beneath his kisses, unable to do anything but close her eyes and just feel. "I think it's time to finish it."

Michael raised his head to gaze at Jessy, who lazily opened her eyes and smiled at him. "Are you sure?"

"Yes," she said, kissing him again, a sweet, brief kiss on the lips. "I've never been more sure of anything in my life."

THE REST OF THE HOUSE was silent and dark. It seemed impossible to her that they were going to do what they were going to do. After so many years of yearning and wishing and hoping and fantasizing, the moment was finally upon her.

All of her bravado disappeared. The closer they got to Michael's bedroom, the more apprehensive she became. This wasn't just kissing or making out or even heavy petting. She and Michael were about to make love. Have sex. Do the deed.

Her stomach churned. Maybe she wasn't ready for this.

Michael looked down at her and smiled, and every hormone in her body flared to sudden, burning life.

Or maybe I *am* ready, she thought, remembering the way his hands had felt on her body, the way his mouth moved so wet and hot over her bare skin.

"After you," he said as he opened the door. Jessy nervously glanced up at him again, then looked into the room. For just a moment, all she could see was the bed. The big, quilt-covered, four-poster bed.

Michael closed the door, discreetly locking it. For a moment, he looked as nervous and awed as Jessy felt. His eyes caught hers, holding her gaze for a few long, silent moments.

"Are you sure?" he asked softly.

Jessy shook away the clinging remnants of her own nervousness and took his hands in hers, holding them loosely as she stood on tiptoe and kissed his throat, his chin, his lips. She felt him tremble even as his body tensed against hers.

"I'm sure," she said and looked up to his eyes again.

Without hesitation, Michael wrapped his arms around her, surrounding her with himself, kissing her as if they had been apart for years instead of hours. His sudden ardor caught Jessy off-guard, as thrilling as it was frightening—especially as she felt herself responding to him, as she felt her own body pressing harder against his, trying to get even closer.

Somehow, moving more gracefully than two entwined bodies should move, Michael maneuvered Jessy backwards to the bed, breaking their breathless kiss just long enough to ease her back against the pillows. He stretched out beside her, holding her close as his mouth found hers again. He deftly unbuttoned her blouse, easing his hand beneath the material, cupping her breast through her bra—

And Jessy suddenly realized what was truly happening. What

was going to happen. Despite the pleasure, despite the intimacy, Jessy felt a sickening wave of self-consciousness, all too aware of how bright it was in the room, even in the dim light of the bedroom lamp. All too aware of how vividly the scars and imperfections of her less than perfect body would appear. Michael would take one look at her and—

Jessy involuntarily jerked away from him, raising her arms to cover herself as she pulled her blouse together again. Her reaction was purely instinctive, the impossible-to-shake remnants of a lifetime spent hiding behind loose clothing and dark shadows. She still wanted Michael as intensely as ever—but could not bear the thought of seeing the disgust in his eyes when he saw her body.

Michael fell back against the pillows, one leg bent at the knee, the other straight out in front of him. He rubbed at his mouth, then ran a hand through his disheveled hair, taking his time before raising his gaze back to Jessy again. For a few long moments they just silently stared at each other, still breathing raggedly, still dazed by the intensity of what they'd shared. Michael remained silent, simply looking at her with a mixture of confusion and disappointment in his eyes.

Jessy couldn't stand it, too humiliated by her own actions, by her own body, to face him.

"Michael—I don't know—I mean—" She sighed, releasing her frustrations in a soft curse. "I don't know if I can do this," she finally said, raising her gaze to his again.

"You were doing pretty good there for a while." Michael didn't bother to close his shirt, and lying there—a sheen of sweat on his bare chest and his eyes hooded with barely restrained desire—he made Jessy's entire body tremble with the need to touch him, to feel him so close to her again. "What's wrong?"

Jessy sat up beside him, still clutching her blouse together, hiding herself from his eyes. "My body—" Her voice caught, each word a torture. This was the last hurdle, the last fear, and she had to face it, even though she was terrified of Michael's reaction.

"Jessy—" Michael scooted closer to her, taking her hand. "I've told you—that doesn't matter to me."

"But it does to me." Jessy managed to look into his eyes. The passion that had filled them only moments earlier remained, but now it was tempered with a tenderness that touched her to the soul. "I've got scars—stretch marks—"

Michael touched her cheek, lifting her face so that he could look into her eyes. He saw the tears shimmering in them and was too confused to speak for a moment. How could she ever believe that he would possibly reject her because of something like that?

"Jessy," he whispered, "I could tell you for the rest of our lives that none of that matters to me—"

"But—"

"But nothing." Michael traced the shape of her lower lip with his thumb, loving the feel, the warmth, of her skin. As she gazed up to him, he felt an overwhelming sense of completeness, a contentment he thought he'd never know. He just wished he could help her feel that same peace of mind.

"Jess," he continued, his voice softer than a caress, "when I look at you, I see a woman who is kind and gentle and compassionate. I see a woman who makes me smile, who makes my children smile."

Tears trickled over Jessy's cheeks. Michael smiled, sweeping the tears away with a gentle touch.

"When I look at you," he whispered, "I see a beautiful woman. I don't know what else I can say to make you believe me—except that I love you."

Jessy gazed at him, then slowly, shakily smiled. "I love you, too—and I want to make love to you—"

Michael said nothing for a moment, leaning away from Jessy, never looking away from her eyes as he gently opened her blouse again. Jessy cringed, as if to hide herself, but Michael stopped her with a faint shake of his head.

"No," he breathed. "I want to see you."

Jessy fought the urge to close her eyes. She didn't want to see him try to hide the disgust, the disappointment, when he finally saw her body. As he eased her blouse away, she felt with exquisite awareness every bulge, every scar, every imperfection. She wanted to turn her face away, but couldn't. She wanted to trust Michael's promise.

Michael finally looked away from her wide-eyed gaze, allowing himself to see her full breasts, to see the milk-white skin that was faintly etched by pinkish striations. For a moment, he had to fight the impulse to smile—*this* was what she was so worried about? He saw absolutely nothing wrong with her; in fact, he couldn't imagine how anything about her could be anything less than beautiful. But he didn't dare smile. Jessy needed to know beyond a shadow of a doubt just how much he loved her, how much he wanted her.

He gently trailed his fingertip over the lacy edge of her bra, tracing the upper swell of her breasts. Her breath caught as he dipped his finger into her cleavage then continued his tortuous circuit. He watched her close her eyes for a moment, watched her gather her courage, and loved her all the more for it.

"Look at me," he said quietly, shrugging out of his shirt as Jessy opened her eyes again. He kept her gaze as he carefully slipped the straps of her bra over her shoulders, then reached around to the back and easily undid the clasp. In her eyes, he could see the struggle to keep her arms at her sides, to resist the urge to cover herself.

Then he allowed his gaze to travel the length of her naked torso. And he allowed himself to finally smile as he met her eyes again.

"Jessy—" he whispered, shaking his head slightly in wonderment. "You're *beautiful*."

His acceptance destroyed the last of the barriers that she had hidden behind for so long. Jessy felt herself blushing to the roots, felt a smile tugging at the corners of her mouth, and realized with a bit of a shock that no matter what might happen between them, this was still *Michael*. This was still the man who made her laugh, the man who talked to her and listened to her and held her as she wept. This was the man she trusted with her life. The man she loved with all her soul.

The small smile finally broke through, and as she touched his chest, stroking the soft, wiry hair, she actually *felt* beautiful. And loved. More than anything, she felt loved.

He cradled her in his embrace as they lay back against the pillows, kissing her so gently, so tenderly, that she thought she might die of the sheer pleasure of his touch. She had that odd sensation of feeling drugged once again; time slipped away from them as they kissed and touched, palms skimming over hard muscle and soft curves, stroking, caressing. The rest of Jessy's clothing seemed to fall away in a few deft motions, and she watched wide-eyed as Michael stood beside the bed, undoing his jeans as he stared unrelentingly into her eyes.

Jessy felt a little dazed as the rest of that magnificent body was revealed to her. Michael's legs were as finely muscled as an athlete, the same ripened peach shade as his chest and arms. Wearing only his underwear, he seemed as sheepish and shy as Jessy had been.

Then, with a bashful smile, he sat beside her once again. With a quick tug, the underwear came off and he was as naked and vulnerable as Jessy.

At the sight of him, Jessy felt the heat rising in her cheeks, spreading throughout her entire body. She glanced back to his eyes and recognized the expression on his face; he was every bit as anxious and nervous as she had been. But even as she gazed at him, that first uneasy moment of vulnerability was passing. And now there was nothing left to fear.

Michael smiled again and moved over Jessy, holding her tightly against him as he kissed her again. Jessy gasped against his mouth at the feel of his long, slender fingers moving over her skin, at the brush of his silky hair against her breasts as his mouth explored her body. She followed his example, touching him as he touched her, marveling at the reaction of his body. He moved so that he covered her body with his, and she could feel the hardness of his arousal pressing against her stomach. The thought that she could inspire such a fierce reaction was as startling as it was empowering.

After what seemed an eternity of soft caresses and gentle kisses, Michael reluctantly rolled away from Jessy, breathing hard as he fumbled through the drawer of his bedside table. Jessy blinked as if coming out of a daze, watching as Michael withdrew a small foil square from the drawer. He looked up, saw her watching, and weakly smiled as he returned to her side.

"I had hoped this might happen," he said softly, ripping open the foil. "I just didn't know where or when."

Jessy slowly smiled, feeling the faintest twinge of embarrassment as she watched Michael slip the condom onto himself, but relieved. She hadn't even thought to consider it.

He returned to her, folding her into his arms as his lips nipped and suckled at hers, and in that moment the last of Jessy's fears were eased. She loved him. She trusted him. And he loved her. Nothing else mattered.

"I'm a little out of practice," Michael whispered as he moved over her again, bracing himself on his elbows as he settled against her. Jessy welcomed his weight, relishing the feel of his body pressed into hers.

She smiled up at him, lacing her fingers through his soft hair as she kissed him again. "Then I guess that's something else we have in common, isn't it?"

Michael's smile lasted only a moment before he dipped his head and kissed her again, communicating his desire, his hunger, in long, thorough kisses that stole their breaths away. He explored her body with his hands, his mouth, and invited her to do the same. Jessy felt her shyness melt away, replaced by burning curiosity. Time faded, measured only through the beating of their hearts, the soft exhalations of their breaths.

When he knew that she was ready for him, Michael raised his head and gazed into her eyes, seeing the need, the passion—the uncertainty. He hesitated, almost ready to stop, to let her regain her courage, when she whispered one word that changed everything: "Please."

Almost unable to restrain himself, Michael eased into her slowly, wincing at her soft whimpers of pleasure and pain, and wrapped his arms completely around her, cradling her close as she adjusted to the feel of him. "I'm sorry," he breathed into her ear, hating himself for causing her any kind of pain.

Jessy took a deep, shuddery breath and looked into his eyes once more. A faint smile curled the corner of her mouth and she moved beneath him, relaxing as she accepted him inside her. "Don't be sorry," she whispered. "I love you."

Michael's eyes closed for a moment as he settled into her, feeling with exquisite clarity a sense of completeness. They would never again have this moment of discovery, but Michael knew that this was only the beginning. And he knew that Jessy felt the same way. She had given herself to him, had given him a gift that he would treasure for the rest of his life.

"I love you too," he said quietly, gazing into her eyes. And he knew, in that shared moment, that they would have the rest of their lives to keep proving it to each other. "I love you—"

Jessy welcomed him with another slow kiss, and as the first light of dawn peeked through the bedroom window, she gazed into his dark eyes and watched as her pleasure was mirrored in his expressions, echoed in his throaty growls and her softer cries. She had never known a man could be so tender; he touched her as if she were made of spun glass, so gentle as he moved over her, inside her. The momentary pain had faded into an almost unbearable pleasure as his breathing grew harsher and his movement gradually quickened. Control slipped away form her as she matched his moves, instinctively growing bolder and more desperate for release with each passing moment.

Finally she could bear no more. She trembled as pleasure rippled through her, then opened her eyes just as Michael shuddered, hovering over her with his eyes squeezed shut and his entire face tight with release. After a moment, his entire body went lax and he opened his eyes to look at her once more, a shaky but tender smile slowly spreading over his lips. Jessy managed to return the smile, gasping as she struggled to catch her breath.

"Out of practice, huh?" She grinned as he laughed softly and rolled her into his arms. The sense of loneliness she had known for so long was gone now, replaced by a happiness, a contentment, that was frightening in its intensity. Michael's hand moved lazily over the length of her back as she burrowed closer to his chest, loving the smell, the feel, the warmth of him. Her entire life had led her to this one moment, this one man.

And she wanted it to last forever.

Chapter Eighteen

"I SHOULD BE OUT doing chores," Michael whispered, bundling Jessy closer to his chest as he slowly stroked the length of her back. She nuzzled into his chest hair, spanning her hand over his stomach as she pressed soft kisses along his throat and shoulder.

"Take the day off."

Michael chuckled. "Tell that to the cows."

Jessy raised her head and kissed him again, loving the way he instantly responded to her touch. She could not get enough of him, could never tire of feeling his hands on her body, of tasting his skin against her lips. And most miraculous of all, she knew that he felt the same about her. There was no question of his feelings for her, no doubts or hesitations.

It was the greatest gift that she had ever known.

Michael rolled Jessy beneath him, cradling her in one arm as he slowly broke away from the kiss with soft nibbles to her lips and chin, trailing his mouth along her jaw, her throat, along the line of her collarbone to her breasts. Jessy gave herself to him completely, unashamed of her body now that she'd shared it with him, smiling in contentment as he traced the curve of her breasts with his hands and mouth. He raised his head slightly, brow furrowed when he saw the smile on her face.

"Am I amusing you?" he asked with a grin, teasing her left nipple with a flick of his tongue.

Jessy tangled her fingers in his tousled hair, watching him as he moved to her right breast. "I just had a vision of my imminent nymphomania, thanks to you."

Michael's grin slowly spread, deepening the lines around his mouth and eyes, and Jessy was struck again by the gentleness, the tenderness, of his gaze. His eyes reflected his every emotion, and at that moment, as he looked at her with such love and affection, Jessy felt as though she were the only woman in the world.

"Imminent nymphomania, huh?" Michael's smile curved wickedly as he returned his attention to her breasts once more, his hand stroking her stomach, moving ever lower. "I've created a monster."

Jessy laughed softly, lifting his face back to hers for another kiss. Her smile slowly melted away as Michael's lips, so soft and warm, found hers once again. The kiss began gently, growing deeper, more desperate with each heartbeat. They wouldn't have much time; soon the sun would be rising and the kids would be waking up and their first night together would be over.

But it was only the first night. The first of many more to come.

Michael moved easily over her body, fitting into her with an ease that took both their breaths away. She held him close as they silently moved together, muffling her cries against his mouth, his throat, as he brought her closer and closer to the edge—

And someone knocked at the door.

"Daddy!" Ben's voice sounded breathless with excitement. "Uncle Frank is here!"

"Come on, Daddy!" Marie chimed in, pounding on the door. "Why's the door locked?"

Michael stopped moving, burying his head in Jessy's hair for a moment as he groaned. Jessy laughed softly, despite the interruption, and kissed his temple as Ben and Marie kept knocking and calling for him.

"You'd better answer them," she whispered.

Michael raised his head, keeping his face so close to hers that she could see her reflection in his eyes. "Sorry, baby—"

Jessy just smiled. "More unfinished business for later."

"Definitely, darlin'." Michael framed her face in his hands, gently stroking her hair away from her eyes, and gazed at her for a few moments. And for Jessy, the rest of the world—the rising sun, the knocking at the door—faded away.

"I love you," he said simply, brushing his lips against hers in a brief, sweet kiss.

Jessy nodded, her eyes shining with tears. "I love you, too," she managed to whisper.

Smiling, he kissed her again, making this one last, and Jessy surrendered to him, melting into him as he enveloped her in his arms. It felt unbelievably good to be so close to him. For the first time in her life, she felt cherished, adored, loved.

Unconditionally, unquestionably, loved.

FOR PROPRIETY'S SAKE, Jessy waited a while to leave Michael's bedroom, making sure the coast was clear before scooting down the hall to her own room. She felt giddy and excited and so alive that the entire world seemed to have been remade just for her. She even sang as she took a shower, belting out every Christmas carol and show tune that she could remember. All of the romance novels she'd ever read could never have prepared her for the stunning reality of actually being in love.

It was more than she'd ever dreamed possible for herself. Much, much more.

By the time Jessy had dressed and followed her nose downstairs to the kitchen, the family reunion was already in full swing. Frank sat at the breakfast nook, Ben and Marie on his lap, laughing with Lyssa and Libby as Michael busily scrambled eggs and made toast.

"Morning, Sunshine," Michael said as Jessy entered the kitchen, flopping a dishtowel over one shoulder as he spooned eggs onto plates. Grinning, he stopped to plant a kiss on Jessy's lips before carrying the plates to the table. Jessy felt herself blushing, feeling as if everyone in the room knew what they had been up to last night.

Jessy joined Lyssa and Frank at the table. "So when's your new book coming out, sweetie?" Lyssa asked, pouring Frank a fresh cup of coffee.

Frank shrugged. "Your guess is as good as mine. I haven't exactly been in the 'romance writer' mindset lately."

Jessy slowly smiled. *"You* write romances?"

"Yup. Hot, sweaty, sticky ones." Frank grinned as Lyssa and Jessy laughed. "My pen name is Janessa DeFleur."

"Seriously?"

"Seriously." Frank sipped at his coffee and grimaced. "Good God, Mike—did you boil a boot in the coffee or something?"

"Bite me, Sheriff Lobo." Michael sought out Jessy's gaze and smiled, saying everything by saying nothing at all.

And for the first time in years, Jessy finally felt as if she were a part of something bigger than herself. She had found her family.

THAT FEELING grew stronger throughout the day, as she caught quick glimpses of Michael doing his chores, as she helped Lyssa and the kids prepare Christmas cookies in anticipation of the big Christmas party that night, as she fielded excited questions from Ben and Marie about Santa Claus and his elves. She remembered all the Christmas Eves of her childhood, and how that one day seemed to last a million years, and wondered at how quickly this magical day seemed to pass.

The house seemed even more alive than before. Christmas music filled every room, and the scent of freshly baked cookies and homemade fudge drifted throughout the house. To Jessy, it felt as though she had stepped into a dream: Everyone laughed and hugged and smiled, happy to be reunited if only for a while.

It was a perfect day, filled with laughter and joy and longing gazes from Michael, but it wasn't until the family began to decorate the Christmas tree that Jessy realized that for the first time in so very long, her heart felt absolutely at peace. She paused as she hung a small Santa ornament on a branch, taking a moment to look around her, capturing memories like snapshots.

There was Frank lifting Marie high overhead as she hung a blue glass ornament on the upper branches of the tree—

And Frank's daughter, Claire, and Ben, sitting on the floor around the coffee table, decorating Christmas cookies almost as quickly as they could eat them, laughing as they dotted frosting on each other's faces—

And Lyssa and Libby, singing along with the Christmas carols, warbling "Santa Claus Is Coming to Town" as loudly and as off-key as they could as they hung tinsel and stockings on the fireplace mantle.

And always, there was Michael, who stood in the doorway with a soft smile on his face, watching her as she helped decorate the tree. She hadn't known he was there, but at the sight of him, tears filled her eyes. For a moment, she felt almost overwhelmed by the sheer joy of it all. The lights of the tree shimmered in her vision, blurred by her tears. As she stood there, surrounded by the love and laughter of Michael's family, she understood that Michael had given her far more than his love. He had given her hope.

She knew that no matter what else she experienced in her life, that this moment—this perfect, peaceful moment—would live in her heart forever.

Michael seemed to sense her fragile state and joined her at the tree, slipping his arms around her waist as he pulled her close to his chest. For a few moments, Jessy had to close her eyes to stem the flow of tears. Michael turned her in his arms and tipped her face up to his, smiling as he gently wiped her tears away with soft strokes of his thumb. In the uproar of the room, he silently mouthed "I love you" and kissed her forehead.

For Jessy, there was no more precious gift than that.

Michael rested his forehead against hers for a moment longer, his smile widening. Then, with a wink, he slipped away from her, sneaking out of the room without drawing attention to himself. Puzzled at first, Jessy watched him go as Marie tugged at her sleeve.

"Jessy? Where's Daddy going?"

Jessy realized that whatever he was doing, it was to be a secret from the kids. "Um—I think he had to go out to check on the animals," she said and smiled. "They get special attention on Christmas Eve, too."

"Oh, okay." Curiosity satisfied, Marie went back to the box of ornaments, rummaging through until she found a snowman. Jessy, more than a little curious herself, made her way over to Lyssa, who sat on the couch sipping eggnog and smiling brilliantly at the sight of all the happy activity. Lyssa looked up to Jessy and patted the spot beside her.

"Are you having a good time?" Lyssa asked, taking Jessy's hand. Her skin felt as smooth as the finest parchment paper, soft despite the years of hard work, and the warmth in her smile, in her touch, made Jessy feel as though she had been part of the family all her life.

"Oh yes," Jessy finally managed to say, her smile faltering as she took a deep breath and looked around the living room. "O, Holy Night" played softly in the background, and for the first time in years Jessy felt in her soul the true meaning of the lyrics: forgiveness, love, hope. At that moment she knew in her heart that miracles could happen, *did* happen, every day—and that she was experiencing the most wonderful miracle of all right now.

"Honey, are you okay?" Lyssa touched Jessy's cheek, gently smoothing away an errant tear. Jessy looked back to her, smiling even as she took a shuddery breath and helpless, happy tears trickled over her cheeks.

"I'm just so glad to be here with you all," she said softly. "Thank you so much—for everything."

"Oh, sweetheart—" Lyssa pulled Jessy into her embrace, accepting her as a daughter, filling the emptiness that she had known for so long. Jessy squeezed her eyes tightly, trying desperately not to cry again, but couldn't help it. It felt too good to be held, to be comforted. It felt too wonderful not to be alone anymore.

The sudden jingle-jangle of sleigh bells echoed from outside and Ben and Marie were instantly on their feet and running for the front door. Jessy wiped at her eyes and stood, smiling at their sudden excitement as she and Lyssa followed them to the door.

And there in the driveway, in a horse-drawn sleigh, was Santa Claus himself.

Santa leapt nimbly from the carriage with a huge bag slung over one shoulder. Ben and Marie gasped in awe, watching with wide eyes as Santa trudged through the snow and joined them on the porch, his huge belly shaking in a jubilant "Ho-ho-ho!"

The kids were on him in a heartbeat, hugging his legs and chattering excitedly with questions about Rudolph and the other reindeer and the elves.

Santa laughed again. "One at a time, kids!" he boomed, a smile in his voice. "Let's get old Santa inside where it's warm. I'm freezing my jingle bells off."

Jessy had to bite back a laugh as Santa's eyes met hers. She'd know those crinkles anywhere.

They followed Santa into the house, laughing as he tried to walk with both Marie and Ben clinging to his legs. He slung his canvas bag onto a chair and rooted around inside it, making a fuss as he hemmed and hawed and shook his head.

"I know I have your presents in here," he said to himself. Ben and Marie were beside themselves with excitement, as Claire and Libby watched with indulgent smiles. "I don't think the elves would let me forget you guys—"

"We were real good this year!" Ben said. "Weren't we, Gramma?"

"Perfect angels, Santa." Lyssa said as she gave Ben a quick squeeze. "We're real glad you could stop by this year."

Santa smiled through his beard. "Well, it's my pleasure, Mrs. Forrester."

"Are you really Santa?" Marie asked, gaze narrowing as she scrutinized him. "Jessy told us that sometimes the elves take his place."

"And Jessy is absolutely right," Santa said, turning to flash a quick wink in Jessy's direction. "But I can assure you, Marie, that I am the real, grade-A, no-substitutions Santa Claus. How else would I know that you made straight-As on your report card this year? Or that when you found a five dollar bill on the playground, you were honest and took it to your teacher?"

Marie's eyes widened as she gasped and turned to Jessy. "He *is* Santa!"

"Where's Rudolph and the reindeer?" Ben asked. "I thought they pulled your sled for you."

Santa straightened up from the bag, an elaborately wrapped gift in each hand. "They do—but I haven't started making my rounds yet. This is a special stop, because you guys have been so good this year."

Ben beamed at Jessy. "I knew he'd come to see us!"

Jessy watched, unable to stop smiling, as Santa handed out gifts to everyone, taking a moment to give Frank a playful cuff to the back of the head. He kissed Lyssa's cheek as Claire snapped photos with her new camera, and danced with a happily embarrassed Libby when "Jingle Bell Rock" played on the stereo. And finally, when Ben and Marie could stand it no more, Santa reached deep into the bag and pulled out their presents. They thanked him with eager politeness and then tore into the wrappings.

Santa watched them for a few moments, smiling beneath his thick white beard, and laughed as they shrieked with delight when their toys were unveiled. Ben and Libby jumped onto his lap, hugging him fiercely, then scrambled down to play with their toys.

Jessy was watching everyone unwrap their gifts, smiling at their happiness, when Santa gently touched her hand. Startled, Jessy turned to him, her smile slanting slightly when she met his eyes.

"Now," Santa announced, giving Jessy a wink as he stood. "I'd better get back to the North Pole so I can get started this evening. I've got a lot of little boys and girls to see to before morning."

Ben and Marie rushed to his side to give him one last hug, and Jessy could see the pure joy in Michael's eyes as he held them tightly.

He headed for the door, the now empty bag slung over his shoulder, and suddenly stopped at the front porch, turning back to them.

"Why, I almost forgot," he said, voice rumbling with laughter. "I need to borrow someone to help me sort through some presents. Miss? What about you?"

Before Jessy could answer, Lyssa was helping her into a heavy parka and gently pushing her onto the porch. "We'll leave a light on for you," she said and smiled. "And Santa, if you see that wayward son of mine, tell him to get his behind home."

"Yes, ma'am," Michael said, grinning behind the beard as he took Jessy's hand and led her out to the sleigh. He helped her climb aboard, taking a moment to tuck a heavy flannel blanket over her legs, then jumped in beside her. With one last wave to his family as they stood on the porch and watched, Michael turned the sleigh around and headed down the driveway. Jessy half-expected it to take flight and zoom them into the stratosphere.

"Where are we going, Mr. Claus?" she asked, snuggling in close to Michael as he slipped his arm around her shoulders.

"Call me Santa, baby," Michael said in a playfully seductive voice, able to maintain a straight face for approximately two seconds before bursting into laughter with Jessy. "And we're going for a sleigh ride."

"As in, 'Oh, what fun it is to ride—'?"

"Exactly." Michael leaned over and kissed her quickly, tickling her with the beard and mustache.

He guided the two horses drawing the sleigh around the house, heading back to the barns. Jessy leaned against his shoulder and gazed up to the starry sky, looking for the Christmas Star. The contentment she felt just being with him at that moment was almost frightening in its intensity. Everything was just too good, too perfect.

Michael finally stopped the sleigh at the frozen pond, releasing the bridles as he leaned back on the bench and smiled at Jessy. The glow of the moon gave his face a bluish cast, but his eyes sparkled like diamonds as he gazed at her.

"That was wonderful, what you did for the kids." Jessy took his cold hand and held it to her lips, pressing a warm kiss against his palm.

"My dad always used to play Santa for us. Every year." Michael tugged off the hat and beard and scratched at his chin. "Itches like you wouldn't believe."

Jessy laughed and stroked his cheek, guiding him close for a quick kiss. "I missed being alone with you today," she said softly.

"I don't know if I could've been trusted alone with you," Michael said with a devilish smile. "We wouldn't have gotten a single thing done."

Jessy smiled and nuzzled up to his throat. "And that would be a bad thing?"

"Lord help me," Michael said softly, giving in to her soft, sweet kisses. "I *have* created a monster."

"Shut up and kiss me, Santa."

"Whatever you want, babydoll." Grinning, Michael settled in closer to Jessy, wrapping them both in the blanket. They kissed as if it had been months instead of hours since they were last together.

"I didn't forget your gift, Jessy," Michael finally whispered, pulling away from Jessy long enough to reach behind the seat and withdraw a large, beautifully wrapped box. "Merry Christmas, baby."

Jessy smiled as she held the present on her lap, looking up to Michael and seeing the anticipation in his eyes. "Michael—you didn't have to—"

"I know. But I wanted to. Open it."

Jessy undid the ribbons and bows, tearing the paper carefully to reveal a plain white box. With a quick glance up at Michael, she lifted the lid.

It was a collection of "Bridal Tree" ornaments, each one cradled in a nest of tissue paper. And in the center, a small velvet box.

Jessy's breath caught for a moment, her heart hammering in her chest as she looked up to Michael's eyes again.

"I realize that we haven't known each other for years," Michael said softly, gazing at Jessy with a tenderness that made her feel almost dizzy, "but I love you so much—and I honestly don't know what I would do without you in my life."

"Oh, Michael—" Jessy's voice trailed away as tears raced hotly down her cheeks. She didn't even bother to try to stop them.

Michael's smile slanted slightly as he gazed at Jessy, his own eyes shining in the moonlight. "I want you to stay here, with me and the kids, forever." He touched her cheek, still smiling. "And if you'll have me, I promise I'll never stop trying to make you happy." He paused a moment, gaze never wavering from hers. "Will you marry me, Jess?"

Jessy couldn't find her voice for a moment. She nodded sharply, smiling and laughing and crying all at once. "Yes," she finally managed to whisper.

"Open the box," Michael whispered, and Jessy managed, with trembling hands, to raise the lid of the tiny velvet box. Tucked within the folds of velvet was the most beautiful ring Jessy had ever seen: a gold band with a small diamond and pearl setting.

Michael held her trembling hand in his, gently slipping the ring on her finger, then turning her hand to press a soft kiss against her palm. She met his gaze again, saw the tears shimmering in his eyes, and knew that wishes could come true. Miracles could happen.

"So how do you feel about kids?" he asked, surprising her into a laugh. "I say we have at least five more, give or take."

Jessy grinned and snuggled in closer to him, pulling his arm around her shoulders so that she could gaze at their intertwined hands, at the ring sparkling on her finger. "And how many of these kids will *you* be carrying?"

Michael grinned. "Heck, I'll carry all of 'em—it's just the delivery part that makes me nervous."

Jessy craned her head back to look up at him. "I can see the next fifty years with you are going to be fun."

"Lady—" Michael waggled his eyebrows and grinned devilishly. "You ain't seen nothin' yet."

"Good," Jessy murmured, managing a quick smile before Michael kissed her again, cradling her in his arms as he pulled the blanket up to their shoulders and they shared the silence of the starry night.

Chapter Nineteen

AN HOUR LATER they returned to the house to find that Lyssa had dinner on the table, waiting for them. The scent of baked ham and fresh bread filled the room, the table laden with even more food than there had been for Thanksgiving.

"It's about time you two got back for dinner," Lyssa said as she entered the dining room. "I thought I'd have to send Frank out to track you down."

"Jessy and I had a few things to discuss," Michael said and smiled, lifting Jessy's left hand to show off the ring.

Lyssa gasped softly as she saw the ring. Her gaze went from the ring to Michael and then to Jessy, her eyes suddenly glistening.

"Oh, sweetheart—welcome home." Lyssa embraced both Michael and Jessy at once.

"It's about time, Monk-boy!" Frank said as he gave Michael a playful shot to the shoulder and swooped Jessy up in a hug.

No one noticed Ann standing in the doorway.

"Michael?"

Her voice was unnaturally soft, unusually meek. Michael turned, his smile fading as soon as he saw her standing there, holding bags of wrapped gifts in her arms.

Ann tried a weak smile. "I rang the bell, but no one answered."

The room fell into a deadly silence. Lyssa began to speak, then thought better of it and walked away, disappearing into the kitchen. Frank glowered for a moment, then joined Lyssa.

Jessy glanced over Ann's shoulder, suddenly afraid that she had brought the Child Protective Services to take the children.

"I'm alone," Ann said quietly, sensing Jessy's worry. Her gaze ticked back to Michael. "Can we talk?"

"I don't know what's left to say," Michael said tonelessly.

"Please, Michael."

The pleading tone in her voice hit its mark. Michael glanced to Jessy and she could see the indecision in his eyes, the anger tempered with sadness. She gave him an almost imperceptible nod.

"Let's go into the living room," Michael said, taking Jessy's hand before she could object. Michael and Jessy sat together on the couch. Ann remained standing, awkward as she studied the ornaments on the tree.

"I remember this one," she said, gently touching a glitter-covered blue dove. "Libby made it in third grade—she swallowed the glitter and scared us half to death, remember?"

Michael sat stone-faced. "What do you want, Ann?"

Ann took a deep breath, releasing it in a deep sigh. "I just—I thought I'd stop by. To see the kids before I go."

"Before you go?" Michael said, his expression dark, unreadable. "So you're taking off again?"

"I just found out today—a magazine in New York is looking for an editor. They want me. I'm leaving for my interview with them tomorrow." Ann's voice faded away as she turned her attention back to them. Jessy saw her gaze go to their entwined hands, saw the almost imperceptible tightening of her mouth when she saw the ring.

"Do the kids like her?" Ann refused to look at Jessy, keeping her eyes on Michael only.

"The kids love Jessy," Michael said quietly. "*I* love Jessy."

Ann nodded, a quick jerk of her head, and finally looked away from Michael back to the decorations on the tree. She touched a gingerbread man made of salt-dough, smiling faintly.

"We made these before—before I left," she said softly. "Libby helped mix the dough and Marie painted the buttons on. Ben couldn't understand why we couldn't eat them—"

She looked back to Michael and Jessy again, her eyes shining with tears. "I never knew," she said, voice little more than a whisper. "I had everything but—I never knew—"

Michael's grip on Jessy's hand tightened, but he didn't get up to comfort Ann. He simply watched her, a muscle jumping in his jaw as he clenched his teeth.

"I shouldn't have done it," Ann said softly. "I shouldn't have threatened you like that. I don't know what I was thinking." Her gaze found Jessy's again. "I'm sorry. I'm truly sorry."

Jessy nodded, not trusting herself to speak. It was the best she could do.

"I'll be moving to New York," Ann said, turning her attention to Michael again. "It's a wonderful opportunity for me—"

"Of course it is," Michael said tightly.

"Can't you at least be happy for me?"

"What about the kids, Ann?" Michael's voice rose for the first time since Ann's arrival. "What am I supposed to tell them when they ask about you?"

"You tell them that I love them—"

"No."

Ann flinched slightly. "What?"

"I'm not making excuses for you any more, Ann." Michael released Jessy's hand and stood, stalking over to Ann. "It has always been about you. What you wanted. What you needed. Your job. Your career. Your life."

"And what was I supposed to do, Michael? Settle for a life here on this farm? Never going anywhere or doing anything or making anything of my life? That might be good enough for you, but I deserved better!"

Michael visibly recoiled. He said nothing, and for a few long moments he and Ann simply stared at each other, as if daring the other to look away first. Jessy saw the pain in his eyes, knew that Ann's words had cut even deeper than she'd intended. And she saw that Ann realized it as well.

"Michael—" Ann spoke just as he turned away from her. He sat stiffly beside Jessy, bracing his forearms on his knees, keeping his head down. Jessy hesitated for a moment before touching his arm, expecting a rebuff, but he took her hand almost eagerly, holding it tightly between both of his.

"I wasn't meant for this," Ann said softly. "I wasn't meant for this kind of life."

"Because you deserve so much more," Michael said bitterly, looking up again.

"Because I *wanted* more." Ann looked around the room, shaking her head slightly. "I'm sorry, Michael."

"What do we do about the kids?" Michael asked quietly. "Obviously we can't share custody—"

"I want you to have full custody."

Michael studied her for a moment. "Do you realize what that means?"

"Yes."

"You're willing to give them up?"

"Well, I'd hope you'd let me borrow them occasionally." Ann tried a small smile, but couldn't sustain it. "They belong with you, Michael," she said softly. "You've made a home for them here. You've given them all the things that I never could."

Michael nodded, that muscle still ticking in his jaw.

Ann laughed bitterly. "Hell, I didn't even know that my own daughter had food allergies. Does that make me mother of the year or what?"

Jessy could see tears shining in Ann's eyes. Michael still seemed unmoved, as still as stone.

"I hope we can work out a good visitation schedule," Ann continued, her voice trembling slightly. "I'll come here, of course, if you'll have me. And maybe I can take the kids to visit New York once I get settled—it could be like a vacation for them—"

"We'll see," Michael said quietly, looking up to Ann again.

"Good—great—" Ann nodded, awkward again.

"When are you leaving?"

"Tomorrow night." Ann smiled thinly. "Nobody likes to travel on Christmas day, so it's a cheap flight."

Michael looked at Jessy and she knew exactly what he was thinking. She gave his hand a squeeze.

"Why don't you—" Michael hesitated, sighing as he looked up to Ann again. "Why don't you come over in the morning. Spend Christmas with the kids before you go."

Ann's smile bloomed, then faltered as she glanced at Jessy. "Are you—I mean, is it okay? Are you sure?"

"I'm sure," Jessy said quietly. She gave Michael's hand one last, quick squeeze and went over to Ann. "You're their mother. The kids will never forget that. I will never forget it. I'll love them and take care of them when you're not here, but you'll always be their mother."

Ann nodded, her eyes shining with tears again.

"I'd like for us to be friends someday," Jessy said softly. "Not just for the kids' sake, or for Michael's sake—for *our* sake."

"Even after everything—?" Ann's voice trailed away, tears trailing over her cheeks.

"Especially after everything." Jessy slowly smiled. "We'll start slow, though. See if we can get through Christmas without a cat-fight or hair-pulling and then go from there."

Ann laughed quietly. "I think I might be able to restrain myself."

"Me too." Jessy's smile brightened a little. "Would you like to stay for dinner?"

"Yes," Ann said softly, nodding. "I'd like that very much."

Michael stood and joined Jessy, slipping his arm around her shoulders as he pressed a quick kiss against her temple. "Merry Christmas, Ann," he said quietly.

"Yeah," Ann whispered, managing a faint smile through her tears. "Merry Christmas."

THE LIGHTS of the Christmas tree blinked in its own rhythm, casting shadows of red, blue, and green over the darkened room. Curled up together on the couch, wrapped up in one of Lyssa's afghans, Jessy and Michael watched the lights of the tree in silence. Everyone else in the house had long since gone to bed.

The grandfather clock chimed, struck twelve.

"It's midnight," Michael said softly, kissing Jessy's temple as she snuggled closer to his chest. "Merry Christmas, baby."

Jessy raised her head to smile at him. "Merry Christmas."

They kissed again, lingering sweetly, taking all the time in the world. As Jessy settled against Michael's shoulder again, she marveled at the realization that this was only the first of many Christmases together.

And that she finally belonged somewhere, with people who loved her as much as she loved them.

"I wonder what Charlie will say when I tell him we're engaged." Jessy smiled, idly unbuttoning the top button of Michael's shirt to stroke his chest. She loved the feel of his skin, the wiry softness of the dark hair.

Michael laughed quietly, a rumbling sound that widened Jessy's grin and sent a pleasant shiver down her spine.

"He'll probably kick himself for losing you," he said, smiling down to Jessy again. "And then I'll kick his ass for hurting you."

Before Jessy could speak, soft footsteps scuffed down the hall to the doorway of the living room. Ben, Marie, and Libby peeked into the room.

"Can we open presents now?" Marie asked.

"It's Christmas morning," Ben added. "Libby said that after midnight means it's morning."

"*Technically* morning," Michael said as he smiled and waved them over. "C'mere, guys. Jessy and I have something to talk to you about."

Ben and Marie ran over to the couch and climbed onto their laps, squirming as they settled comfortably against them. Marie leaned against Jessy, one arm around her neck, as Ben sat between them, half on Jessy and half on Michael. Libby, much more ladylike and adult, perched on the edge of the cushion beside Michael. Laughing, he wrapped his arm around her shoulders and hauled her back, until the five of them were all jumbled on the couch.

Jessy's heartbeat pounded so fiercely she could feel it in her temples. Before this moment, she hadn't even considered the notion that the kids might not *want* her to marry their father. What would she do then? What *could* she do?

"What would you guys think," Michael said, looking from Ben to Marie to Libby, "if Jessy and I got married?"

Silence. The kids looked at each other, then back to Michael. Jessy thought her heart might stop.

"Would she live with us?" Marie asked softly.

Michael nodded, eyes solemn. "Yes, she would."

Ben shyly smiled. "Would she make us cat pancakes in the morning?"

"I sure would," Jessy said, smiling as she kissed the top of Ben's head. Suddenly she could breathe again.

"Would you expect me to be a babysitter for more rugrats?" Libby asked, trying to sound smart-alecky, but betrayed by the smile in her eyes.

"Yeah!" Marie shouted, grinning brightly. "Can we have a baby sister? A baby brother would be okay, but I'd rather have another sister."

Michael looked to Jessy, barely able to control his broad smile. "We'll see what we can do."

"Good!" Marie gave Jessy a hug and a sloppy kiss on the cheek. "I'm glad you're going to stay."

"Me, too," Jessy said as Ben joined the embrace and kissed her other cheek. She met Michael's gaze and wished she could freeze the moment and keep it in her heart forever. "I love you guys," she said quietly.

"We know," Libby said, smiling as she leaned against Michael in a hug. "Ditto to you."

The grandfather clock chimed the quarter-hour, and Michael glanced at his watch, frowning slightly. "Uh-oh," he said, keeping his expression deadpan and serious. "I hope Santa hasn't decided not to stop because you guys are still awake."

Marie and Ben stared at him with wide, disbelieving eyes. "He might not stop?" Ben asked quietly.

Michael shrugged, exaggeratedly nonchalant. "Gee—I don't know. I thought I might have heard something on the roof tonight—like reindeer hooves. But maybe it was just the wind—"

BEN AND MARIE didn't need to be told twice. They scrambled off Michael and Jessy's laps and ran for the stairs. As Libby trailed along behind them, almost embarrassed by her own excitement, Michael and Jessy followed the kids up the stairs, holding hands and exchanging delighted glances. Jessy thought she might never stop smiling.

They tucked the kids into bed with a kiss and a tickle, even though they knew it would be a long night of excited whispers and giggles before Marie and Ben settled down enough to fall asleep.

"Can we stay up and watch for Santa?" Marie asked as Jessy smoothed the curls away from her forehead and kissed her cheek.

"Nope," Michael answered, folding his arms over his chest in an attempt to look authoritative. "He won't stop by if you're awake."

"What if we hide?" Ben asked.

"Santa knows," Michael said sagely. "He always knows."

Jessy laughed; she could remember being that age, so excited about Santa's visit that sleep was impossible. They would probably be up and opening presents by five in the morning. And she could hardly wait.

Once the last minute drinks of water were fetched and the night-lights were plugged in and the closets were checked (because the Boogeyman might not take Christmas Eve off, Ben pointed out), Michael and Jessy were finally able to duck out of the bedroom and close the door. They immediately heard the sound of footsteps as Ben and Marie scrambled out of bed and headed to the window for their Santa watch.

Michael and Jessy looked at each other and smiled.

"Every year," Michael said, chuckling. "Like clockwork."

"But Santa always stops anyway," Jessy said as she stepped into Michael's open arms. She wrapped her arms around his neck, and they simply held each other, relishing the embrace, enjoying the precious moment. "Old Santa's a very forgiving soul."

"Who are you calling 'old'?" Michael asked with a grin. He kissed the tip of Jessy's nose. "Want to help Santa haul in the presents?"

"Don't you have elves to help you with that?"

"The elves don't let me pinch their butts," Michael said as he gave Jessy a healthy pinch. She yelped before she could catch herself and collapsed in giggles against him.

"Okay, okay," she said between laughs. "But only if I get equal opportunity." She gave his backside a grope and Michael started in surprise.

"Better not start something you're not prepared to finish," he said in a low, utterly sexy voice, pulling her closer.

Jessy smiled up at him, batting her lashes, nuzzling in close to his ear. "We'll see who's ready to finish," she whispered, breathing softly against his earlobe. She could feel the effect of her words on him as his embrace tightened. "*After* we bring in the presents."

Michael groaned good-naturedly. "After?"

"*After.*" Jessy kissed him quickly. "Duty calls."

"I guess you're right—" Michael rested his forehead against hers. "But when we're finished, can I unwrap an early present?"

Jessy smiled. "Only if I get to unwrap one, too."

With a mischievous grin, Michael chuckled and dipped his head down, kissing Jessy so slowly, so thoroughly, that she felt her entire body melting against his. When he raised his head and gazed at her again, Jessy had to catch her breath.

"Deal," he said, kissing the tip of her nose again.

Epilogue

"WHAT COLOR EYES should the fairy queen have?" Jessy asked as she studied the mural. Michael had left the coloring decisions up to her and the kids, having done all the hard labor of sketching a gorgeous fantasy world of fairies and gnomes and magical creatures on the bedroom wall.

"Green!" Marie said, handing Jessy a tube of forest green paint. Her cheeks were smudged with dabs of blue and pink, the same shades as the otherworldly sky of the mural.

"Then green it shall be." Jessy grinned as she squeezed a dime-sized blob of green paint onto her palette. "How's it going on the ogre, Ben?"

Ben carefully finished painting in the purple spots on the ogre's orange skin and looked over to Jessy, a huge smile on his face. "I'm done!"

Jessy carefully filled in the fairy queen's green eyes and then handed Marie the palette and brush, bracing the small of her back as she stretched.

"Have you *really* got a baby in there?" Marie asked, eyeing Jessy's belly.

Jessy looked down at her swollen stomach and smiled. "I sure do. And she's awake—I can feel her doing her exercises."

"Can I feel it?" Marie asked, flattening a hand over the curve of Jessy's stomach. The baby chose that moment to give a fierce kick, sending Marie into a gale of giggles. Laughing along with her, Jessy moved over to the small couch in the corner of the nursery, care-fully easing herself down and sighing with relief as she sank into the cushions. Ben—copying what he'd seen Michael do a hundred times—helped her tuck a smaller pillow behind her back before climbing up beside her.

"Are we going to have a brother or a sister?" he asked, pressing his ear against the worn denim of Jessy's workshirt. Marie clam-bered up on Jessy's other side and did the same.

"I don't think the baby's going to be able to tell you yet," Jessy said, grinning.

"It's going to be a girl," Marie said. "And I'm going to help take care of her."

"I want it to be a boy," Ben said and looked up to Jessy again. "I don't want another yucky girl."

"We don't know what the baby's going to be," Michael said from the doorway, smiling as he walked into the nursery and sat beside Jessy and the kids on the couch. "But we're going to love the baby no matter if it's a boy or a girl. Right?"

Marie and Ben nodded emphatically and Jessy smiled over their heads to Michael, almost dizzy with the tremendous rush of love she felt for all of them. She couldn't remember her life before meet-ing Michael. It seemed hard to believe that it had only been eight months since the wedding. Even harder to believe that in another three months she would be having a baby.

Their baby.

"I think Gramma and Libby are going to fix brownies," Michael said and grinned. "If you two hurry, Gramma might let you clean the batter bowl."

Ben and Marie looked to Jessy first—they were her special help-ers, after all—and she nodded. "Take off, you guys. You've both done a great job today."

In a heartbeat, Ben and Marie were off the couch and out of the room, racing down the hallway to the stairs. Michael watched them go, then scooted closer to Jessy, slipping one arm around her shoulders and flattening his other hand against the rounded slope of her stomach.

"Hey, hot mama." The gentle smile on his lips pushed Jessy's precarious emotions over the edge, bringing tears to her eyes. "Hey—what's wrong?"

"Nothing," Jessy said and swiped at her eyes, leaving a streak of green paint on one cheek. She smiled and sniffed, but couldn't help the tears that continued to flow. "I'm just happy and these stupid hormones are driving me crazy."

Michael chuckled as he gathered Jessy into his arms, holding her close as she helplessly wept against him. He smiled and kissed her hair, her hot tears soaking through the thin cotton of his T-shirt, holding her until the storm had passed.

When she finally got the worst of it out of her system, Michael tipped her chin up so that he could look at her again, gently wiping the tears from her cheeks. His smile was the gentlest thing that Jessy had ever known. Just seeing it made her feel cherished, unquestionably loved.

"I'm sorry," she managed to say, smiling despite her still hitching breath. "I just never thought I'd be this emotional. Of course, I never thought I'd be having a baby, either."

Michael flattened his palm against her belly again, his smile widening. "Personally, I think we should be congratulated for waiting as long as we did."

Jessy smiled and leaned into his shoulder, closing her eyes as she covered his hand with her own and felt three heartbeats merging into sync. The baby shifted position and Michael sat up straighter, a huge grin on his face.

"She just kicked!"

"I know. I was there." Jessy laughed as Michael flattened both hands on her belly, waiting for another flutter. "She just can't wait to meet her daddy."

The baby began kicking again, and Jessy and Michael watched in fascination as her stomach jumped and bounced. Michael unbuttoned the bottom of Jessy's denim blouse and kissed her bare belly.

"I love you, kid," he murmured to the baby. He lifted his head and smiled at Jessy. "And I love you, too," he said softly, raising up to kiss her with a tenderness that made Jessy's entire body melt against him.

"I love you, too," Jessy whispered.

Michael's eyes shone with unexpected tears. Jessy reached out to him, cupping his cheek in her hand as they smiled to each other, amazed and awed by what they had created. It was a moment Jessy had never dreamed she might experience. It was a dream come true, an answered prayer.

It was her life, *their* life, and it was a miracle.

About the Author

REBECCA BROCK is the director of a small
library in southern West Virginia. She is also the author of a collection of short horror stories (*Abominations*) and a variety of other
horror stories published in anthologies and online since 2000.

When not cleaning up after her cats, Rebecca enjoys books and
movies in a variety of genres (romance, horror, true crime, sci-fi)
and attempts to be crafty by crocheting, sewing, and cross-stitch-
ing. *The Giving Season* is her first published novel; all the others are
hidden away in drawers somewhere.

FEEDBACK IS always welcome! Please check
out Rebecca's blog (http://horror-hack.blogspot.com) and website
(http://www.rebeccabrockonline.com) to leave messages and see
what's coming up next.

About Pearlsong Press

PEARLSONG PRESS is an independent publishing company dedicated to providing books and resources that entertain while expanding perspectives on the self and the world. The company was founded by Peggy Elam, Ph.D., a psychologist and journalist, in 2003.

PEARLS ARE FORMED when a piece of sand or grit or other abrasive, annoying, or even dangerous substance enters an oyster and triggers its protective response. The substance is coated with shimmering opalescent nacre ("mother of pearl"), the coats eventually building up to produce a beautiful gem. The self-healing response of the oyster thus transforms suffering into a thing of beauty.

The pearl-creating process reflects our company's desire to move outside a pathological or "disease" based model of life, health and well-being into a more integrative and transcendent perspective. A move out of suffering into joy.

And that, we think, is something to sing about.

PEARLSONG PRESS endorses **Health At Every Size,** an approach to health and well-being that celebrates natural diversity in body size and encourages people to stop focusing on weight (or any external measurement) in favor of listening to and respecting natural appetites for food, drink, sleep, rest, movement, and recreation. While not every book we publish specifically promotes Health At Every Size (by, for instance, featuring fat heroines or educating readers on size acceptance), none of our books or other resources will contradict this holistic and body-positive perspective.

WE ENCOURAGE YOU to enjoy, enlarge, enlighten and enliven yourself with other Pearlsong Press books and products, which you can purchase at www.pearlsong.com or your favorite bookstore. Keep up with us through our blog at www.pearlsongpress.com.

Measure By Measure
a romantic romp for the fabulously fat
by Rebecca Fox & William Sherman

Fat Poets Speak: Voices of the Fat Poets' Society
Frannie Zellman, Ed.

FatLand
a novel by Frannie Zellman

Ten Steps to Loving Your Body
(No Matter What Size You Are)
& *Something to Think About:*
Reflections on Life, Family, Body Image
& Other Weighty Matters
by the Queen of Rubenesque Romances
by Pat Ballard

The Program
a novel by Charlie Lovett

Off Kilter: A Woman's Journey to Peace
with Scoliosis, Her Mother
a memoir by Linda C. Wisniewski

Splendid Seniors: Great Lives, Great Deeds
inspirational biographies by Jack Adler

The Singing of Swans
a novel about the Divine Feminine by Mary Saracino

Beyond Measure:
A Memoir About Short Stature & Inner Growth
by Ellen Frankel

Unconventional Means:
The Dream Down Under
a spiritual travelogue by Anne Richardson Williams

Taking Up Space:
How Eating Well & Exercising Regularly Changed My Life
by Pattie Thomas, Ph.D. with Carl Wilkerson, M.B.A.
(foreword by Paul Campos, author of *The Obesity Myth*)

Romance novels and short stories featuring Big Beautiful
Heroines by Pat Ballard, the Queen of Rubenesque Romances:
The Best Man
Abigail's Revenge
Dangerous Curves Ahead: Short Stories
Wanted: One Groom
Nobody's Perfect
His Brother's Child
A Worthy Heir

& Judy Bagshaw:
At Long Last, Love: A Collection